Grace and Marigold is an engrossir̶ ̶̶̶̶̶̶̶̶̶̶̶̶̶̶̶̶̶ ̶̶̶̶̶y ̶̶̶̶ ̶̶̶̶̶̶̶̶̶̶̶̶̶̶̶̶̶ ̶ ̶̶̶̶ ̶ ̶̶̶̶̶̶̶ ̶̶̶̶̶ ̶̶̶̶ ̶ ̶̶̶̶ ̶̶̶̶̶̶̶̶̶̶̶̶ ̶̶̶̶ ̶̶̶̶̶̶̶ ̶̶̶̶̶̶̶̶̶̶ read, filled with unforgettable characters. It is an intelligent and evocative study of a tumultuous time and place, and a moving and thought-provoking portrait of self-discovery.
 —Michelle Wright, author of *Small Acts of Defiance*

Mira Robertson is like a perceptive street photographer, but with words, capturing dazzling snapshots of remarkable people in a fleeting moment and place. We slip into a pitch-perfect London in the seventies alongside Grace, as her life swirls with squatters and strikes, casual encounters and shifting alliances, fears and freedoms, and those too-familiar feelings of the outsider. If you were there, then, you'll remember. If you weren't there, *Grace and Marigold* will bring it vividly to life before your eyes.
 —Kelly Gardiner, author of *Goddess*

A vivid, irresistible portrait of a young Australian adrift in eccentric 1970s London. Taut and beautifully crafted, Mira Robertson writes with a tender understanding of the waywardness of youth.
 —Carrie Tiffany, winner of the Stella Prize for
  Mateship with Birds

I want to live in this novel. A vivid Sapphic coming-of-age romp through bohemian 1970s London. Witty, moving and utterly real.
 —Kate Davies, author of *Nuclear Family*

Mira Robertson's debut novel, *The Unexpected Education of Emily Dean* was published in 2018. Her short stories have won prizes and have appeared in various literary magazines and journals. Her screenwriting credits, written with director Ana Kokkinos, include the award-winning films *Only the Brave* and *Head On*.

Mira lives in Melbourne.

Other books by Mira Robertson

The Unexpected Education of Emily Dean (2018)

Grace & Marigold

Mira Robertson

SPINIFEX

We respectfully acknowledge the wisdom of Aboriginal and Torres Strait Islander peoples and their custodianship of the lands and waterways. The Countries on which Spinifex offices are situated are Djuru, Bunurong and Wurundjeri, Wadawurrung, Gundungarra and Noongar.

First published by Spinifex Press, 2024

Spinifex Press Pty Ltd
PO Box 200, Little River, VIC 3211, Australia
PO Box 105, Mission Beach, QLD 4852, Australia

women@spinifexpress.com.au
www.spinifexpress.com.au

Edited by Susan Hawthorne, Renate Klein and Pauline Hopkins
Cover design by Deb Snibson
Typesetting by Helen Christie, Blue Wren Books
Typeset in Horley Old Style
Printed and bound in Australia by Pegasus Media & Logistics

A catalogue record for this book is available from the National Library of Australia

ISBN: 9781922964045 (paperback)
ISBN: 978192264052 (ebook)

MIX
Paper | Supporting responsible forestry
FSC
www.fsc.org   FSC® C008194

For Ana,
and Judy and Peter

1

Grace was on the verge of snapping up Mayfair when Gerald pounded up the stairs, shouting that the Pewsey Street squatters were about to be evicted. It wasn't unexpected – they'd been under threat since the issuing of a court order. Moreover, a week ago, Special Branch had conducted a raid on the grounds of suspected IRA connections, which Gerald said was bullshit; they were just fishing for general information, harassing anyone on their left wing hit list. Now word had spread that the eviction was imminent, and supporters were needed to man the barricades.

'We're in the middle of a game,' Grace said.

Gerald was having none of it and told her not to be a fucking pillock. They had to leave straight away. To make sure, he kicked over the Monopoly board and went off to round up the others.

Soon, everyone was crammed in the back of his transit van. Everyone, that is, except Marigold, whom Grace had not seen since their awful confrontation in the kitchen two nights earlier. She had ruined their friendship and could see no way to repair the damage. She tried to convince herself that Marigold's absence was a relief and to ignore how hollow and drained she felt, how everything had become an act, a pretence, like trying to win at Monopoly, when it was a game based on capitalist greed, something they all deplored.

The convoy from Belton Road set off, horns blasting in solidarity. Gerald parked in a nearby street, and they walked the rest of the way with a group of other Beltonians, drawn towards their destination by the sound of drumming, a tribal call to arms. A group of street theatre performers ran past dressed as villain landlords and bailiffs. There was a festive vibe in the air, testament to the idea that resistance to the fascist forces of capitalism, the ruling classes, the pigs and so on, was cultural as much as anything. Taunting the cops and the hired henchmen of the council with songs and street theatre was an essential part of the squatters' resistance. *Our resistance*, Grace thought, as she forced herself to stop thinking about Marigold and to focus instead on the coming confrontation, the anger she felt towards the fascist authorities who would rather smash up houses and throw people out on the street – for what? What bastards they were. Galvanised by outrage, she began to look forward to what was to come, even the threat of arrest. Instead of hanging back on the fringes, she was determined to throw herself into it.

The barricades, made from sheets of corrugated iron reinforced with timber struts, stretched across both ends of the street. Behind the tin, the squatters had created a bulwark of broken furniture and old mattresses, tree branches and rusty cyclone wire. Among the chaotic piles of junk, Grace spotted a bathtub and a cracked toilet. To her eye the barricades looked impenetrable, but Gerald said the pigs would knock them down in a matter of minutes. It was more important to have a big crowd – a measure of support and solidarity to show those in power that the squatters were not going to go quietly, that they were taking a stand.

'If there's violence, let everyone see who started it,' he said.

The Beltonians soon dispersed, catching up with people they knew. Grace found herself alone among the drifting crowd, scanning the faces for Marigold. She couldn't help it. Along the street, people huddled around bin fires, warming their hands, passing joints. Some carried placards with hand painted slogans: *Fuck the rich. Housing for all, squat the lot. Freedom is a full-time career.* A guy in a surplus military jacket shoved a leaflet in her hand urging her to join the workers' revolution and oppose the imperialist something or other which she didn't catch. She remembered hearing the same sort of slogans from the Spartacists at Melbourne University where they were known as the Sparts or, more often, the fucking Sparts, despised by everyone for the way they turned up at all the demos and meetings and tried to take over, shouting their revolutionary war cries with zombie-like intensity. Being on the left was taken for granted, but the Sparts were as reviled as the right-wing Christian Union.

Further along the street, she joined others who had gathered around Annie, as she strummed a guitar, singing 'Mr Tambourine Man'. Her voice, pure and clear as spring water, caught Grace in the chest. She listened until the song finished and then wandered away.

It grew colder and there was a dampness in the air. Peering at her watch, she saw that hours had passed. It was two in the morning.

'They won't come until dawn.'

Grace looked up to see a waif-like girl wrapped in a threadbare blanket.

'Coppers, bailiffs an' all,' the girl said. 'I've been evicted three times. Bastards always come at dawn. Do you live here?'

'No,' Grace replied. 'We came in support. What about you?'

The girl pointed at a house opposite. A large 'no evictions' banner hung out of an upstairs window. She said her name was Maggie, and that she was from Belfast. Being Irish meant the pigs gave her a hard time, she was Irish trash to them, a dirty tart. She'd been raped by a copper, but it was no use reporting it. Who was she going to tell? She talked non-stop, relating everything that had happened to her since leaving Ireland. Rough sleeping under railway arches and living in squats with people who were off their heads, going hungry and stealing food. She was high on something. Speed, or perhaps coke. Grace felt sorry for her while simultaneously wanting to shake her off; the ceaseless flow of words weaving a sticky trap. Maggie was

3

telling her too much, even if it was the drugs talking. She let her chatter on until she could bear it no longer.

'Sorry Maggie,' she said, 'I have to go. Friends are waiting.'

She saw the collapse of the waifish face and almost relented, but the girl didn't try to detain her and gave in immediately, as if she was used to people brushing her off. Grace knew that her excuse was not believed. A memory of her own neediness surfaced – that first meeting with Marigold, who had rescued her and taken her in. She quickened her step, overtaken by the need to get away.

Hours passed and the revelry subsided, the street theatre and singing fizzling out along with the bin fires. Those who got in first huddled together on mattresses dragged onto the footpath, while others hunkered down next to the dying fires, or stood quietly in groups, smoking cigarettes, sharing joints. The whole assembly of protestors gradually sank into semi-hibernation, including Grace who, after leaving Maggie, had run into Vanessa. They found a spot on one of the footpath mattresses with enough space to curl together like spoons in a drawer.

She woke to groans and sighs as around her people stirred with the first glimmerings of dawn. After retrieving her legs, which were entangled with Vanessa's, she sat up. Every part of her ached; she was stiff and cold. A slow turn from night into day had begun, the sun invisible behind lowering banks of cloud that smothered the tops of the chimney pots. How different from the shimmering red ball that bolted up from the horizon. *The dawn coming up like thunder*, her father would say, adding, as if he didn't say it every time, *Mandalay, one of Kipling's finest poems*. Kipling, whom she had discovered at university, was a despised imperialist.

As the darkness thinned, an air of anticipation began to grow. Mattresses were dragged back inside the houses, tea was brewed and handed around, and tactics were discussed. There was to be no violence – at least, not from the squatters. The whole strategy was about passive resistance. Lie down, go limp. Refuse to move.

4

Where were the press? The photographers? There had to be photographers. Pictures didn't lie. Someone was sent off to ring a press contact. In general, the press was the enemy but getting photos of squatters being roughed up by the rozzers could also generate sympathy from the public. At least, that was the theory. Then the word came through, spreading like wildfire. *They're coming, they're coming,* and Grace and Vanessa were swept up in a rush towards the barricade at the northern end of the street. Someone crashed into Grace from behind and she stumbled, setting off a chain reaction of mini collisions. By the time she'd regained her footing, Vanessa had melted into the crowd.

Police sirens wailed as three large removal trucks roared into view, stopping inches from the corrugated iron in a show of aggression. Moments later, sirens still blaring, four paddy wagons pulled up beside the trucks. Already, the so-called removalists were pouring from the rear doors of the vans, sledgehammers and crowbars in hand. The crowd tightened up, everyone jostling and shouting as those behind pressed forward while those in front tried to resist being catapulted into the barricade. From the other side, the hired heavies were ripping it apart and, as Gerald predicted, it soon gave way.

A male voice shouted instructions through a megaphone. Everyone was to link arms and sit down to create a human barrier that would stop the bailiffs and goons reaching the squats. As people began to follow the instructions, cops were already moving in. Scuffles broke out amid shouts of police brutality. A path was forced open, the cops stationing themselves in a row to stop the protesters from swarming back, allowing the hired henchmen to enter the squats on that side of the road.

Then came a loud crash and a collective cry from the crowd. The door to the first squat had given way. A chant began: *shame, shame, shame.* From ground level, Grace could only catch glimpses of what was happening. More immediate was the energy swirling around her, the press of bodies, shouts of shame, and the sound of wood splintering as another door was smashed to pieces. To the tune of 'Wouldn't it be Loverly' a lone voice rose above the general hubbub. Others soon joined in, and the massed voices rang out, joyful, strong, and defiant, adapting the words, turning it into a song of resistance about needing a home somewhere, a home without a landlord there. It was spine-tingling and uplifting, yet Grace couldn't stop the tears that welled, remembering how she and Marigold had sung 'On the Street Where You Live', and how different things had been back then.

After two verses the singing died away and the mood changed. It began with a woman's scream, followed by shouts and curses and people jumping to their feet. The crowd, which had been unified, was suddenly no longer a single organism, turning instead into a chaotic jumble of individuals pushing in every direction, some wanting to get close to the action, while others were equally keen to escape it. Grace leapt up too, not wanting to be trampled underfoot.

The guy with the megaphone shouted that the press had arrived, urging them to report the truth, that the squatters were peaceful and only wanted somewhere to live. She let herself be carried with the dominant current, towards the line of cops where a committed group of protesters were attempting to break through. Each time they surged forward, the cops forced them back. Arrests were made, and people were hauled off to the waiting paddy wagons. Meanwhile, the ransacking and destruction of the squats was well underway. Doors were smashed in, the possessions of the squatters were thrown out into the street, creating bonfire piles of furniture, bedding, and clothes. Front doors were boarded up and large padlocks attached. Somewhere in the crowd, a child wailed.

Up ahead, Grace caught sight of Gerald as he hurled a missile at the police line. The target clapped hands to his face as egg yolk dripped through his fingers. Gerald raised his fist in gleeful triumph. Moments later he was tackled to the ground, his arms pinned behind his back, while a press photographer snapped furiously. As the cops dragged him away, she tried to follow, an instinctive reaction that had no practical purpose. What could she do? She couldn't stop the police from bundling him into the open maw of a paddy wagon. Nor did she get far, there were too many people pushing and shoving.

The megaphone guy was calling for calm while the Spart from earlier, who had tried to hand her a leaflet, began to shout slogans through a loud hailer, urging people to rush the police, to resist by any means necessary, to take up the armed struggle.

'Defend yourselves against the violence of the state,' he screamed.

Grace could feel the anger rising around her, the press of bodies grew more intense and without warning she began to tremble. She couldn't catch her breath, her vision blurred, and her heart began to race. She had to get out of the crowd and with a strength borne of desperation began to burrow through the pack, praying that she was heading towards the edge and not back into the centre.

She emerged to find herself on the opposite side of the street, beside a shabby row of terraces that had yet to be broken into and where the front doors opened directly onto the footpath. Reaching the wall of the nearest squat, she sank down beside it. The panic that had overwhelmed her now seemed out of proportion. She fumbled in the pocket of her jacket and found a cigarette. With the smoke flooding her lungs, she grew calmer, her strength returning, grateful that the others from Beltonia hadn't witnessed her ignominious flight.

She took a last puff of the cigarette when a door to her left opened, followed by the sound of hurried footsteps. A female figure rushed past, leaving behind an after-image of a black and green cloak – the cloak, Grace belatedly realised, for which she had been the dressmaker's dummy. She jumped up, spontaneously calling out to Marigold, who was already some way ahead and did not stop.

2

Four months earlier, Grace lay on a couch in the same communal room where, subsequently, she would play Monopoly. She was waiting for Marigold who'd promised to cut her hair. The couch, like almost everything in the Free Republic of Beltonia, had been rescued from a skip. Marigold was late but Grace wasn't ready to give up hope. Half an hour late was hardly late at all. And what did it matter anyway? They were not slaves to the arbitrary division of time like the masses who repeated the same things in the same way every day, day after day, clocking on and off and giving up their freedom in exchange for a few pounds and a shitty gold watch at the end of it. Which was how Gerald put it. To be honest, Grace had never imagined that kind of life for herself, but the details weren't important. In the Free Republic of Beltonia they were forging something new, that was the important thing.

She picked up *The Dharma Bums* that Martin had left lying on the floor and read the first sentence before letting it slip from her fingers. She wasn't in the mood for Kerouac and sat up to roll a cigarette. The smell of coriander and cumin begun to permeate the house, a sign that Alan was cooking a curry. The aroma of the spices wafted up the stairs and into the front room while, from below in Martin's bedroom, came the throb of drums and bass guitar and Neil Young's yearning, cracked falsetto. Now and then, the shrill whine of a drill broke through. Grace assumed it was Gerald who, when not fighting the fascist authorities and their anti-squatting henchmen was always making and repairing things, using whatever was to hand.

The Neil Young record came to an end. The drill stopped a few seconds later. Footsteps clattered on the stairs and Raymond, who was from Lyon, poked his head into the room.

'You have seen Annie?' he enquired.

'Busking,' Grace replied. 'I think she said Holland Park. You haven't seen Marigold?'

Raymond shook his head and disappeared. His departure was followed by a faint peal of feminine laughter that Grace attributed to Vanessa, knowing that Ingred rarely laughed and was likely to be locked in her makeshift darkroom. Ingred, Raymond, Annie, and Alan lived next door, where the kitchen had been gutted beyond repair. It was the reason Gerald and Martin had knocked a hole in the dividing wall, turning the two houses into one big squat.

The only person not accounted for was Marigold. Where was she? Had she forgotten after all? Grace crossed to the window and propped it open with a piece of wood before leaning out, keen to catch sight of her approaching. A few Beltonians drifted past and waved. She took a final puff on the cigarette and flicked it into the street.

The haircut was not even her idea in the first place. When the letter arrived from Primo Press with the offer of an interview, Marigold had insisted. Grace needed a fresh look. 'Something a bit less—'

'Less what?' she'd asked. Marigold had deflected the question. Projecting her own fear, Grace suspected she meant less Australian. It was the spur she needed to agree. Added to which, Marigold said she was brilliant at cutting hair.

'You can ask anyone,' she said, waving around a large pair of dressmaking scissors. She had a knack for making clothes out of almost anything and was in the process of transforming a curtain

9

into a dress. It was due to her that Grace had an interview in the first place.

Two weeks earlier it had been their turn to 'shop', an activity that involved scavenging for left-over fruit and vegetables at the North End Road market. It was winding down when they'd arrived, the air ringing with the sound of cockney voices as the barrow boys spruiked their wares. At the sight of the girls, a weedy barrow boy picked up a large marrow.

'Very filling, my lovelies,' he crooned, stroking it suggestively.

The barrow boys were always making sexual innuendoes, using courgettes and carrots and bananas. There was hardly a vegetable they couldn't turn into something sexual. Marigold enjoyed flirting with them, pretending she was keen to get the best deal before walking away with a laugh to rummage through the boxes and crates at the rear of the stalls. There, she gathered the produce that had been thrown out – bruised or overripe fruit, and vegetables no longer at their best. At the end of the day when the stall holders and barrow boys were desperate to get rid of everything, they gave up bargaining with her and gave her stuff for free, suggesting what she might give in return. Some of the young men were handsome, with curly hair and dark, inviting eyes. When they smiled, Grace was shocked at how often she saw rotten crooked teeth.

'Cheer up, darlin'', the world hasn't ended,' the boy with the marrow phallus called. Grace gave him a smile to compensate for the fact that Marigold had chosen to ignore him as she hoisted a bag of foraged produce onto her shoulder.

'Come on,' she said. 'We've got enough and I'm sick of it.'

They adjourned to their usual post-market haunt, a greasy spoon caff near the tube station. On the café table lay an abandoned copy of the *Evening Standard*. Marigold flicked over a page.

'What about to this? Girl Friday wanted for vanguard publishing company. Must be self-starter, office experience essential.'

'I don't have any office experience,' Grace had replied. She was thinking about what to order and not really listening. Marigold, however, was undeterred.

'You're penniless Grace. And frankly, you don't have much experience of anything. I don't see why it should be an obstacle. A first-class degree in English Literature is far more important.'

'I don't have a degree in English Literature.'

'Pff. I doubt anyone will check the records of an obscure university in the colonies.'

'Australia's not a colony,' Grace said, feeling protective of her country and its status, ignoring the irony of defending it when she was its harshest critic and had declared on more than one occasion that she was never going back.

'You graduated, didn't you? That's all that matters.'

Which was true, though her academic career had been far from stellar, scraping through an Arts degree in European history with a bare pass. A year later, the French Revolution had faded to a single image of Marat, stabbed to death in his bath.

'Trust me,' Marigold went on, 'a job in publishing is perfect if you're ever going to write a novel. It means there'll be literary parties. You're bound to meet hordes of famous authors. Doris Lessing, Margaret Drabble—'

She continued to name literary lions, although Grace had stopped listening, cringing instead at the memory of how she had babbled on about wanting to write. It was in the first days of their friendship when she'd been desperate to impress. Yes, she'd thought about writing a novel once or twice – an ambition banished almost as soon as it had arisen. She had no ideas and nothing to write about.

'And Simone de Beauvoir—'

The name cut through the chatter in her head, and she glanced at

11

Marigold, alarmed by the possibility of meeting the famous French writer at a London literary soirée.

'I thought Simone de Beauvoir lived in Paris.'

Naturally, she agreed with everything in *The Second Sex*, it was just that she hadn't got around to reading it.

'Anyway, they're not going to choose me,' she said, realising, ex post facto, the meaning of her words.

A week later, a letter arrived with the offer of an interview, the result of an impressive application in which Marigold had convincingly conveyed Grace's many and varied imaginary skills. She was jubilant; the job was Grace's for the taking. The successful applicant, however, wondered if she really wanted the job or whether she had gone along with it because Marigold had rescued her from the abyss in those dark weeks when everything was hopeless and bleak. Not that it had been that way at first.

Arriving at Heathrow, Grace had felt exhilarated. Australia was far behind her and London, with all that it promised, beckoned.

The black cab slipped into the stream of traffic leaving the airport.

'Where to, princess?' the cabbie enquired.

You're only twenty, she heard her mother say, *you're too young. At least let me contact my old friend, Eve, in Sussex. She'd love to put you up.* She remembered how she'd laughed at her mother, a sarcastic, pitiless laugh. Wild horses would never drag her to Sussex. In the departure area, before boarding the plane, she'd ripped the page from her address book and tossed it away.

Faced with the cabbie's question she was seized by a moment of regret. He caught her eye in the rear vision mirror.

'Earl's Court?'

She hesitated, unsure what to reply.

'All the Aussies go there.'

Hearing this, her heart sank. The last place she wanted to go was where the Aussies went. Still, it was a destination, and she was in urgent need of one. He took her silence for assent and, as they sped towards London, began to talk about all the Aussies he'd met. Her exhausted body subsided into the seat, the cabbie's monologue rolling over her, while through the window, rows and rows of redbrick houses unfurled under a grey, cashmere-soft sky. 'London,' she repeated to herself, 'London, I'm actually here.' She was entering the city and wanted to experience every moment.

She woke to realise they were no longer moving. The cabbie turned and winked at her.

'Slept like a baby,' he said.

'Are we there?' she asked, straightening up, suddenly aware that she did not know where or what the *there* was. Once again, he came to her rescue.

'Earl's Court Youth Hostel, sweetheart,' he said. 'Your home away from home.'

The cab driver was right. Earl's Court Youth Hostel was filled with Australians, all convinced that everything English was *shithouse*, and that Australia was the best place in the world. On her second night, she allowed herself to be swept up with a group and taken to the local pub where one of the boys – Gazza from Perth – bought her a pint of the shithouse English beer. Everyone was talking about where they were planning to travel and where to buy a *grouse second-hand combi*, or if they were going to get a job in a pub first, at which point she had a distressing vision of herself driving to Kathmandu with Gazza and his mate Bruce. She took it as a warning that she had to get out of Earl's Court. She hadn't escaped Australia to end up with Gazza and Bruce and the claustrophobia of familiarity. Of assumptions about who she was, because she wasn't that person – whoever it was they assumed her to be. Somehow, she'd stopped thinking of the Australian boys and was railing against her mother. She couldn't bear it a minute longer. In London she had a chance to be truly herself, without the weight of … of … expectations.

The word *expectations* filled her with sudden fury, and at the same time, her mind veered away from interrogating it further. What expectations? She didn't want to think about any of it.

'Are you okay?' asked one of the girls from the youth hostel.

'No,' she replied, 'No, I'm not.' She brushed aside the girl's consoling hand and pushed through the crowd of revellers and out of the pub, impelled by a single thought. She had to find somewhere to live, somewhere with real Londoners.

Soon enough, a *Time Out* magazine left lying on the table in the youth hostel kitchen came to her rescue. There, in the accommodation for rent section, she found a room in Shepherd's Bush for eight pounds a week.

Joel, the young live-in landlord, showed her around. The room was cold and damp and smelled of blocked drains. A set of rickety wooden steps led up to a lumpy double bed mattress on a raised platform, under which she glimpsed a jumble of tea chests, suitcases, and miscellaneous items of furniture.

'What's that?' she asked.

'Don't touch it,' he warned, explaining in a cursory way that he rented out the space for people to store their stuff. 'It's just the space under the bed. You don't need it.'

She didn't want to live in a room filled with other people's stuff but gave in, not wanting to sound petty. And technically he was right – it was just the space under the bed. She'd begun to breathe through her mouth to avoid the drain smell and the sweaty, unwashed pong of Joel's clothes. His hair was so tangled and matted that she half expected to see a small animal, a mouse or gerbil, appear from within its depths.

Still, she told herself, *except for the smell and his hair, he's not bad looking, and all I need is a bed.* It was the kind of justification made by someone determined to ignore even the most inauspicious signs, an indication of how desperate she was for her London life to begin.

And the signs were everywhere. The squalid rat-infested kitchen and the ancient toilet with its slimy, stained bowl and malfunctioning cistern. Worse, Joel was prone to violent outbursts of rage against his mother, outbursts that he directed at Grace. She was the sole lodger – previous tenants sensibly having fled.

'How could you have sent me to that fucking school!' he screamed. 'They destroyed me.' Sometimes he agreed that Grace was not his mother, although it didn't stop him. She kept the door to her room locked which didn't stop him either. He banged on it, raging about how she had fucked up his whole life. Or else he pleaded to be let in, he wanted to fuck her. Was she his mother then, or was she Grace? Terrified that the lock would break she began to leave the house early in the morning, wandering the streets like a vagrant.

Looking back, she couldn't bear to think about those four weeks at Joel's. She couldn't understand why she'd stayed so long, why she hadn't walked out, foregone the rent paid and found somewhere, anywhere else. It was easy to forget how beaten down and hopeless she'd felt.

That fateful afternoon she was trudging along in her usual aimless way, feeling sorry for herself, not caring where she was going because it was all the same – dreary rundown houses and concrete footpaths. The London of Buckingham Palace and Westminster Cathedral, the Houses of Parliament, the art galleries and museums, the glamour of the West End, was a world away. She was too depressed and anyway, she hadn't come to London to be a tourist. But even in the midst of her misery, she was determined not to admit defeat and go home. She had to soldier on. Sometimes she cried as she walked, not caring who noticed. Nobody ever spoke to her anyway, which was why, when a female voice called, *watch out*, she muttered *fuck off* under her breath, only to feel something squelch under her shoe, followed by the unmistakeable reek of dog shit.

'Don't say I didn't warn you.'

The shit on her shoe and the criticism of the girl who made it were the last of many straws and she burst into tears.

The critical girl introduced herself as Marigold. She was twenty-five and said *girl* was infantilising, she was a woman, although that discussion came later when she and Grace had got to know each other. With long reddish hair and pale, translucent skin, she reminded Grace of a pre-Raphaelite painting – Ophelia in her watery grave or The Lady of Shallot. The resemblance, as she soon found out, was superficial because Marigold was the opposite of a palely loitering heroine. Nor was she draped in flowing robes, wearing instead black tights and a man's long striped shirt, tied at the waist with a silk scarf. Chunky black work boots completed her outfit.

The dog poo incident had taken place outside a shabby terrace house. Marigold made Grace take off the offending shoe and come through to the back garden. She filled a bucket with water and found a twig for scraping off the shit, which she gave to Grace, as there were limits to the help she was prepared to offer.

'Bravo,' she said, when it was done.

Embarrassingly, Grace couldn't stop crying. 'It's not the poo,' she croaked. 'It's all the other things.'

'What other things?' Marigold demanded.

In normal circumstances Grace would never have blabbed to a complete stranger but circumstances were not normal and once she began, it was impossible to stop. Marigold listened and didn't say anything, the expression on her face becoming more and more severe.

'I'm really sorry, I know I've bored you with my tale of woe,' Grace said, feeling mortified that she'd gone on for so long and regretting the phrase *tale of woe* which made her sound weirdly old-fashioned. She felt sure Marigold was judging her.

'Don't be so stupid, I'm not bored,' she said. 'We're going there right now to get your belongings. You're moving in here.'

'But Joel …'

'... will do exactly as he's told.'

They went straight upstairs to Grace's room, where Marigold instructed her to pack everything. She had almost finished when Joel appeared and blocked the doorway, demanding extra rent as compensation for the lack of notice. Grace was ready to capitulate immediately.

'Oh, I don't think so,' Marigold said. She smiled at Joel in a friendly way and wandered across to the platform bed. 'Gosh, what a lot of storage you have.'

'So what?' he said. 'I told you. You're not leaving until she's paid the rent.'

'Fire hazard I would have thought,' she said, turning towards him.

As Marigold lunged at Joel, Grace heard the metallic click of a zippo lighter. A blue flame shot up, hair sizzled, and an acrid stench filled the air.

'What are you doing, you mad bitch?' he screamed. 'You've fucking burnt my hair.'

'And you're a fucking slum landlord.' She followed him flicking the lighter on high as he backed away. 'It's us should be demanding the rent money.'

At the door, he screamed that he was going to fucking break her fucking legs, before bolting up the stairs to his top floor flat.

'And don't come back,' she called.

Outside on the pavement, she grabbed Grace by the hand and pulled her along. They ran down the street, Marigold whooping. Grace wanted to join in, but her pack was thumping up and down, hitting her in the small of the back and all she could do was gasp for the next breath.

3

After her escape from Joel's, the summer finally arrived. Days of glorious sunshine were followed by long balmy evenings when the sun hung suspended in the hazy sky, as if Helios had abandoned his chariot, leaving it to drift above the London chimney pots. Flowers appeared in the cracked footpaths and new growth pushed through gaps in the hoardings of boarded up houses everywhere. In the communal garden, foxgloves, giant fennel fronds and dope plants grew leggy, clamouring for space amongst a tangle of weeds and climbing vines, along with the increasing numbers of naked bodies as Beltonians abandoned their dark Victorian squats for the sunshine.

They had spread an old rug over a patch of weeds. When Grace saw that Marigold wasn't undressing, she wished she could retrieve her own casually discarded clothes, unable to think how to do it without revealing that she'd stripped off thinking Marigold would do the same. Compelled to go on with it, she lay down and pretended to be relaxed.

'You don't mind, do you?' Marigold said, immediately commandeering her stomach as a pillow.

'No,' Grace replied, closing her eyes. In fact, she didn't mind at all and was secretly thrilled, interpreting it as a sign of their closeness. It wasn't always like this. Marigold was often distant and uncommunicative. She hated to talk about herself, and weeks had passed before revealing to Grace that she'd gone to Oxford and had a first-class degree in modern languages. Now she was freelancing for some sort of company, translating reports which she typed up in her bedroom. It was a stop-gap arrangement – she never said what for. Nor did she ever speak about her past, brushing aside tentative enquiries. She said it was boring and irrelevant which made Grace feel boring and irrelevant for wanting to know. Marigold was right. Why talk about the past and the people they had sloughed off? Only the present and future were important.

Gerald believed she was hiding the fact that she was an aristo, slumming it for her own entertainment before returning to the world of wealth and privilege. Marigold didn't bother to confirm or deny his assumptions, though it was obvious that she came from a different world. The way she spoke, her air of casual confidence, her occasional haughtiness, infuriated him, while for Grace, the same qualities were an indispensable part of her charisma.

Before she'd understood how much they disliked each other, Grace had let slip that she was attracted to Gerald. Since then, she'd pretended to lose interest, and hadn't protested when Marigold said his confidence was arrogance and that he was not worth it.

She was beginning to feel too hot. Marigold's head was surprisingly heavy and her mass of hair, spilling over Grace's belly, had trapped the heat like a mohair blanket. It was uncomfortable, but she didn't ask her to move; the intimacy was too precious. And what did it matter if Marigold came from money, or if her parents were upper class, even aristocrats? Nobody chose their parents; it was not her fault.

Squinting up at the sky, she tried to work out the time by the placement of the sun. Later, they planned to go flâneuring, which

Marigold had explained was a French word for wandering aimlessly. She said flâneuring was essential if Grace was ever to know London. It was only by getting lost that one discovered anything.

Grace thought about the early weeks at Joel's and how London had seemed dingy and grey, the streets she'd tramped indistinguishable from one another, treeless, the houses all crammed together. She remembered how overwhelmed she'd felt by the buffeting, surging crowds that poured into the underground, the rancid smell of so much humanity. People looked old and drab and the weather was awful.

Flâneuring with Marigold, her eyes were opened to new worlds and a city of extremes. Yes, it was dismal and decaying. But also grandly, glitteringly opulent. The reek of history was everywhere and though her knowledge of London's past could have fitted on the head of a pin, what mattered was the sense of being part of something so layered and complex. The city had been there for hundreds of years and would endure for hundreds more. It made Grace think of the tiny town near her parents' farm, and the flimsy weatherboard houses that seemed to rest so lightly on the earth, ready to be blown away in a hot wind. Even Melbourne with its endless suburbs, wide streets, and the great blue bowl of the sky, seemed insubstantial by comparison.

London in summer was greener than she had ever imagined, the trees in the parks, enormous. The light was different, mellower, and more diffuse. And streets crammed with houses and buildings of two storeys or more, unlike the single storey streets of the Melbourne suburbs.

How strange it was to walk down Pall Mall and stand in Trafalgar Square, to window shop in Oxford and Regent Streets, wander past the Eros fountain at Piccadilly Circus – all names she'd only ever seen on the Monopoly board. And then Baker Street, Cheapside, Rotten Row and Grub Street – how they rolled off her tongue, bedazzling her, conjuring visions of Dickensian squalor and the murder mysteries of Conan Doyle and Agatha Christie.

Setting out on the long summer evenings without a plan, they strolled along high streets and into side streets, past rows of seedily genteel terraces, through bleak housing estates and across parks where lovers lay in the grass and Grace saw her first squirrel and once, was attacked by a goose. They meandered beside canals where barges slid by silent as ghosts, and wandered down Charing Cross Road, peering in bookshop windows. Venturing into Soho, they saw working girls totter on platform shoes, their pimps loitering in doorways. In Covent Garden, they crossed the market square, littered with empty boxes and vegetable scraps, before ambling into Bloomsbury where Virginia Woolf once had a room of her own. Sometimes they stopped for a pint of beer in pub rooms of tallowy light and dark wood, the smell of winter fires still lingering.

On their first outing, Grace had assumed that Marigold was being kind, extending a hand to her because she was alone and didn't know anyone. She thought Marigold would get sick of her and she'd be discarded. But it hadn't happened.

Lying in the garden under the rug of hair, Grace was overcome by a surge of gratitude, and broke the silence.

'I owe you everything.'

'No, you don't,' Marigold replied. Without lifting her head, she felt for Grace's face and stroked her cheek. 'And I don't want you fawning over me or thinking I'm marvellous because I'm not.'

Grace had laughed then, certain that Marigold was wrong. Laughed, too, in order to dispel the idea that she would ever fawn, while secretly resolving that she had to be vigilant with herself.

The haircut had been forgotten. It was galling to be of so little consequence, and she made a vow that it was the last time. She wasn't going to hang around for Marigold ever again.

'That's it,' she said aloud, just as the offender rushed into the room, exclaiming, *there you are*, as if she'd been searching everywhere.

'Of course, I'm here,' I've been waiting forever,' Grace replied. 'Where have you been?'

'I've had an awful day, Gracie,' Marigold said. 'Don't be angry with me.'

Gracie was the name her father sometimes used and, secretly, Grace saw Marigold's adoption of it as a sign of their special bond, though there were times – for instance, the preceding hours – when the special bond began to seem like an illusion. As for her father, she had turned her back on him, banishing him from her life.

'You could at least say sorry,' she said, unable, in the end, to resist the alluring tenderness of *Gracie*.

'Profoundly sorry,' Marigold said. 'Begging for your forgiveness.'

'Okay, that's enough,' Grace said, trying to be stern.

They retired to Marigold's room where she sat on an upturned tea-chest while the brilliant hairdresser went to work. They did not talk, as Marigold said she needed to concentrate. The only sound came from the regular click of the dressmaking shears and the rustle of clothing as she moved around, creating puffs of air that dispersed her distinctive smell – earthy and a little musky – sending Grace into a dreamy state until, glancing down, she noted with alarm the numerous clumps of pale hair littering the floor.

'Don't cut too much,' she said.

'Don't worry,' Marigold replied. 'You can trust me.'

But she couldn't get the sides even and had to keep cutting. By the time she allowed Grace to look, her hair was no more than an inch long.

'Like a blonde Jean Seberg,' Marigold enthused, reminding Grace that they had seen *Breathless* together at the Electric.

She peered at her image, trying desperately to see a likeness to Jean Seberg, but the reflection in the mirror looked far more like an escapee from a mental institution.

'It's very chic, very French,' Marigold said, fiddling with a patch that was almost bald.

'Are you sure?'

'Absolutely,' she replied.

4

Grace pulled out a chair and sat down at the kitchen table.

'What's happened to your hair?' Ingred said in her blunt way, a characteristic Grace had decided must be typical of the Danes. Not that she knew for sure, as Ingred was the first Danish person she'd met.

'Nothing's happened to it. I cut it, that's all,' Marigold said.

Ingred raised her eyebrows and shrugged, her reaction confirming what, in her heart, Grace knew: that Marigold's depiction of French chicness was a lie. Even with the disaster of the haircut weighing on her, she hadn't wanted to miss out on Friday night dinner when the household came together. Gerald had instituted the tradition which he insisted was not a rule because there were no rules, although he had a way of making everyone feel that they ought to attend. If, sometimes, others felt the weight of this, Grace did not. These were her people now; this was her new life. She was determined to mould herself into a Beltonian and wanted nothing more than to immerse herself in the ideas and opinions that ricocheted around the kitchen table. She didn't want to appear ignorant and listened avidly to the talk of squatters' rights and the necessity of opposition to the hegemony of the ruling class. That marriage and the nuclear family were the foundation stones of capitalist oppression was obvious.

The past was rotten, and they were remaking things, a way of living together where monogamy was scorned. The belief that nobody owned anybody was a basic tenet, which was not to say everyone agreed with each other about everything, something Grace was only beginning to discover.

At first, she thought of her new home as Marigold's squat because of how Marigold had invited her – ordered her – to move in. She'd assumed that her new friend was somehow in charge of things, the head of the household, before realising that Marigold didn't aspire to be the head of anything in Beltonia. At house meetings, she kept in the background, letting others make decisions. Grace was surprised, remembering how she had taken over when they'd first met, marching her back to Joel's, ordering her to pack everything and when Joel tried to stop them, setting fire to his hair. At the squat, she was a more shadowy presence, and not the leader that Grace had expected. Gerald was always going on about equality and she wondered if Marigold was placating him, although that seemed unlikely. Ironically, he was the one who acted like a leader, while advocating for the death of such roles. He was doing it at that very moment.

'We must reject established structures of control,' he said.

The meal was over, and everyone was smoking except for Ingred, who said smoking was a waste of time and made them stink.

'The idea of a single leader is reactionary. We are all leaders,' Gerald went on.

Grace glanced at Marigold and saw her smile – a small, private grin that gave her away. Gerald saw it too.

'What?' he said. 'You don't agree?'

'Whatever you say, Gerald,' she replied, as if it wasn't worth arguing.

'Ah, yes, the poor little rich girl, slumming it in a squat until Daddy orders her home.'

'Unlike you,' Marigold replied, 'play-acting with meetings and leaflets and calls to action. Do you really think you're going to change anything?'

'Oh, shut up you two,' Annie said. 'Why can't you get on?'

Grace wished they would, too. They rubbed each other up the wrong way over almost anything, as she had found out.

She'd been crammed between them in the front seat of Gerald's transit van on the way to Primrose Hill where a spate of renovations promised rich pickings. Marigold joined them at the last minute and although Gerald didn't object, he emanated a prickle of antagonism. He was explaining to Grace how he and Martin were the first squatters in Belton Road when it was a squalid row of abandoned Victorian terraces. They were given the address by Rough Stuff, the squatting estate agency run by people with names like Crow and Psycho Kid. Grace had read their witty bulletins featuring such opportunities as *mansion, currently no roof, would suit astronomer.* Buckingham Palace was often listed as a potential home for the homeless with more than six hundred rooms. Behind the satirical façade, Rough Stuff was a serious enterprise and had helped many hundreds of people find houses to squat.

After Gerald and Martin moved in, dozens more people turned up and soon, the whole street was occupied. The council ignored them for a while until the tide turned and the press started a campaign against squatters everywhere.

'We were painted as drug addicts, hippies and anarchists, sponging off the government,' Gerald said, unable to keep the outrage from his voice.

'Of course, there's never been a drug addict, hippie, or anarchist in Beltonia,' Marigold observed with a wry grin.

'What's that got to do with it,' he snapped. 'They were calling for us to be cleaned out, like we were vermin. Anyway, it was before you came. You weren't even there.'

'No need to get heated,' Marigold said mildly.

He ignored her and continued with his potted history. How the fascist press didn't care about the housing crisis. They never bothered to report on the scandal of streets full of empty houses left to rot by local councils and capitalist landlords. All they cared about was making money, selling newspapers with fake stories about squatters invading the houses of people on holiday. Fantasies about Mr and Mrs Bloggs coming home from their two weeks on the Costa del Sol to find the locks changed and junkies inside.

Marigold had looked away by then and was gazing out of the passenger-side window to emphasise that she wasn't listening. They were passing a long stretch of abandoned houses, boarded up behind corrugated iron hoardings that were graffitied with slogans. *Homelessness, whose crime? The council is guilty. Fuck the rich, house the poor.* On the hoardings in a street near Beltonia, Martin and Vanessa had painted *corrugated iron is the character armour of the council* – an enigmatic sentence that Vanessa said was a reference to the theories of the psychoanalyst, Wilhelm Reich, and his revolutionary ideas about sexual repression. Grace was keen to know more about the revolutionary ideas, but she hadn't asked. She didn't want Vanessa thinking she was sexually repressed.

Turning into Abbey Road, they'd approached the famous pedestrian crossing and Gerald began to calm down, recounting how he'd convened a meeting of the street after the Greater London Council threatened them with mass evictions. A working group was formed and Ingred, who was from Copenhagen where squatters had taken over a complete neighbourhood and declared themselves a mini-state, said they should follow suit.

'So that's what we did,' he said. 'The Free Republic of Beltonia, set up with a proper constitution and formal independence from the rest of Britain.'

'What does it mean?' Grace had asked. 'You can't really secede.'

'Exactly,' Marigold said, revealing that she had been listening all along.

'Exactly,' Gerald echoed, triumphantly. 'It was a tactic, a publicity stunt.'

Newspapers and magazines suddenly wanted to run feature articles about Beltonia. Instead of being parasites sucking the city dry, they were creative and hardworking and best of all, photogenic. For a time, the street swarmed with press photographers, journalists and even tourists, who came to see what was going on. The council had to back off and was forced to abandon its mass eviction plan.

'The proclamation of the Free Republic of Beltonia turned the tide,' Gerald said. 'But it's not like we've won the war. The enemy is still out there.'

In Primrose Hill they found a couch in a skip. It was the same couch on which Grace had waited for Marigold to arrive and cut her hair.

Ingred was no longer in the kitchen. She had retreated to her dark-room when Raymond began talking about schizo-analysis and how they had to harness revolutionary desiring machines that would destroy capitalism. He was quoting from Deleuze.

'Impressive but incomprehensible as usual,' Vanessa said.

The others felt the same and were always teasing Raymond about his French philosophers. He took it in good spirit, telling them it wasn't his fault if the English were a bit stupid.

'There's a party tonight at number twenty Martin said, distracting them from any further analysis of capitalism. 'Are you girls coming?'

'Women,' Marigold corrected. 'Maybe.'

Later, Grace and Marigold walked along the street to the party house. They could have gone the back way, given that the boundary fences had been removed to create a large, communal garden. Beltonians didn't believe in private property. Gardens were meant to be open areas, used by everyone, where children could run free and old people could gather and warm their bones in the sun, although, so far, the latter had proved irrelevant. Nobody over thirty had shown any desire to live in the Free Republic. In any case, going the back way was easier said than done. Some areas were overrun with brambles and weeds and building rubble, making them almost impenetrable.

In theory, everyone was responsible for maintenance, and for planting and harvesting vegetables and building benches in sunny spots for the old folk (should they unexpectedly arrive) and creating play areas for the children. In practice, some of the squatters were not as committed to the principles of the Free Republic as others. They'd gone along with it simply because they were desperate for somewhere to live. They weren't interested in turning up for working parties or having a say in the decisions that needed to be made. Others, like Tina and Dave next door, were drug addicts and too busy trying to score. The lack of commitment was annoying, but as Gerald reminded everyone, Beltonia wasn't paradise; it was a work in progress. There were no rules and no bosses. Everyone had an equal say, which didn't mean that having a say was compulsory. After all, it was a free republic.

Approaching number twenty, Grace could see people clustered on the street. Laughter and voices carried on the night air along with wood smoke from the fire in the communal garden and the smell of Moroccan hash and home-grown weed. Music throbbed from open windows, setting up an answering beat inside her, drawing her forward, leaving behind Marigold who had stopped to greet friends. She made her way inside, down the passage and into the crowded kitchen where joints were passing from hand to hand. A man with a wispy goatee offered her a mug.

'Scrumpy,' he said, 'it's got a kick to it.'

Someone pushed past as the goatee wandered off into the throng.

'Grace,' a voice called.

She sculled the contents of the mug and turned to see Vanessa.

'Come with me.' Vanessa took her hand and tugged her towards the door.

Already the scrumpy was making her feel light-headed.

Outside, people had gathered around a fire, sitting on broken-down couches and kitchen chairs and rugs spread out on the grass. They found a space on a rug and sat down. A girl passed her a joint. She drew the smoke deep into her lungs and held it for a few seconds before blowing out a plume. She handed it to Vanessa and lay back. Someone threw more wood on the fire, old floorboards and joists, sending firecracker sparks into the night sky. Vanessa lay down beside her.

'I've decided to become an astrologer,' she said. 'Pearl gave me a reading and says it's definitely what I should be doing.'

By turning her head, Grace could see the side of Vanessa's face and strands of her long, hennaed hair.

'Really? What about your acting?' Vanessa had been taking classes with a community theatre group.

'Pearl thinks my true vocation is astrology. She says I can act as a side-line. You should meet her, she's amazing.'

Vanessa continued to talk about how Pearl had studied astrology from some world-famous guy and gave readings to equally famous people, and she was so lucky because Pearl didn't take just anyone on as a student. The problem was money because Pearl's classes were expensive.

Grace was half listening, wondering if she believed in astrology. She knew that despite their many differences, Gerald and Marigold agreed that it was rubbish, and remembered how Marigold had suggested it would be better to read the entrails of a chicken, in imitation of the ancient Romans. At least that way they could eat the chicken afterwards. She tuned in again to hear Vanessa offering to draw up her chart.

'I'll do it for half price,' she said. 'I need the practice. Do you know the exact time you were born? Otherwise, I can't do the proper calculations.'

As it happened, Grace knew she'd been born at four o'clock in the afternoon.

It was school holidays, and she was home from boarding school, lying on her parents' bed, watching her mother as she sat at the dressing table, putting on her make-up. Her mother never went anywhere without her *face* on, even if there was nowhere to go, and Grace, her brother William, and their father were the only people she saw. They lived miles from the nearest town and the neighbours on the adjoining farm were two ancient bachelor brothers who kept to themselves. In those days, before she had seen the truth about her parents, Grace loved to spend time with her mother, keeping her company while she got on with chores, their conversation roaming over novels her mother had read and wanted to discuss, and plans for doing up the spare bedrooms and the latest ideas for the garden.

She'd been absorbed in a daydream about getting her hands on a denim skirt, and whether she could persuade her mother to make one for her when something landed beside her on the bed.

'I found it when I was cleaning out my drawers,' her mother said.

It looked like a little luggage tag for a doll's suitcase, with a piece of string attached. Examining it more closely, she saw her surname and the date and time of her birth, written in faded fountain pen ink. Apparently, in the era in which she'd been born, the newborns were carted off to the nursery each night so that the mothers could sleep. The luggage tags ensured that mistakes were not made, and the babies and mothers were correctly reunited each morning.

'That's awful,' Grace said.

'How so?'

'The babies, abandoned like that.' She was thinking of herself, of course.

31

Her mother had shrugged; she didn't think it was so terrible.

'Here, give it to me,' she said, 'and I'll throw it out.'

But Grace refused. She wanted to keep it and was shocked at her mother's lack of sentimentality.

'Well, what do you think?' Vanessa said. 'It's not about predicting the future. It's psychological. About coming to know who you are. You should read Jung, he proved that it works.'

Grace was sure that the phrase *coming to know who you are*, belonged to the amazing Pearl and imagined telling Marigold, knowing she would find it hilarious.

'I'll think about it,' she said, closing her eyes. The joint, in combination with the scrumpy, was making her sleepy. I must read Jung, she thought, and Wilhelm Reich too.

She woke to find Vanessa gone and Gerald sitting beside her, eating dhal from a wooden bowl.

'Want some?' he asked, 'now you've woken up.'

She sat up, pretending to look unconcerned that Gerald had found her napping. It wasn't the kind of image she wanted to project, especially to him. She wanted to say that she hadn't been asleep and had only closed her eyes, before it occurred to her that she might have been snoring, and that it was safer just to smile. He handed her the bowl in which there was nothing more than a blob of dhal stuck to the bottom. Rather than feeling disappointed, she interpreted the offer as a signal that he wanted to make a connection. At last, the moment had arrived when something was going to happen between them. She poked at the lump of dhal, hoping he would make the next move, thinking of the earlier conversation and his view that they must all be leaders and reject – what was it they had to reject? She couldn't remember, except that it was obvious he was a leader and it made him desirable. A catch, as her mother might have said, though not about someone like Gerald. Why was she even thinking of this, when the whole concept of a *catch* was so awful and outdated, implying manipulation on the part of the woman. She would never be like that.

'Sorry, he said, 'there's not much left.'

'Why give it to me then?' she replied, sounding angry and not playfully sexy. It was the result of thinking about the *catch* thing, but she couldn't bring herself to explain.

An uncomfortable silence followed until Gerald leapt to his feet, waving at someone on the other side of the fire. 'Boris,' he called and with a cursory smile at her, strode away.

Grace watched as he disappeared into the further reaches of the communal garden without greeting anyone. There was no Boris.

The party swirled around her, oblivious to her solitary figure. She replayed the encounter with Gerald in her head, hoping it would sound different. An invitation rather than an accusation. It did not. She had blown her chance with him.

In this defeated mood, she abandoned the party and walked home, punishing herself, knowing it was pointless and unable to jolt herself out of it.

The house was empty. She climbed the stairs to her bedroom and threw herself down on the bed, a mattress on the floor. The faint sound of laughter and music filtered into the room and Grace half-wished she hadn't rushed home. What choice had there been after that bungled encounter? Tomorrow she'd find an excuse to seek Gerald out and laugh about it.

Sleep proved elusive and she was still awake hours later when people began returning. The front door banged a few times; muted voices and the clatter of footsteps on the stairs. And then, just as the house had settled again, and her internal ruminating voice had stopped, the quiet was broken by the unmistakable sounds of sex.

It wasn't uncommon to hear others fucking. Some nights the entire squat echoed with cries and groans of pleasure, leaving her with the suspicion that she was the sole person in Beltonia not screwing their brains out. She was sick of masturbating; her fantasies had become boring and repetitive and while believing, in theory at least, that there was nothing wrong with wanking and that women ought to take control of their sexual pleasure, it made her feel depressed.

She pulled the eiderdown over her head and wondered if it was Gerald with someone he'd picked up at the party. Or was it someone from the house? Vanessa or Ingred, or even Annie although she and Alan were a couple. Not that being a couple precluded having sex with other people as nobody believed in monogamy. Grace hoped it was not Marigold, feeling reassured by the antipathy between them, until she remembered Mr Darcy and Elizabeth and the possibility that mutual dislike could turn out to be a prelude to passion. But that was fiction. She didn't want to think of Gerald fucking anyone who lived in the house, especially Marigold.

The eiderdown provided no protection from the sound of escalating pleasure, the cries and moans rising to a crescendo before eventually subsiding. They seemed to have reached simultaneous orgasm and she couldn't help comparing it to her own unsatisfactory experiences.

She'd lost her virginity to Sam, a funny, clever law student who said he was in love with her. She had tried to persuade herself that she felt the same way. The first time was painful and perfunctory. Her friend, Clara, said it was like that for everyone and not to worry, it got better, which turned out to be true. Even so, it was nothing like the experience she'd imagined it would be. She never had an orgasm with Sam and found his sweaty, grunting climaxes rather disgusting. Their relationship fizzled out, leaving her with an unrequited longing for passion and romance, for her life to be radically transformed by it, and to feel that she couldn't live without him (whoever he was).

The most important thing was to fall in love with a man. She would give herself another chance with Gerald. Surely, all was not lost.

5

The weekend passed without a chance to speak to Gerald, there were too many people around. It was never the right moment and she couldn't decide what to say, justifying her inaction with the excuse that she was too worried about the looming Girl Friday interview.

On Monday morning, she staggered out of bed at seven o'clock in order to have the kitchen to herself. The bathroom, a makeshift affair tacked onto the rear of the house, had been unusable for months. The plumbing had collapsed, and the rusty bath was a health hazard. For weeks, Gerald and Raymond had promised to plumb in a bathtub they'd rescued from a skip. Instead, it remained dumped in the garden, filling with rainwater and pond scum. In the meantime, they made once-weekly trips to the council bath house. On her first visit, Grace had expected it to be bleak and institutional with slimy floored shower cubicles, cold water, and drain holes clogged with hair. Instead, hot water gushed promiscuously into a bath so deep that she'd floated. Wisps of steam rose from the surface of the water and drifted up to the sea-green ceiling far above. Pipes clanged and hissed and sometimes she heard voices and laughter from adjoining bathrooms, imagining couples, head to toe, their limbs entwined.

Nevertheless, the inconvenient reality of menstruation remained, with the only option a *bird bath* at the kitchen sink. Bird bath was a phrase her mother used, invoked during periods of drought when the tank water got low. There, it had involved the privacy of an actual bathroom, whereas standing naked in the kitchen of the squat, pretending to be relaxed about washing her cunt in public was another thing altogether. Using the word cunt was because of Marigold, who said they had to reclaim it.

'No more front bottom, pussy, or fanny. A cunt is a cunt,' she decreed.

Grace agreed wholeheartedly, yet when an occasion arose where she might use the word, it stuck in her throat. She hoped Marigold hadn't noticed and practiced saying it to herself. *A cunt is a cunt.*

She entered the empty kitchen and slung her towel over a chair, glancing at her reflection in the window, hoping that her hair might have grown. It had not and if anything, appeared to have shrunk. She tried not to think about it and turned on the taps at the sink. Whispering the cunt mantra, she began the awkward task of washing herself without flooding the floor. Her period was not due for a week, but she couldn't face the interview with the suspicion that some part of her – she was thinking of the reclaimed cunt – might smell.

After dressing in her bedroom, she returned to the kitchen to wait. The interview was not until ten. Over time, others arrived, including Alan, who had a job with computers that nobody understood. It marked him out as suspicious and probably a capitalist. He was accepted, reluctantly, because of his relationship with Annie who, as a busker, had cachet to spare. Raymond said Annie had a voice like *La Môme Piaf*.

'I thought you were going for an interview,' Alan said, looking sceptically at her apple green cheesecloth shirt, red velvet flares and Indian leather toe sandals.

'Don't listen to Alan, he's got the fashion sense of a travelling salesman. You look splendid,' Marigold said. 'Perfect for a vanguard publishing company.'

At the entrance to Primo Press, a woman appeared and introduced herself as Rita, giving Grace a startled glance before a mask of politeness descended. Grace knew it was to do with her hair and had an urge to abandon the interview. Too late, for Rita, somewhat impatiently, was already ushering her inside with an authority she was unable to resist.

As the front door closed, Rita turned and proceeded to lead the way up the stairs. Her bottom, encased in a form-fitting skirt, swayed slightly from side to side, filling Grace's field of vision. Their ascent seemed to go on for ages although it couldn't have been longer than a minute or two.

On reaching the second floor, they entered a spacious, light-filled room. Two canary yellow sofas faced each other across a glass-topped coffee table, while underfoot, scrubbed floorboards were partially covered by a white shag-pile rug. Framed posters depicting rock psychedelia, swirling flower power and otherworldly dreamscapes, hung on the walls, creating an intimidatingly groovy vibe. An image of a woman with a fox face, like a Beardsley drawing on acid, caught her eye and for a moment Grace felt quite disorientated.

'One of our best sellers,' Rita said, motioning for her to sit down.

Grace wanted to ask if the poster was a blow-up of the book cover. Before she could enquire, a heavily pregnant woman entered the room, faltering briefly as she took in the sight of Grace's near-bald head.

'Elizabeth is going to interview you too,' Rita said. 'She's leaving to have a baby.'

For the second time, Grace wished she could make a run for it but inventing an excuse was beyond her. And Rita had already begun.

'So, Grace,' Rita said, 'we've read your job application and we're impressed.'

'Really?' she exclaimed. 'I mean, really good. I mean, that you're … happy.' She forced herself to stop speaking and smiled.

'Touch typing, reception experience, filing.'

Rita ticked off the items on her fingers, the nails of which were painted deep red and perfectly manicured. She exuded an air of sharp sophistication, her narrow face saved from plainness by well-shaped lips, and eyes with irises so dark they were almost black. Like falling into a well, Grace thought, before hauling herself back from the brink. Rita's hair was also black, and cut in a (genuinely) chic bob, the opposite of her own tow-coloured tufts.

Looking at Rita's immaculately made-up face, it was obvious to Grace that she was the kind of woman who bought lingerie not undies, a woman who would not be seen dead in a cheesecloth shirt and velvet flares. It made her aware of the gulf between them and of how Rita was the embodiment of femininity in a way that she could never be. Not that she aspired to such an embodiment, yet, paradoxically, it made her feel inferior.

'And shorthand,' Elizabeth added. 'Simon will be pleased about that.'

Elizabeth's reference to shorthand jolted Grace from her reverie about Rita. She gave a strained smile, remembering the shorthand discussion with Marigold. It was stressful enough to pretend she could touch type fifty words a minute when she struggled with twenty. How could she possibly get away with claiming to know shorthand? *Just scribble away*, Marigold had said. As long as she got the gist of it, everything would be fine. There was no need to transcribe each and every word. Including shorthand in her application was essential.

The interview unfolded with neither Rita nor Elizabeth questioning the fake resumé. Nor did they ask any difficult questions, scarcely focusing on the job at all. To her surprise, they didn't mention the first-class English literature degree. Instead, they spent the time plying her with questions about Down Under. Had she ever been bitten by a snake or a redback spider? What crimes had her convict ancestors committed? She hadn't finished telling them that her ancestors were not convicts, when Rita began to imitate her accent, despite Grace's certainty that she'd managed to get rid of it. There were even some people who'd been surprised to learn she was Australian. Admittedly, it was not people but a person – Ingred – who was unfamiliar with Australians and guessed that she was South African, which, because of Apartheid and the risk of being taken for a racist, was actually worse.

'G'day cobber. Fair dinkum,' Rita said, hooting with laughter. 'Don't give me the raw prawn.'

Elizabeth laughed too. They were finding the whole thing hilarious. Grace wanted to tell them that nobody used words like that, and the phrase was *don't come the raw prawn*, not that anyone she knew had ever said it. But she was feeling crushed and couldn't bring herself to say anything. Eventually Elizabeth must have seen the look on her face.

'Sorry, Grace, we're just teasing,' she said.

'You've got the job,' Rita added. 'If you still want it.

In an attempt to retrieve some self-respect, she almost refused and had to remind herself that she was already in debt to Marigold and could not ring home for more money. They wanted her to start next week as Elizabeth had been ordered to rest. Friday was her last day.

On her way home the humiliation of the interview faded, and she began to look forward to regaling Marigold with her success and how impressed they'd been. How she'd blown them away.

Annie and Raymond were in the kitchen.

'Did you get the job? Annie asked.

'Think so,' Grace replied, brushing the enquiry aside. 'Have you seen Marigold?'

'She went out. Didn't say where.'

'You know how she is,' Raymond said.

There was nothing unusual about people coming and going, staying with lovers, or getting out of it and needing a bed for the night, or, in the case of Alan, visiting parents. Things like that were taken for granted. Raymond was alluding to the way Marigold never revealed where she was going or when she would return. There was no reason why she should, but it created a coolness towards her, a perception that she didn't quite belong. Grace suspected she had a lover and wished Marigold would confide in her. She wanted to be supportive and prove her loyalty, while at the same time, she didn't want the lover to exist and was relieved that, thus far, he was only a figment of her imagination.

Gerald considered Marigold's secrecy an affront to the spirit of Beltonia and one more black mark against her. *Back to the family bank,* he sneered, and it was true that she seemed to have more money than a part-time translating job suggested. Grace wished Marigold would defend herself. Instead, she said she couldn't care less what anyone (particularly Gerald) thought. She was impervious to the opinions of others. It made Grace feel ashamed of her own weakness, always changing her views to fit in with everyone around her.

With Marigold not there to share the news about the job, she wished she hadn't been so monosyllabic with Annie. Unable to change course and gush about her success, she waved away the offer of tea and went upstairs to change out of her velvet flares. The day was already quite hot.

From the pile of clothes on the floor, she retrieved a pair of orange-tinted jeans that had been hacked off at the knees and which Linda, the previous occupant of the room, had left behind in the bottom of the rickety wardrobe that nobody had wanted because of the way its doors swung open at random. Vanessa was sure there was a poltergeist at work, despite Marigold pointing out that the floor sloped and the catches on the wardrobe doors barely functioned.

Early in the summer, Grace had joined the others in the garden where Marigold had noticed she was wearing Shanti's cut-off jeans.

'Who's Shanti?' Grace had asked. 'I thought you said they were Linda's.'

'They were. She changed her name.'

'Oh?'

'She joined the Orange People and went off to the ashram in India.'

Grace looked at her blankly.

'Sannyasins. Followers of the Bhagwan.'

Marigold explained that Bhagwan Shree Rajneesh was an Indian guru whose followers wore orange clothes, hence, the name Orange People (and the reason for the unsuccessfully dyed, orange-tinted jeans). Grace had a vision of shaven-headed devotees in red and yellow robes, dancing and chanting, banging their drums along Bourke Street in the centre of Melbourne.

'You mean like the Hare Krishnas?'

'No. The Rajneeshis are into group therapy and fucking,' Marigold explained. 'Not that I'm against fucking. It's the Bhagwan posing as god on earth that I object to. I tried to warn Linda. Americans are so naïve.'

'Yeah, absolutely,' Grace had said, ignoring the fact that she'd never met any Americans.

Now, once again wearing Linda-Shanti's cut-offs, she returned to the kitchen to find Annie and Raymond gone, replaced by Gerald who was frying bacon and eggs.

'Want some?' he asked. 'Don't worry, you can have half. Not like last time.'

He laughed and she found herself laughing too, the awkwardness of the dhal encounter banished.

'You need to eat before we get stuck in.'

'Get stuck into what?'

'There's a squat needs the floors fixing.'

He put the frying pan on the table and grabbed two plates. The smell of the bacon was making her salivate. Since the demise of the pigs everyone except Gerald had given up meat. The pigs had been nurtured in the communal garden as part of a self-sufficiency thing, until the trauma of killing the first one had converted them to vegetarianism. The second pig, perhaps sensing its impending fate, had escaped. It was rumoured to have been stolen by the gypsies camped under the railway arches, although everyone agreed you couldn't really say stolen, as the pig was on the loose.

'Rough Stuff are sending a family over tomorrow. Up from Manchester, with two kids.'

Without thinking, she picked up a rasher of bacon and popped it in her mouth.

'Knew I could count on you,' he said, as if eating the bacon meant she had agreed to help him.

6

She dragged another load of rotting floorboards into the back yard. The garden was overgrown with thistles and weeds and the long, purple-flowered spikes of rampant butterfly bushes. The fence in between had collapsed, and the house next door was derelict and empty, the garden wild with weeds and suckered elms thrusting up through middens of rubbish.

After dropping her rotting load onto the heap they'd created, she returned to the front room and watched Gerald pulling nails from the boards he'd collected from skips in streets where the houses were not empty and derelict, and where people were renovating at huge expense. He had tied his shoulder length hair in a ponytail to stop it dangling over his face. A week after Marigold's experiment with the dressmaking scissors, Grace's own locks were still tufty. She wondered if Gerald would ever go bald, which reminded her of an article she'd read in a magazine. Given a choice between a small penis or baldness, most men chose the former. The survey results had been a revelation; she'd always thought men were obsessed with the size of their dicks.

Gerald looked up from his work and a rush of heat scorched her cheeks. She had the unnerving sense that he'd caught the drift of her thoughts.

'Come on, he said, 'stop lazing about and help me.'

He showed her how to lay the boards and nail them to the bearers. Her first efforts were hopeless, bending the nails and leaving gaps between each board, so that she had to jemmy them up and start again.

'You're gripping the hammer too tight,' he said. 'Relax, let it do the work.' He took it from her and banged in a nail with two blows. 'See, easy does it.'

Before long, she got the hang of it and worked her way across the room, finding a rhythm, extracting old nails from the bearers, slotting the boards into place and hammering in the square-headed flooring nails. If weighted right, they slipped in smoothly with a few well-aimed blows. She liked the feel of the hammer in her hand, the heft of it, the easy swing, the sound of hammer hitting nail. Doing things that were the province of men was exhilarating. *Formerly the province of men*, she corrected herself.

'You're almost as good as a man,' Gerald said, which got her hackles up until he laughed. 'Got you,' he teased. 'I know Marigold thinks I'm a sexist shit.'

'You are a bit,' Grace said, and laughed too.

After that, he began to talk about himself. He had grown up in Sheffield where his father and uncles worked in the steel mills. He couldn't stomach the thought of a life like his dad's.

'That's why I came up to London. All my mates went to work at the rolling mill. In a few years, they'll be married with babies, whole lives planned out, forty years in the factory and a gold fucking watch at the end of it, bodies wrecked and living on fuck all. That's if they're not made redundant and chucked on the scrap heap.' He sat back on his haunches, facing her. 'See, everything changed for me when I discovered Marxism. Blew my mind. Showed me the reality of what's happening.'

'What do you mean?' she asked.

'It's just a matter of time before the state collapses,' he said, explaining how six months ago, the miners had gone on strike, cutting off the coal supply. And how, in response, the Tory government had introduced a three-day working week to save electricity. For two months, the power went off every evening. The poor copped it as usual, old people and kids froze, and workers got laid off without pay.

'That prick Ted Heath blamed the miners' union when all they wanted was a decent wage.'

Grace tried to imagine the whole city of London in darkness, lit only by candlelight, and wished she'd been there.

'Sort of like the Blitz,' she said, having heard the stories of London in wartime.

'The point is,' Gerald went on, ignoring her interruption, 'squatters like us adapted. We're used to having no services.' It led to a general election and the Tories got dumped. But he had no time for the new Labour government. 'They've thrown a few quid at the miners to buy them off for a while. But change is coming. A revolution,' he said.

She felt a shiver of excitement and had a fleeting image of herself on some kind of front line, striding into battle. 'Does that mean you're a communist?'

He shook his head. 'I never joined the party. Too much sitting on my arse at meetings, passing resolutions. I'm more of an anarchist.'

'Doesn't being an anarchist mean you want to abolish the state?'

'Is that right?' he said with a grin. 'You're an expert on it then.'

'I mean, what about The Free Republic? The constitution. Marigold says—'

'I don't give a tinkers what Marigold says. You should think for yourself, Grace.'

He spoke lightly, which almost made it worse, his words hitting their target. She wanted to protest that it wasn't true, to retaliate with a cutting remark that would turn the tables. When nothing came, she changed tack.

45

'Why do you hate her?'

'I don't hate her. I just don't trust her.'

'About what?'

'Who is she? What do we know about her? She's not one of us.'

'What do you mean? What are you talking about?'

He shook his head and leaned forward, pulling her towards him until their lips collided. His tongue pushed into her mouth and a wave of pleasure rippled through her body.

Back at their squat, Gerald led the way along the dimly lit, ground floor passage. She waited while he fiddled with the lock on his bedroom door, feeling anxious, no longer in the grip of the spontaneous kiss. That he had a bedroom door at all was the exception. Only he and Marigold had doors.

'What if … you know, privacy?' Grace had asked at her first Friday night dinner, disturbed by the possibility of being interrupted in the middle of having sex or even while immersed in a compelling novel. To which Gerald had replied that privacy was the obsession of the dull middle classes, making her feel that she might as well have been decked out in twinset and pearls – an outfit she'd once worn with an air of insouciant sophistication, or so she'd imagined. To cover her blunder – the privacy one, not the twinset – she'd laughed, pretending that her question had been ironic.

'I thought you said privacy was dull and middle class,' she said, to distract herself from mounting anxiety.

'I did, but I don't want undercover agents snooping around,' he replied.

'Undercover agents?' She couldn't help sounding sceptical.

'It's not a game. They know we're a threat to them. To the whole system.'

'Isn't that a bit paranoid?'

'You don't get it yet, Grace. There are things in here that would incriminate me.' The things, he explained, included equipment like crowbars and bolt cutters for breaking into squats, mailing lists of squatting activists, and a gestetner machine for printing flyers and leaflets – the same leaflets about which Marigold was so scornful.

'How would undercover agents be snooping around?' she asked.

'They infiltrate. Turn up with a cover story about being homeless so they can join a squat. All the time they're gathering information to bust us. That's why we need to be careful. Check people out.'

'Did you check me out?'

He laughed and shook his head. 'Of course not. You're Australian.'

There was no time to decide if she felt disappointed or pleased, before the lock turned and he pushed the door open, beckoning her to enter.

A naked bulb dangled from the ceiling, illuminating a skein of cobwebs. The walls were painted black, and on the floor lay a double bed mattress with a scrunched-up duvet. A faint, inky smell emanated from the gestetner machine, but it wasn't unpleasant. She watched as he lit two candles on the windowsill. He'd boarded up the window after members of the National Front had hurled bricks through it, shouting death threats and slogans about *England for the English* and *Blacks out, Jews out, Fags out*. It had happened before her arrival, but she'd heard the story more than once. The National Front were the favoured stand-over men for firms of private bailiffs who couldn't be bothered getting the proper court orders authorising evictions. So far, their forays into Beltonia had been limited and sporadic, just enough to create a climate of uncertainty and fear.

Once the candles were lit, he switched off the light, plunging the room into semi-darkness. The feeling of being in a cave intensified and she had to suppress a flicker of claustrophobia. He put a record on the turntable, crossed the room and sat down on the mattress where he began to unlace his boots. In the background, Leonard Cohen began to sing about half-crazy Suzanne.

'Come and sit down,' Gerald said.

She took off her sandals and joined him on the mattress. He told her she was beautiful which had the effect of making her feel like an object. The sexual desire that had surged through her body on that initial kiss had fizzled out, she felt closed up and there was a buzzing in her head. She offered no resistance when he kissed her again and let him peel off her clothes, wishing she could give in to the feeling of his naked body against hers and be swept away. Instead, she was besieged by a torrent of agitated thoughts. Were the sheets clean and when was her last period, had she forgotten to take the pill, did he use condoms, or should she risk it? What if she got pregnant? She'd have to get an abortion. If only she could relax and abandon herself to his caresses and the feel of his springy cock pressing eagerly against her thigh.

He moved down under the duvet, his tongue circling her nipples and she felt her vagina clench in response. At last, her body was responding. Yet her mind continued to whirr. What if a candle caught fire? Or the National Front thugs returned? Were there really undercover cops living amongst squatters, spying on them to undermine the movement? Why did she feel so tense, and how could anyone enjoy sucking a penis? She would refuse to do it, even if he begged. God, what was wrong with her? She gazed up, remembering the cobwebs she'd glimpsed hanging from the ceiling. What if a spider dropped down on them in the middle of having sex?

'I think we should turn on the light.' She grabbed Gerald by the hair as his head descended past her belly button. 'I need to see.' Her voice had taken on a panicky tone.

'What's wrong?' he said, emerging from under the duvet.

'I'm sorry, I can't stay.'

'What? Why?'

She scrambled up and began to pull on her clothes.

'What have I done?' He sounded almost plaintive.

'It's just … urgent.'

Avoiding his outstretched hand, she grabbed her sandals and stumbled towards the door. As she blundered down the dark hallway, she wondered how she could ever face him again.

Curled under her sleeping bag and the eiderdown left behind by Linda who had become Shanti, she allowed herself a rare moment of secret rebellion against the Beltonian privacy ethos, and wished she had a door to lock. The thought that Gerald might come looking for her was too awful. What could she say? It was impossible to explain. She pulled the bedclothes up around her neck and closed her eyes, convincing herself that he wouldn't come. Going round and round in her head was the knowledge that there was something wrong with her.

Even as she tried to resist it, a memory insisted. A falling-down student house in Carlton, people crammed into every room, the music thumpingly loud and everyone getting drunk on cheap booze. She was drunk too, and Isaac Hayes was blasting from the stereo. Now and then the needle jumped as old floorboards flexed under the weight of heaving bodies. Along with others, she spilled into the back yard, a barren, concrete square with a Hills Hoist in the middle and an outside dunny in a timber lean-to at the boundary fence that in spring was covered with jasmine. The heatwave was in its third day; it was after midnight and the cool change had not arrived. Everyone was dancing. The girl, whose name she did not know, was never to know, grabbed her hands and then she was dancing too. They twirled and turned and shimmied and she felt exhilarated. The girl pulled her in close and murmured something in her ear. Before she could disentangle herself, they were kissing, the girl's body clamped to hers and she could feel the heat of the stranger's body and how they were soldered together, groin to groin and she thought she was going to pass out because they were kissing for so long and because she had turned to liquid.

The music suddenly stopped, and they fell apart – *cleaved in two* were the words that came into her head. A male voice called out *lezzos,* and she saw Frank, whom she'd gone out with a few times, staring at her. *Go on, root,* Frank yelled, the cry soon taken up by others. *Root, root, root.* The girl screamed that they were misogynist dickheads and sexist pigs.

Inside, someone put on Ziggy Stardust and turned it up, drowning out the vile chorus.

She was not a lesbian. A lezzo, like her old headmistress, Miss Moore, with her cap of iron-grey hair and severely cut suits. A butch dyke like Stephen in *The Well of Loneliness* – that doomed love story she had wept over in her final year at school. Stephen, the freak of nature, neither man nor woman. Why had Stephen's parents named her Stephen? Surely, it was tempting fate. Two years later she watched *The Killing of Sister George* at the university Union Theatre, sidling into the back row to avoid being seen, ready to pretend she'd thought it was some kind of mystery murder story. The film was even more depressing than *The Well of Loneliness*, and far creepier. Sister George was a repulsive, raging alcoholic and her lover, Childie, wandered around in a frilly nightie.

'Oh, for god's sake,' she muttered to herself under Shanti's eiderdown. 'It's not like that anymore.' Everything was different now. There was a Women's Liberation Movement and lesbian feminists who were nothing like Stephen or Sister George. In her final year at university, she'd watched from the side-lines as female students began to hold meetings, demanding that the men who ran the Student Union give up their positions of power. Suddenly, everyone was reading *The Female Eunuch* or pretending to, and Germaine Greer was interviewed on television. The patriarchy was oppressive; it was time for women to wake up and demand freedom and equality. Grace absorbed the ideas in a superficial way, convincing herself that she was already free, living her life exactly as she pleased. She couldn't admit to the contradiction – that she was only free to be straight.

Home for the holidays, her father teased her. Had she burned her bra, and was she one of those women's libbers? Provoked, she declared herself a feminist, while back on campus, she kept her distance. There were too many lesbians involved, and unlike Stephen and Sister George, they were all the more terrifying for being real.

No, she couldn't bear to be gay, even if things had changed. Thank god she wasn't a dyke. The thought of a *life lived in the shadows*, a phrase she'd read somewhere and never forgotten, filled her with horror. Though she had kissed that nameless girl, she couldn't be held responsible. The girl had given her no choice.

In the morning, Grace helped Vanessa henna her hair, applying the hot paste, before wrapping her head in tin foil to speed up the process. They sat at the kitchen table, smoking, waiting for it to take effect.

'If you want, I'll do it for free,' Vanessa said.

'My hair?' Grace replied.

'No, silly. The reading. Your chart.'

At the party Grace had said she would think about it, secretly dismissing the offer. She had decided that believing in astrology was stupid. But the Gerald debacle and the memory of the unnamed girl's kiss, had shaken her. She almost wanted Vanessa to be right and that her astrological chart would reveal the truth about her. If it was written in her chart she'd have to accept it.

'Okay,' she said. 'But I don't really believe in it.'

Ignoring Grace's scepticism, Vanessa gathered her instruments, including pens and paper, set square, compass, and an ephemeris – a book recording the placement of the planets in the zodiac for years past, present and future. Drawing up a chart turned out to be much more complex than Grace had imagined. The positions of the sun, moon and all nine planets had to be determined according to the time and place of her birth. She tried to look interested as Vanessa pored over the sheet of paper on which she'd drawn a wheel divided into twelve segments with various markings and squiggles that represented planets and the signs of the zodiac.

'We need to calculate the aspects. Squares, trines, and oppositions first, and then the minor aspects. I'll show you how to do it,' Vanessa said, apparently unaware that Grace had no interest in the mechanics of how to draw up an astrological chart and was waiting with growing impatience for what it could tell her about herself – the *coming to know who you are*, that Vanessa had promised at the party. Not wanting to dampen Vanessa's enthusiasm and risk the possibility of it being abandoned, she tried to appear keen, watching as angles were measured with a set square and a succession of crisscrossing lines were drawn from one squiggle to another. Meanwhile Vanessa kept up an authoritative commentary about the need for accuracy and how astrology was a science. The more Grace thought about it, the less likely it seemed that the position of the planets at the time of one's birth could reveal anything about anything. She didn't voice her doubts, holding on to her hope that something important was going to be revealed, reminding herself that Jung was a believer.

'You're all air and water,' Vanessa said finally, her brow furrowing.

'Really?' Grace replied. 'Air and water.' She couldn't help thinking of the expression *all piss and wind*. It was something she'd heard her father say.

'And look, a trine linking Saturn, sun, and the moon. Interesting. And a square here. And here.' She pointed at a few places on the chart, shaking her head and looking concerned.

'A square. Is that bad?'

Vanessa didn't respond and continued to pore over the chart and the various aspects and angles which were important and revelatory, though it was unclear of what. Now and again, she sighed and look troubled. A few times she smiled and nodded to herself. The moon in the fourth house was interesting and there was the issue of the twelfth house too – it was significant. As Vanessa droned on about the various houses and the ascendant and midheaven, Grace stopped listening, her thoughts drifting to Gerald, and how she'd stuffed things up. If only she hadn't panicked. Should she ask Vanessa to see what the chart said? Was he right for her? Except she didn't want to reveal anything; she wanted her chart to do the revealing without having to tell Vanessa.

'So, what do you think? Grace?' Vanessa's voice had an exasperated edge.

Grace smiled and gave a sort of half nod.

'Does that mean you'll come? I need a definite answer. Places are limited.'

'I'm not sure,' she began, meaning to confess that she hadn't been listening.

Vanessa didn't wait to hear the rest and declared that she'd already decided, she was putting Grace's name down for the weekend encounter marathon. It was going to change her life. 'No arguments,' she said firmly. 'It's obvious. I can see from your chart.'

There was no opportunity to argue or even to ask what such an event entailed for they had forgotten about the henna, which had been on for hours. After unpeeling the tin foil, Vanessa dangled her head over the kitchen sink while Grace filled saucepan after saucepan with water, rinsing the clotted paste from her hair. The henna had taken spectacularly. Vanessa's hair was vermilion.

7

After three days, Grace admitted to herself that the thrill of working for a vanguard publishing company had waned. Since her arrival, all she'd done was sit at her desk in the reception area outside Mr Vandenberg's office. He'd gone to Scotland to sign up an author and she had yet to meet him. So far, there had been no letters to type and three days had passed without a single telephone call. It was increasingly strange and, at the same time, a relief as the mini switchboard looked complicated. She worried that as a professed *self-starter* and *experienced Girl Friday*, she was meant to take the initiative and get on with things. The question was, what things? Rita hadn't provided any instructions and was ignoring her. As usual, she'd gone out to a meeting and Grace had no idea when she'd be back.

From the downstairs office of Eric, the pale and reedy graphic designer, came the sound of a Genesis album. She'd met Eric on the first day, when Rita had given her a whirlwind tour of the building and some brief information about the company. They had only recently begun publishing books.

'One, as a matter of fact. About to publish, I should say,' Rita had added, 'if the manuscript ever arrives,' going on to explain that Primo Press designed and sold posters. Reproductions of album covers and original psychedelic art, transformed into posters with Eric's design skills. The stock was kept in a South London warehouse where Basia, the Polish bookkeeper, oversaw the mail orders and liaised with selected outlets. Grace now understood the bestseller comment about the fox-woman poster that had puzzled her at the interview. It wasn't, as she'd assumed, the cover of a novel. But what did it all mean for her position as Girl Friday with a vanguard publishing house?

'Simon … Mr Vandenberg,' Rita quickly corrected herself, having instructed Grace on how she was to address him, 'has a vision for expansion. Literary fiction and so on. Your speciality,' and she gave a rather dismissive wave.

Grace had nodded in a casual way, attempting to disguise the pressure she felt at the words *your speciality*. Her reading was voracious and indiscriminate, including quite a lot of literary fiction, but hearing it named as her speciality was unnerving. It was one thing to discuss *The Alexandria Quartet* with her mother or argue over who was the better writer, Charmian Clift or George Johnston, (which wasn't really an argument as they both adored Charmian) while deadheading roses and hanging out the washing. It didn't make her an expert like a person in possession of a first-class degree in English literature. She was only the Girl Friday. Surely, they wouldn't expect her to provide critical analysis. Even so, she couldn't help feeling uneasy about her fake degree.

She closed her eyes, deciding that sleep was preferable to enduring another minute of boredom. At university, she'd perfected the knack of dozing through lectures undetected by cupping her chin in one hand, elbow on the desk, the other hand pressing the tip of a pen against the open page of her notebook.

Just as she was drifting off, a door banged and heavy footsteps pounded up the stairs. Her eyes snapped open and on impulse she grabbed the telephone. If the footsteps belonged to Mr Vandenberg, she didn't want him to find her sitting idle.

'Yes, right away,' she said. 'I'll get onto it straight away.' She scribbled the words *straight away* on her notepad as a burly, bear-like figure with a thatch of straw-coloured hair, loomed into view. He strode past her desk, wrenched open the door to the office and stepped inside, closing the door behind him. Just as she put down the phone, the door opened, and the bear peered out.

'Who are you?' he said, glaring at her.

'Grace. I'm the—'

'Where's the other one?'

'Gone ... to have a baby.'

He frowned, looking rather put out. 'If anyone calls, I'm not here.'

'What time should I tell them to call back?'

'Irrelevant. I'll still be out.'

'But what if it's urgent?'

'What happened to your hair?'

Instinctively, her hand flew up to smooth ruffled locks that no longer existed. She had temporarily forgotten the disaster of her hair, lulled into forgetfulness by the English custom of avoiding personal comments – a custom her new boss apparently disdained.

'Oh, nothing,' she said, immediately wishing she'd thought of something witty to say as it was obvious that something had happened to her hair and saying that nothing had happened made her seem stupid.

The bear moved towards her with a laugh, his paw extended in greeting.

'Simon,' he said, squeezing her hand in his big mitt.

'Grace,' she said, flustered, remembering too late that she had already told him her name.

'Ah, like the American princess.'

'Mm,' she replied noncommittally. It was true that she'd once loved her name, half-believing that she was a princess too, whose true identity would one day be discovered. By the time she was a teenager she thought it was old-fashioned and prissy. It was her mother's fault. After all, she was the one who'd chosen it. Only, she didn't want to think about her mother when her new boss was looming inches away.

She let her eyes skim over his face, noticing the plump redness of his lips which, for some reason, she found unnerving. He was at least thirty-five. She'd expected him to be wearing a suit instead of baggy brown corduroy pants and a King Crimson t-shirt. The black leather jacket she'd glimpsed a moment ago must have been discarded in his office. After waiting for him to say something else or leave she broke the silence.

'I hear you've been in Scotland.'

To her dismay, she heard the upward inflection on the word Scotland, turning her conversational statement into an Antipodean question. Under pressure, her newly acquired English accent had collapsed.

'I have,' he replied.

She smiled, waiting for him to continue, inwardly squirming from his scrutiny. 'Is something wrong?' she managed to ask.

'Nothing's wrong, Grace-with-the-mouse-chewed-hair. Nothing at all.' And with a laugh, he departed back to his den.

With only a door and a few dozen feet separating them, snoozing through the afternoon was no longer an option. But sitting at her desk with nothing to do was making her anxious and she wondered if Rita had returned from her meeting. It was time to confront her and demand a proper job description or, at the very least, some verbal instructions.

Finding Rita's office empty, she went downstairs, pausing in the doorway of Eric's work room, where he was perched on a high stool at his graphic design desk like a clerk in a Dickens novel. Stevie Wonder's *Innervisions* had replaced Genesis and was pumping from the state-of-the-art speakers. At least a hundred LPs were lined up in an open shelf above the turntable. Against the opposite wall was a sleek black leather couch and in front of it, another glass topped coffee table, identical to the one in the interview room. She knocked on the open door to let him know she was there.

'Have you seen Rita?'

'Gone to the warehouse,' he replied, turning towards her. 'Come in. Have a fag,' he said, and held out the packet. 'Make yourself at home.'

She sat down on the leather couch. Eric lit her cigarette and returned to his stool. He said nothing, content to observe her which had the effect of making the smoking of her cigarette feel exaggerated and awkward. For the second time that morning, a man was subjecting her to an inspection. She tried to think of something to say to deflect his attention when he got in first.

'So, are you or not?'

'What?'

Eric poked out his tongue and waggled it at her. He began to giggle.

'I don't understand what you mean,' she said, unable to prevent a peevish tone from entering her voice. She didn't want to offend him. It was far too early to make enemies, especially given the Rita situation. Stevie Wonder stopped singing and instead of answering her question, Eric leapt off his stool and bounded across to the turntable.

'What do you want to listen to?' He began to flick through the row of albums.

'Anything. I should probably go—'

'What about Janis? He began to sing the Mercedes-Benz song in a fake croaky voice while removing the album from the inner sleeve and placing it on the turntable. At the sound of Joplin's anguished rasp, he returned to his stool. She could feel him looking at her again. It was time to make her escape.

'Thanks for the cigarette.' She stood up.

'You know what Rita thinks?'

'Rita thinks what?' interrupted a voice behind her.

'Come in,' Eric called, 'we were just talking about you.'

Rita swished past and sat down on the couch. She picked up the packet of cigarettes on the coffee table, extracted one and clicked her fingers at Eric. After he'd lit her cigarette, she looked from one to the other.

'Well?'

'I was about to tell Grace why you thought she was the right person for the job.'

'Oh, shut up Eric. I wouldn't take any notice of Eric if I were you,' Rita said. 'He's a congenital liar.'

'Am I?' Eric replied.

He giggled and Grace tried to laugh too. She felt out of her depth.

'I'm glad you find it funny,' Rita said sharply.

'Sorry,' she replied, and before Rita could direct anything further at her, gave an apologetic grimace and muttered that she had to get back to work. 'Things to do,' she said, and hurried from the room, aware that the abrupt announcement of her departure would have done nothing to improve her standing.

She picked up the phone and held it to her ear, ready to pretend she was busy, in case Rita suddenly appeared. Almost at once, a light flashed on the control panel. She put down the receiver with the result that the telephone began to ring. Someone was finally calling Primo Press. Now that it had happened, she felt panicky and had an overwhelming resistance to answering it. But her frayed nerves couldn't stand the insistent sound and after a few seconds she grabbed the receiver from the cradle.

'Hello.'

'Hello,' a surprised, sonorous male voice replied. 'Is that Primo Press?'

'Grace Manners, Primo Press,' she said, pulling herself together.

'Ah, Grace Manners,' the man repeated, as if he recognised her name. 'Pop me through to Mr Vandenberg, please lovey.'

'Who, I mean, whom shall I say is speaking?'

'Max Meier.'

'I'm very sorry Mr Meier, Mr Vandenberg is not in.'

'Call me Max, lovey. Well, how about you knock on his door, pop your head in and have a butchers, because I think you'll find he's there. Let him know I'm on the blower and need a word.'

'But Mr Meier … Max—'

'I know, puss, he said not to disturb him and if it wasn't urgent, I wouldn't ask you, but it is. Believe me, lovey, it is. All I need is a quick confab.'

She resented being addressed as lovey and puss and would have said it was not acceptable if she hadn't been off kilter. Added to which, it was her first task as Girl Friday and she didn't want to bungle it.

'Hold the line, please, and I'll check to see if he's returned to his office,' she said, adopting an official tone. She crossed the room and knocked on Simon's door.

'Not here,' came the *basso profundo* response.

'It's Mr Meier,' she whispered loudly, face pressed up against the door, so that Max could not hear her. 'He says it's urgent.'

There was no reply. She stared at the door. Did she dare open it and relay Max's message?

Sliding into her chair, she picked up the receiver. 'I'm very sorry Mr Meier, I've checked. Mr Vandenberg is not in his office. Can I take a message?'

A long, disappointed sigh ensued.

'You've let me down Grace, I expected you to do better than that. Never mind. I want you to tell Mr Fatberg that if I don't have his

60

cheque on my desk by early next week, I'm going to nail his bollocks to the wall. I'm going to ruin him. Have you got that, Grace?'

'Yes Mr Meier.' In some part of her brain, she registered that he had abandoned *lovey* and *puss*.

There was a click, followed by the buzz of disconnection. She put the phone down. Max had uttered his threats in the same charming tone with which he had conducted the rest of the conversation. Nevertheless, it was as if she'd been physically roughed up. Attempting to write an edited version of his message on her note pad, she discovered that the pen had a life of its own and skidded across the page. After the second attempt, she gave up. The possibility of another phone call was making her feel ill. She needed to escape, but where to go, given she had already fled from Eric and Rita? The kitchen beckoned as a temporary refuge. She stood up just as Simon's door flew open.

Oh,' she blurted, 'Max, Mr Meier rang.'

'Time for lunch, I'm ravenous,' he said. 'Make sure you get a decent brie this time. The last one wasn't ripe. And some fresh figs if he's got any.'

She felt increasingly at sea. This time? He?

'Where's Rita?'

'With Eric,' she replied, pleased that this was a question to which she had an answer.

'Go on then, off you go.'

'I'm not sure—'

'Gretel, isn't it?'

'Grace,' she responded, feeling annoyed that he had already forgotten her name and that he'd chosen to replace it with the unattractive Gretel.

'Well, don't be dim, Grace, ask Didier.'

Who and where was Didier? Not wanting to appear dim, she resisted the urge to seek further information. She would have to risk it and hope for the best, by which she meant that there would be somewhere to buy brie – whatever that was – and figs, even if she couldn't find Didier.

'French deli across the street,' he called after her. 'Turn left, walk one block. You can't miss it.'

Out on the street, she turned left as instructed and walked for a block to arrive at *La Figue de Barbarie*. The Barbarous Fig, her attempt at a translation, was an odd name for a delicatessen however a glance through the glass shopfront was enough to convince her that she'd come to the right place.

Two sleek blonde creatures pushed their way out as she entered. Behind the long counter stood a portly middle-aged man sporting an extravagant moustache.

'Monsieur Didier?'

'At your service,' he replied.

Grace explained that she was the new Girl Friday at Primo Press and had come to buy lunch. Didier knew exactly what was required and began to gather the various provisions. He was out of fresh figs, and she had forgotten already the name of the other thing. She suspected it was a cheese.

'Eight pounds, fifteen p, and some free *poires*,' Didier said, presenting her with a large brown paper bag filled with French delicacies.

'Eight pounds, fifteen p,' she echoed, feeling stunned by how much a bag of French provisions cost, followed by the even more alarming realisation that she had less than two pounds in her purse. Keen to avoid any more accusations of dimness, she'd rushed off without thinking of payment.

She made a show of scrabbling in her bag.

'Oh gosh, I must have left my purse—'

'Ha,' he interrupted, 'no need for the acting, he has sent you without the money, *oui*?'

She stopped her fake ferreting and gave a shame-faced nod.

'*D'accord*. Tell him I am waiting. Tell him I am a patient man but patient men, they have their limits.'

She took the proffered bag of provisions. 'Thank you very much Monsieur Didier, I'll make sure I tell him.'

First Max Meier, and now Didier. Were they, she wondered, the tip of the iceberg?

8

Like Rita, Simon was often out, which meant Grace could give up the charade of busyness. Instead, she dozed or went downstairs to visit Eric. Occasionally, she made forays into Simon's office, one ear cocked for the sound of the front door. A large desk dominated his room; the walls decorated with psychedelic posters, including one of Jimi Hendrix, rocking out in a green suit, splashes of colour exploding behind him. Books, comics and magazines were crammed into a tall bookcase. The overflow lay in piles on the floor, along with poster tubes, a few crumpled articles of sports clothing, two squash rackets, a baseball glove and other miscellaneous items. Among the books, she discovered half a dozen novels by the writer J. G. Ballard and while his visions of global catastrophe freaked her out, she couldn't stop reading them. Ballard's dazzling yet disturbing tales of apocalyptic breakdown seemed like a warning of what was to come, the first signs already visible on London streets where mountains of uncollected rubbish seethed with rats, and boarded up, rotting houses were everywhere.

Although addictive, the novels of drowned and drought-plagued worlds left her feeling disconnected and in need of human contact, of whom Eric was the only option. From time to time, she wondered if he really was a congenital liar and what he'd been about to tell her

– why Rita had chosen her for the job. She felt unable to ask, afraid that the answer would be insulting as it was increasingly obvious that Rita considered her quite worthless. Eric appeared to have forgotten about it and she decided against bringing it up. He'd begun to call her on the internal line, wanting her to make him coffee, and demanding cigarettes from the off-licence. Marigold told her she had to draw the line somewhere.

'Nip it in the bud or you'll end up as the office drudge.'

'Easy for you to say,' she'd replied, aware that the description was rather too apt. Even so, it had helped to motivate her, and she told Eric that from now on he could get his own coffee and cigarettes.

'I'm not the office drudge,' she said.

She had decided he was rather creepy. His tendency to giggle and the way he looked at her, turning his head and angling his eyes upwards, the hint of a smirk on his lips. It made her suspect he was imagining her in the nude. But was he? Perhaps she was being unfair, misreading his body language and projecting something onto him that wasn't there. And what did it matter anyway? She needed company.

'You know Simon's married, with a horde of brats,' Eric said. 'Not that it stops him.'

'From what?'

Eric gave her a look. 'Come on Grace, you're not that naïve.'

She frowned, put out that she had appeared naïve, while casting her mind over the exchanges she'd had with her boss to date, searching for signs of undue interest on his part. There were none.

'I don't think we should gossip.'

Eric responded with his trademark giggle. 'Yeah,' he drawled, 'wouldn't want to tell tales.'

After a few seconds, she capitulated. 'What's his wife like?'

'Tall, sexy. Dangerous. Marina, she comes in sometimes.'

'What do you mean dangerous?'

'Just don't get on the wrong side of her.'

'Why would I?'

'I don't know. Why would you?' he said, widening his eyes at her in an irritating way.

She had meant her question to be a clear indication that she had no intention of getting on the wrong side of Marina. Simon was her boss; she wasn't interested in him. Annoyingly, Eric had chosen to misinterpret her, as if, once again, she'd been naïve.

The front door banged, rattling the windows, and loosening the ceiling plaster. A shower of fine white particles fell like icing sugar onto Marigold's magenta velvet dress – the one she'd made weeks earlier from a curtain and which she'd been wearing since the sudden onset of chilly autumnal winds and plunging temperatures. She was lying on the couch, listening to Grace.

'Then she said, and I quote, *I'm not here to hold your hand. It's up to you to prove yourself.*'

'Well—' Marigold began.

'I can't ask Simon because I've acted like I know what I'm doing. It's too late. And he's never in and when he is, he's rushing off somewhere. You have no idea what it's like. Making Rita a coffee every morning, then going out to get the lunch things and sorting the mail is not a full-time job. It's not what I expected. I'm dying of boredom.'

Grace had been pacing around the room as she spoke. After pushing Marigold's feet out of the way, she slumped down on the end of the couch. Their conversation was taking place in the communal front room, where the companion curtain to Marigold's dress had been tacked across the windows. It was not wide enough, leaving a draughty gap on either side.

'If you're so bored, why don't you resign?'

'I can't resign. I haven't been paid.'

'That's ridiculous. You've been there for more than a month.'

Marigold sat up, shaking plaster dust from the folds of the curtain dress. Her chestnut hair, which she'd wound into a knot and fastened with a broken chopstick, had come loose, tumbling over her shoulders in a dishevelled tangle. 'You can't let it drag on,' she said. 'It's not your fault you've got nothing to do. He's obliged to pay you.'

She made Grace promise to speak to Simon at the earliest possible opportunity. 'That means tomorrow,' she said.

Simon didn't appear in the office until the early afternoon, by which time Grace had given up practicing her request to be paid and was reading *The Drought*. She heard him pounding up the stairs and shoved the book in the desk drawer.

'My office. Dictation,' he called, striding past her.

She watched him disappear, aware that the hour had finally arrived and now, more than a month into the job, she was about to be revealed as an imposter. Dictation meant shorthand.

With pen poised over her open notepad she waited for him to begin. He lit a cigarette and took a puff.

'A letter to Max Meier,' he said.

She shot him a look, suddenly remembering the phone call from her first week, when Max had threatened to ruin him and nail his bollocks to the wall. She had never relayed the message.

'You know he—'

'My dear Max,' he began, speaking over her. 'If you're going to quote Shakespeare at least have the decency to get it right. *Neither a borrower nor a lender be* is from *Hamlet*, not *The Merchant of Venice*. And you, good sir, *are a most notable coward, an infinite and endless liar, an hourly promise breaker, the owner of no one good quality.*'

She scribbled furiously as he rattled off a further volley of insults from Shakespeare before turning to the 'bogus claims' which he utterly and comprehensively refuted, and which, if not abandoned, would be put in the hands of his solicitors. References to previous correspondence and the ins and outs of the dispute between them continued in rapid succession. It was all to do with money and what was owed or not, and the agreement between them, the terms and conditions, and Max's unreliability, not to say treachery. It was impossible to keep up and she soon lost the thread, the marks in her notepad turning into a hotchpotch of meaningless symbols. She continued to make random squiggles, flicking over successive pages of her notepad with a flourish, feeling powerless to put an end to the performance and admit that she was out of her depth. She was still scratching away when she realised he was no longer speaking and that it was quite possible he had stopped some time ago. After a final dotting of an imaginary i, she closed the notepad and looked up.

He was observing her.

'Cigarette?'

He held out a packet of Gauloise Bleu from which two cigarettes protruded. She took one and leaned forward for him to light it. His fingers brushed hers and she couldn't prevent the twitch that jerked the cigarette away from the flame. She noticed that he had noticed and how they both pretended not to. He leaned back in his large leather chair, his t-shirt riding up to reveal a strip of pale rounded belly, covered in gingery fuzz. Strangely, she didn't find the sight of it repulsive, though in her discombobulated state, she hardly knew what she thought or what she was feeling.

'So how are you finding us?'

'Great.'

'Rita's filled you in?'

'Yes,' she lied.

'Excellent,' Simon said.

He looked at her in an intense way with the promise that he had more to say, which he did. 'Off you go then.'

She turned on the typewriter, pushed the paper release lever and fed in a piece of paper, snapping the lever into place. The humiliation of his summary dismissal continued to rankle. She'd been caught off guard by that intense look, only to be shooed out like a child and resolved that, next time, she would get in first and announce her departure before he was ready. It crossed her mind that the next time might be her last and opened her notepad with a sinking feeling. How on earth was she going to type up the letter to Max?

Marigold had said that fifty words a minute was the bare minimum for a Girl Friday, doubling the actual speed Grace had attained during the four-week course she'd attended in Melbourne after graduating with her less-than-stellar arts degree. She'd been at a loose end that was drifting into depression and immobility and although she had no intention of ever working as a secretary, she had taken up her mother's offer to pay for the course. It was something to do, while waiting for the future to arrive.

It had been ages since she'd typed anything and was alarmed at the sensitivity of the electric typewriter. Letters doubled and tripled with disconcerting rapidity under the pressure of her stuttering fingertips, forcing her to begin again. After multiple attempts she was able to complete the first sentence without mistakes, followed by the quote from *Hamlet*. At that point her shorthand had descended into random scribble, confronting her with the problem of what to write next.

The afternoon was slipping away, the wastepaper basket filling up with error-ridden pages. She was beginning to feel desperate. Her approach in trying to replicate Simon's longwinded ramblings was a dismal failure. She cast her mind back to the discussion with Marigold. What had she said? Not to worry about the actual words and to get the gist, which in this case was Simon's assertion that he owed Max nothing. That was it; she had to focus on the gist. The fewer words she used, the less opportunity there'd be for typing errors. It was time to be ruthless.

At five-thirty she knocked on Simon's door. There was no reply and imagining what Marigold would do, she entered and briskly crossed the room, aware that a cursory perusal of the letter would reveal its brevity. Worse still, it was apparent that the correction tape had been in high usage. The single typed page was grubby.

She reached his desk where he appeared to be asleep, arms folded, and chin slumped towards his chest. She put the letter down and began to beat a hasty retreat.

'Wait!'

The single word rang out and she lurched to a halt.

'Do you always do what you're told?'

'Do you?' she heard herself say, turning to face him.

'Touché.'

He laughed and reached across the desk, seizing the letter and, to her astonishment, signed it without a glance.

'Stay for a minute. Unless you've something urgent to do,' he said.

She squinted at him, unsure if he was being ironic. If so, he was disguising it.

'Come, sit. So, you're from Oz. Love the place. Are you a Sydneysider? My first visit to Sydney, James took me to King's Cross and got me stonkingly drunk.'

'No, Melbourne.'

'Ah, marvellous Melbourne. Not that I've experienced it. Next trip, you must show me around.' He jumped to his feet, surprising her with his agility. 'How long has it been, Grace? A month? More? Either way, we should mark the occasion.' He opened the cabinet next to the bookcase and returned with two glasses and a bottle. 'A wee nip,' he said, pouring a generous tot into each glass. 'Bottoms up.'

In less than a minute, she had downed two glasses of the delicious peaty whisky.

'Tell me then, how are you finding our fair city?'

'I love it.'

'Not homesick?'

She shook her head.

'Got yourself a nice little bedsit?'

'Actually, I live in a squat,' she said, disappointed that he saw her as the kind of girl who would live in a nice little bedsit. To emphasise how far removed she was from that kind of boring individual, she told him that they were experimenting with new ways of living; the family was repressive, and they had rejected bourgeois individualism.

'Anyway,' she said, trying to wrap it up because it was becoming garbled, 'it's like a community.'

'A commune,' he said.

'Sort of. We don't call it that.'

'What do you call it?'

'The Free Republic of Beltonia.'

'Ah,' he said. 'And is there free love in the free republic?'

'Love is never free,' she replied, in a moment of inspiration.

He laughed and told her she was a breath of fresh air and that with a decent haircut she could turn heads.

'Don't grimace, I'm serious,' he said. 'We're going to shake things up, you and I. So, tell me, what have you been reading?'

'You mean, novels?'

'Exactly. Novels. I'm relying on your expertise and youth to get ahead of the pack, break new ground. Capture the zeitgeist.'

For the life of her, she couldn't remember a single thing she'd read except for the Ballard novels which she was reluctant to mention, not wanting to reveal that she had been raiding his room.

'Barbara Pym.' The name popped out before she could censor it.

'Never heard of her. That's why you're here. Someone up to the minute.'

'I mean, not Barbara Pym now. Before, when she was, you know, ahead of the pack. She's not ahead anymore.' Why on earth had she mentioned Barbara Pym? Her mother claimed *Excellent Women* was brilliant and very funny, but it was written ages ago and set in the past. It wasn't even something she'd read. A novel about a clergyman's daughter sounded horribly dull regardless of her mother's enthusiastic recommendation.

'Alright, if you say not,' he replied, looking a little surprised at the vehemence with which she'd declared Pym to be out of bounds.

'I meant someone else,' she said.

'What do you think about sex?' he enquired.

'It's, um ... it's good,' she mumbled, flustered by his rapid change of topic. She wasn't expecting to talk about sex and remembered Eric's warning. Her cheeks felt hot.

'No, no.' He laughed. 'Think of Lady Chatterley. Upper class totty with her bit of rough. The publishers made a bomb even though most people only ever read the steamy bits.'

'I didn't realise all you wanted to do was make money,' she responded, determined to claw back some ground.

'I didn't say that. But if we can ...'

'It's just that Rita said literary fiction.'

'Did she indeed?'

'Yes.'

He was smiling at her, and she returned his gaze, feeling surprisingly relaxed and confident. That it was a result of the whisky and not some radical transformation of her personality, escaped her notice.

'As a matter of fact, I've been sort of wondering ...'

'As have I,' he said with a sly grin.

'... about my job.'

'Ah. Your job. Have you ever been to the Frankfurt Book Fair?'

'No.'

'Time you did. We'll aim for that.'

If the telephone hadn't rung, Grace was positive she would have been able to speak about the job and that she wasn't sure what she was meant to be doing and it had probably just slipped his mind, it was not a big deal, except that she hadn't been paid. However, the telephone did ring, and she couldn't let it go unanswered.

As it turned out, it was only Basia from the South London warehouse with a query about a mail order, and though she'd missed the chance to ask for her wages, Grace was heartened, feeling that she had made a good impression on her boss, and that he liked her.

9

Her bedroom was freezing. She wrapped herself in Shanti's ancient eiderdown and lay down on the bed, intending, once warm, to go and find Marigold. Goose down escaped through one of many holes and tickled her nostrils. She wondered what Shanti's parents were calling her now and whether they knew where she was and what she was doing. She imagined telling her father that she'd changed her name and was a devotee of an Indian guru. Imagined his shock and incomprehension followed by ridicule and derision. He would never understand her. Hadn't they always come to grief? It was unbearable. Why was she tormenting herself when she had no plans to become a sannyasin? Why tell him anything?

She sat up and reached for her tobacco pouch when Marigold sauntered in and threw herself down on the mattress.

'Gosh it's cold.' She grabbed the ancient eiderdown, releasing a cloud of goose down into the air. 'Honestly Grace, this thing is moulting. You need to get rid of it. Roll me a cig, will you?'

As Grace went to work on the cigarettes she noticed that Marigold looked different. 'Why are you wearing those clothes?' she said.

'What's wrong with them?' Marigold wrapped the eiderdown around her shoulders.

Instead of her artfully designed homemade clothes, she was dressed in a pair of baggy woollen trousers and a navy-blue jumper that was unravelling at the neck. Russet hair sprang out from under a black beret. Grubby sandshoes completed her outfit. Grace knew that similarly dressed she would have looked drab and poverty stricken whereas Marigold could have been the star of a French film about occupied Paris. A partisan. Or a black marketeer like Violette Leduc, two of whose novels she'd found on Clara's bookshelf and devoured during her last year at university when she should have been studying. *My mother never gave me her hand* was the first line of one of those novels and at odd times it popped into her head and sometimes she couldn't get rid of it for ages.

'Nothing's wrong with them. It's not what you usually wear, that's all.'

'Marigold, Grace,' Gerald's voice boomed from the bottom of the stairs. 'Come on, hurry up.'

'Oh fuck,' Marigold groaned.

'Hurry up, we're waiting,' Gerald yelled again.

Marigold jumped to her feet.

'Coming Gerry,' she shouted, making a face.

Grace smiled in complicity, knowing how he hated to be called Gerry, yet unable to rid herself of the feeling she'd betrayed him. It made her remember that she had never told Marigold what he'd said. How he didn't trust her, and she was not one of them. Not telling her was also a betrayal. Since that day in his room, she and Gerald had avoided each other, and she had tried not to think about what had happened.

'What are they waiting for?' she asked.

Marigold was halfway down the stairs and didn't reply.

They entered the kitchen, where the funky smell of hash hung in the air. Martin was smoking a joint. On the table, a Tilley lamp flickered, the sole light source since the local electricity board had disconnected them two days ago. Vanessa had reconnected the rest of the house in an illegal and ingenious manner, learning her skills from her ex-boyfriend Terry. It meant they were not paying anything, but the wiring in the kitchen had gone wrong and she'd yet to fix it. In the eyes of the law, they were stealing electricity. Gerald said the law could get fucked; it was only there to protect rich cunts. Marigold continued to correct him – they were rich pricks.

Grace squeezed past Gerald who was standing in the doorway with an impatient, coiled energy. She had expected everyone to be there, but Martin and Ingred were the only ones sitting at the kitchen table. Martin took another puff on the joint and handed it to Ingred who passed it straight to Grace who sucked the hash-laden smoke into her lungs, holding it for as long as she could, enjoying the sense of her body dissolving at the edges, her head floating. Ingred was so straitlaced; she didn't know what she was missing. The joint continued to circulate and after taking a puff Marigold offered it to Gerald. He shook his head.

'You should relax,' she said, 'you look nervy.'

'I'm not nervy,' he replied. 'Why the fuck would I be nervy?'

'I don't know,' she said with a laugh. 'Maybe you're scared.'

'What are you on about? You're talking shite.'

As usual, they couldn't resist sniping at each other.

'Right, let's get on with it,' he said, addressing everyone.

'Get on with what?' Grace asked Martin.

'The break-in. Gerald's staked out an empty house.'

'And if we don't get in now, we'll be too late,' Gerald said. 'The council's started sending in goons. They're smashing up places so's they can't be squatted. Fuckers would rather destroy everything than let people have a roof over their heads.'

Discovering that they were about to conduct a break-in, Grace regretted her enthusiastic puff on the joint and wished she had copied Ingred by passing it on without indulging, her head suddenly spinning with panicky images of squatter-bashing thugs wielding iron bars. It wasn't just paranoia – Gerald had friends who'd been beaten up and thrown out of their squat in Brixton. She tried to listen as he outlined the plan and issued instructions. There was an unlocked window on the first floor that could be reached with a ladder, one of which he'd left against the rear wall on his initial reconnaissance visit.

'Soon as I've climbed in I'll open the front door,' he said. 'That way, the cunts ...' he glanced at Marigold, '... pricks can't do us for criminal damage.' It was a conciliatory correction.

By the time they reached the end of the street and turned the corner, excitement began to overtake Grace's trepidation. Her breath quickened, alert to every sound and sensation: the smell of wood smoke drifting in the air, the drone of the traffic on the overpass and the rustle of their clothing as they walked, the dull thud of their footsteps. The street they'd entered was dark and deserted, some way ahead a single streetlight blinked and flickered, summoning up lines from a poem –

Half-past one,
The streetlamp sputtered,
The streetlamp muttered,

– and she was transported to a stuffy classroom, sweltering in summer heat while Mrs Murchison read T. S. Eliot aloud, giving them a glimpse of another world. Now, here she was in that world, or at least, in London, on a mission to break into an abandoned house, part of a movement fighting for squatters' rights, resisting the fascist capitalists and the National Front. It was all rushing through her head, while conscious of the fact that she was glorifying her role. At best, she was an accidental participant. Distracted by this insight she stumbled on the uneven footpath, bumping against Ingred who, instead of the censorious glance that Grace expected, grasped her by the arm, steadying her.

'Sorry,' Grace whispered.

'Okay, this is it.' Gerald, who had been leading the way, stopped in front of a terrace house at the end of a row of identical houses. 'Wait here.' Having issued his instructions, he slunk down the side lane.

'Wait here,' Marigold repeated, mimicking Gerald's tone. 'Seriously, why do we let him get away with it?'

'We must unite,' Ingred said.

Grace was about to ask her what she meant. Did she mean we, the women, must unite, or we must all unite with Gerald, but there was no chance to speak. The front door was already opening.

Ingred entered first, shining her torch. Marigold and Martin followed with Grace shuffling behind them as they picked their way along the passage, avoiding the gaping holes where floorboards had rotted. The smell of mould was overpowering, and she was beginning to wish that she hadn't volunteered to stay the night, consoling herself that Marigold was staying too.

'We will sleep here,' Ingred announced, shining her torch into a downstairs room, empty except for a three-legged chair.

They left Gerald fixing a new lock on the front door and set off back to their squat for candles, blankets, and a double bed mattress. Time was of the essence because Gerald couldn't stay for long – there was a meeting in Brixton and he was speaking. Marigold said it was typical of him to bugger off, which was ironic given how often she was the one who went missing. Grace waited for one of the others to say something, but nobody did.

On their return, lugging the mattress and assorted things for their overnight stay, Gerald reminded them of the need for a round-the-clock presence.

'If the council turn up and nobody's here, they can board it up and evict us. It's a legal technicality.' That he hadn't organised for new squatters to move in straight away seemed like a flaw in the plan. 'Cheers, then,' he called, loping off down the street and into the darkness.

Grace and Martin dropped the mattress on the floor of the temporary bedroom to an explosion of dust. It swirled into the air, covering them in a sticky layer.

'I said not to drop it,' Ingred scolded.

'Why didn't you carry it then,' Martin replied.

Grace sat down on the mattress and wrapped a blanket around her shoulders. She watched Ingred arrange the candles on the mantlepiece and window ledge. The flickering yellow flames softened the bleakness of the room but could do nothing to relieve the cold which had infiltrated the foundations.

'Just remembered something,' Marigold said. 'Sorry.' She gave an apologetic wave and vanished into the hallway.

'Where are you going?' Grace called, getting tangled in the blanket as she tried to rise. 'Are you coming back?'

'Soon,' came the faint reply.

'She will not,' Ingred said, adding in a sardonic tone, 'Like Gerald.'

'Yes, she will,' Grace countered, unable to prevent a sinking feeling.

'Doesn't matter. There'll be more room on the mattress,' Martin said, sitting down beside her.

He took out his tobacco pouch and extracted a ready-made joint. Ingred was shining her torch through the window.

'What're you looking for, Ingred?' asked Martin. 'Come and huddle up with us.'

'No thank you,' she replied.

'Is there someone out there?' Grace asked, nervously. She was thinking of the National Front thugs who'd thrown bricks through Gerald's window. Ingred didn't answer and left the room.

'Now they've both gone,' Grace said.

79

Martin shrugged and lit the joint. After a few drags, he held it out and she took it, despite her earlier misgivings. They lay side by side under a mound of blankets, passing it between them until the roach burned her lips. She had accepted that Marigold was not going to return and wondered where she'd gone, feeling hurt that she hadn't confided in her. It was stupid to feel like that. No one was beholden to anyone. They were free to do whatever they wanted, and Grace didn't want to be constrained by anything either. Their friendship existed on a pendulum of intimacy and distance determined by Marigold, and she wondered why she gave her that power. Was it because she didn't want to cling? It was too close to fawning. *I don't want you fawning over me or thinking I'm marvellous because I'm not*, Marigold had said.

Ingred's candles began to gutter and the flickering shadows on the ceiling provoked the unflattering idea that she was a moth to Marigold's flame, fluttering in her orbit. Which made her think of their first meeting and the torching of Joel's hair. What if he'd caught fire and been seriously burnt? Had Marigold even thought of that? God, she had to stop worrying about things that hadn't happened and remind herself of how tender-hearted Marigold could be. The unofficial guardian and defender of stray cats, no matter how mangy and flea-bitten. Stray cats and stray people too, like Vincent, the mad violinist who frequented Beltonia and slept rough in the shell of a house in a nearby street. She looked out for him, leaving food on his doorstep, and giving him money. *Charity is the guilty conscience of the rich*, Gerald said. *It changes nothing.* Which Grace thought was probably true, but so was the fact that Vincent needed help.

A single candle continued to flicker, setting up a vibration in her chest. The joint she'd smoked with Martin was stronger than expected. She closed her eyes, wishing the buzzing sensation would stop, and that it was Marigold lying beside her and not Martin. Marigold, with all her confusing contradictions, her secrets and mystery. The tremor in her body quietened, and she began to sink down towards sleep, through layers of memory, of people and places.

Fitzroy, and a ramshackle double-storey Victorian mansion with a leaking roof and a dozen bedrooms inhabited by a floating population of university students. Her official address was a women-only university hall of residence, insisted upon by her parents, against her pleadings and lamentations. The friends she'd made there had abandoned college for shared student houses at the end of the first year, leaving her with the homely and studious, the girls who still wore cardigans and knee-length skirts and joined madrigal groups and debating societies; who never got pissed or smoked dope or participated in demos and sit-ins; who believed in the value of a university education. The same university education to which Grace gave barely a thought as she threw off the shackles of her boarding school years, intoxicated by new-found freedom.

In her third year, even the minor restrictions imposed by the college felt unbearable. Clara came to her rescue, inviting her to camp at the Victorian mansion; there was usually a mattress going spare. And if the spare mattress was already taken, they slept together in Clara's bed, which meant talking most of the night, getting stoned and laughing like loons. They talked about everything, except the one thing Grace couldn't say. Sometimes Clara stayed with her boyfriend Mike, and Grace had the bed to herself.

Clara was calling herself a feminist by then, and so was Grace, but only because her father had teased her, whereas Clara was serious about it. She went to Women's Liberation meetings and tried to get Grace to come too. She didn't understand Grace's reluctance and Grace couldn't explain.

Clara, she really missed her. She wanted to write, find out what she was doing now. But she'd made up her mind. She was starting again, reinventing herself, and had to be ruthless.

Perhaps she sighed then or made some kind of small movement that encouraged Martin to speak.

'Are you awake?' He turned towards her. 'Grace, are you awake?'

She felt his breath on her face as she struggled to the surface. 'Mm.'

'Have you ever fucked in public?'

'What?'

'You know, at a party, or in a train.'

'What are you talking about?'

'Fucking, in public.'

'With people watching?'

'Right under their noses but nobody sees. They haven't got a clue.'

'No.'

'You should try it.' He spoke in a dreamy monotone, almost as if he was talking in his sleep.

In the silence that followed, she reflected on the fact that she'd never had a proper conversation with Martin. She knew he was into a personal enlightenment thing and attended weekend courses at a centre in north London. Whatever it entailed, it was unlikely to involve fucking in public places.

'Nobody expects it, so they don't see you,' he said. 'We only see what we expect to see.'

'Why bother if nobody sees you?'

'But they might. That's the point. The risk. The excitement. Sex without risk is boring. Honestly Grace, you should try it.'

She tried to imagine a public place where she would be prepared to have sex. Not with Martin, who was too skinny and had the wrong smell. He was not her type. What did that mean? What or who was her type? An intangible quality, a vibe that would tell her, this is the one. She'd hoped Gerald might be it. Maybe he was and she should try again. She wanted to be swept off her feet, to fall madly in love. What did she know about love? It seemed to strike people at random and in strange configurations. Annie and Alan for example. She was a busker, and he had that job with computers. They seemed to have nothing in common.

How did Martin find girls who wanted to do it, she wondered? Were they in love with him? Did they fuck standing up, ready to make a quick get away? She had never had sex standing up. Once, at an anti-Vietnam moratorium in Melbourne, she'd become wedged in the crowd and a man had stuck his hand up her skirt and goosed her through her underpants. The crowd was so tightly packed that she couldn't get away, couldn't even move her arms to fend him off. She'd been trapped and unable to stop him. Telling Clara about it later, she questioned why she hadn't shouted for help. Or yelled at him to stop. And then wished she hadn't told her anything because Clara just looked at her and said she didn't know in an ironic voice, as if the answer was obvious. Grace understood it as a message that she was weak and if she'd really been a feminist, she would have told the man to fuck off.

A few weeks later she began to think about it while masturbating. Getting off on it was disgusting, but she was powerless to change the tape in her head and remembering this now, she experienced an unwelcome kinship with Martin. Were they both perverts?

'I wonder where Ingred is?' she said, desperate to distract herself.

Martin didn't reply. He had fallen asleep. She closed her eyes and waited for sleep to claim her too.

She woke to feel him curled against her with his arm draped across her body. She pushed him away, fumbling for the torch beside the mattress and after switching it on, peered at her watch. It was five past eight and still dark.

'What time is it?'

At the unexpected sound of Marigold's voice, she gave a yelp of alarm, flashing the torch onto the shape in the bed that ought to have been Martin.

'Fucking hell,' she cried. 'What are you doing here? Where's Martin?'

'You were dead to the world, and he woke up and wanted to go home, so I took his place.'

'But you left. You were gone.'

'Oh ye of little faith. Come on, get under the blankets before you freeze.'

'Little faith is all you deserve,' Grace said. She lay down and let Marigold tuck the blankets around her neck.

'I know. It was the thought of being squeezed onto the mattress with Martin and Ingred.'

'Ingred left after you.'

'She must have come back because I almost stepped on her. Can you believe she slept on the floor?'

'Shh, she'll hear you,' Grace whispered.

Marigold assured her that Ingred had already gone home. 'It's always coldest just before dawn,' she said, snuggling into a more comfortable position.

'Don't you mean darkest,' Grace said to cover the pounding of her heart.

'Hmm, maybe you're right,' Marigold murmured. 'I think I might snooze for a bit.' She fell asleep in seconds, leaving Grace unable to move for fear of waking her, thankful for the layers of clothing between them. Far from being cold, she was burning up.

Dawn – the real not the metaphoric one – had broken by the time Gerald returned to check that all was well. The new squatters were due to arrive later in the day. Until then, someone had to hold the fort.

'Right then,' he said, 'I'll leave you to it.'

'No, you won't,' Marigold said. 'We've done our bit, it's your turn now.'

He protested that he had things to do and couldn't spare the time, but Marigold was insistent. They had things to do too and there was no use him arguing that his work was more important because, frankly, she did not give a shit.

'Cheers then,' she called as they departed, echoing his words of the night before.

10

They arrived home to a kitchen buzzing with activity. It was Saturday when breakfast continued for hours as people drifted in and out. Alan was stirring a pot of porridge on the hob, while Annie fried eggs, and Martin buttered the toast. Soon, Raymond arrived with a bag of croissants from a recently discovered French bakery. Ingred made a brief appearance from her dark room, pouring herself a cup of coffee only to disappear again. Terry, Vanessa's ex-boyfriend wandered in, naked except for Vanessa's Japanese bathrobe which floated out behind him, revealing everything.

'I thought you'd split up,' Martin said.

'Except for sex,' Annie commented with a wry grin.

Later that afternoon, Grace agreed to be Marigold's dressmaking dummy which meant standing still, draped in pieces of black and green tartan as Marigold measured and pinned. She was part-way through making a cloak from a swag of material salvaged from a charity shop. Afterwards, they were going to see a film at the Gate cinema. As she maintained her pose, Grace let her eyes wander, taking in the messy vibrancy of the room. Clothes and pieces of material overflowed a tattered armchair and spilled onto the floor beside an old Singer sewing machine. A cracked mirror leaned against the wall and, near the window, a pot plant sat on a plinth of bricks. A few dozen books were stacked in a pile beside the bed – the usual mattress on the floor. Perched on the mantlepiece, surveying its domain, was a bedraggled stuffed crow with a single beady eye, that Vincent had given to Marigold, and which she'd accepted so as not to hurt his feelings. Grace found the bird vaguely sinister, the way its eye always seemed to be staring at her.

'Finished,' Marigold announced. She helped Grace take off the cloak before rummaging through the pile of clothes on the armchair to find a coat and scarf. 'We should hurry,' she said, 'I don't want to be late.'

In Melbourne, Grace had seen the occasional film where comparing the style of one director with another had never occurred to her. In fact, she'd barely registered the director's existence. Marigold, on the other hand, was passionate about the cinema and had introduced Grace to the work of the major auteurs, criss-crossing London to see their films. Soon, Tarkovsky, Bertolucci, Godard and Bergman had become familiar names.

On the way to the Gate, Marigold explained that Z, the film they were about to see, was directed by Costa-Gavras, based on a famous novel by a Greek writer. It was a fictional depiction of events that happened in Greece in the 1960s, events which led to the downfall of the democratic government and the installation of a military junta.

'I saw Z when it was first released, and it's just as important now,' she said. 'You know the military junta was only deposed a few months ago.'

'Mm,' Grace said, implying, falsely, that she was au fait with the Greek situation. 'It sounds amazing.'

At the cinema they discovered that the screening had been cancelled. The projector had broken down. It was disappointing, and having taken the trouble to go out, they didn't feel like returning home straight away.

'Pub,' Marigold said. 'I'll pay.'

She was still paying for everything, and Grace vowed to herself that she would tackle Simon tomorrow. It could not go on.

They ordered pints of bitter and found a table for two in the corner. The pub soon filled up. Enclosed in their bubble, Grace was no longer disappointed about the cancelled film, barely noticing the crush of customers and rising babble of voices. A group of middle-aged women were singing, their table littered with bottles of Babycham. To make Marigold laugh, she turned her job into a joke, imitating Eric's creepy giggling and Rita's imperious manner. She made fun of herself too, miming her approach to Rita, cup of coffee in hand, like an obsequious butler from an Ealing Studios comedy.

Returning from the bar with another round of drinks she saw a man in a dark blue donkey jacket standing at their table, gesturing as if reprimanding or warning Marigold about something. They were involved in a heated conversation, and, curious to hear what was happening, Grace sped up. Just as she arrived, the man departed. As he brushed past her on his way towards the exit, she caught a glimpse of a saturnine middle-aged face.

'Who was that?' she said, sliding into her chair.

'No idea,' Marigold replied.

'What did he want?'

'A cigarette.'

'You looked like you were arguing.'

Marigold shrugged. 'He wanted a cigarette and I said no. That's all.'

'Oh, come on,' Grace said, emboldened by the alcohol. 'You weren't arguing about a cigarette. Why can't you tell me?'

'There's nothing to tell.'

'Why are you so secretive?'

Marigold frowned. 'What are you talking about?'

'Well, for a start, you're always going off for days and never say where. And you never talk about your family. I don't even know if your parents are alive. I hardly know anything about you, and you know everything about me. And Gerald told me he doesn't trust you,' she added, a strategy designed to distract her from the obvious untruth of the last statement, because Marigold did not know everything about her. Not at all.

'I'm devastated.'

'He thinks you're not one of us.'

'One of us? Which us? Are you one of us? I don't even know what it means.'

'Yes, you do. He says you're an aristo.'

'Oh, so I'm damned because I didn't grow up in a council flat and my father isn't a coal miner and my mother a domestic servant? He knows nothing about me.'

'That's the point. Neither do I.'

They stared at each other across the small table. Grace refused to look away.

'Alright,' Marigold said, a steeliness in her voice. 'You want to know about my parents. First of all, I've had nothing to do with them for years. They live in luxury and believe they deserve it. If you met them, I'm sure you'd find them charming, as long as you didn't get in their way. Because they're ruthless. They don't give a shit about anyone except themselves and their kind. I loathe everything they stand for.'

'What do you mean? What do they stand for?' Grace asked, thinking of her own parents, and feeling shaken by the ferocity of Marigold's speech.

'Upholding the system that allows them to profit while oppressing workers and ordinary people. I don't just mean British workers. I'm talking about the British Empire and its legacy. That's where their money comes from. Oh, they're very good at justifying their wealth, they even make contributions to worthy causes to keep up their benevolent façade. My parents and their kind are everything that's rotten about this country. Nothing will ever change until we get rid of them. In one way Gerald is right, I do come from privilege, but I've rejected it utterly.'

The conversation had gone further than Grace had ever imagined and, now that it had, she was consumed by a hunger for more. 'Where do you go then if you don't go home?'

'Friends. A surprise, I know,' Marigold said, with a grin, 'I do have them.'

'Who? That guy you were arguing with?' Grace asked, ignoring Marigold's attempt to lighten the conversation. She didn't want to be distracted. 'You knew him, didn't you?'

Marigold didn't reply. She seemed to be making up her mind – whether to speak at all, and if so, what to disclose.

'His name is Ed. We had a thing for a while.'

Her revelation was so surprising that Grace couldn't think what to say. Ed was old and ugly. In her mind's eye, she saw his dour angry face as he stalked past. How could anyone, especially Marigold, find him desirable? Was the thing they'd had, over? She was about to ask when Marigold turned the tables.

'Speaking of which, what's happening with Gerald?'

Too late, Grace wished she'd never mentioned how she found him attractive. 'Nothing,' she said with a shrug.

'Now who's the secretive one.' Marigold reached across the table and grabbed her by the hand. 'You must tell this Gerry, you are mine,' she said in a silly accent.

Grace knew she was fooling around to avoid further questions. She was avoiding things too, such as the way she'd bungled things with Gerald, and how the statement, *you are mine*, was like a silent bomb exploding inside her. She pulled her hand away with a smile and picked up her pint glass.

They left the pub, giddy with laughter and a little drunk. A cold wind stung their eyes, blowing them into a side street where the noisy bustle of Notting Hill was soon replaced by an almost eerie silence, broken only by the tattoo of their footsteps on the pavement. Grace had to force herself to slow down, to stop racing ahead of her friend who didn't seem affected by the fact that they were two women alone on a dark, empty street.

'Well then,' Marigold said, 'I've told you about my parents. Now it's your turn.'

'There's not much to say. They live in the country, on a farm. A sheep station. They're not enormously rich or anything. Not like yours.' She paused for a moment, remembering the conversation in the pub. 'I hate what they stand for too,' she added.

'Forget them, Grace. We don't owe them anything. They're utter bastards,' Marigold said, linking arms as if to cement their united front.

They strode on, buoyed by a shared contempt, while Grace thought of everything she hated about her parents, determined to convince herself they were utter bastards and that she didn't owe them anything. With Marigold by her side, the last vestiges of ambivalence soon subsided.

A block of flats loomed on their left and as they approached the entrance, a woman ran onto the street, closely pursued by a man. He caught up with the woman and pushed her against a parked van, shouting abuse. In return, the woman screamed at him that it was over, she was leaving him for good this time. The man began to pace in an agitated way, yelling and jabbing his finger at her for emphasis. Suddenly, he picked up a length of something from the gutter and swung it, catching the side of her head. She sagged against the van, and he raised his weapon again. On impulse, Grace stepped forward.

'Hey there,' she shouted. 'Hey.'

The man turned and she saw that the weapon was a piece of wood. Blood was running down the side of the woman's face, and behind her, Grace heard Marigold calling for her to come away, but she was already committed.

'Listen to me,' she said to the man. 'Put it down. She's hurt.'

She saw the wild look in his eyes, and it occurred to her that he was completely out of it and that she ought to be frightened. Instead, she took two more steps towards him, her eyes seeking his, knowing it was important not to threaten or scare him; that she had to speak evenly, without emotion, and continue without a break.

'Don't hit her anymore. You're angry now, but you'll regret it. You don't want to hurt her.' She went on repeating the same things, that he would regret it, that he didn't want to hurt her anymore. Whatever had happened between them, don't make it worse.

The woman's screams had turned to angry sobs, and the man had stopped pacing. His body twitched intermittently, as if afflicted by a misfiring electrical current. A kind of stasis had been reached. Grace continued to speak, telling the man that he was a good person; that everything would be okay. She didn't know how long she could keep it up when he dropped the lump of wood and, at the same instant, the woman bolted down the street. At first, it seemed he was going to go after her. Instead, he turned and lurched away though the entrance of the flats.

Now that it was over, Grace's legs felt shaky, adrenalin was flooding her body and her heart was racing. Marigold hurried to her side, grabbing her roughly by the arm.

'What the hell were you thinking?' she said. 'He could have killed you. Couldn't you see he was off his face? How could you be so stupid?'

'Sorry. I wasn't …'

'Oh, fuck,' she interrupted, 'I'm the one who should be sorry. You scared me. I really thought he was going to bash you.' She looked towards the entrance of the block of flats. 'Come on, let's get out of here before he decides to come back.'

They didn't speak again until they'd turned the corner and were halfway along the next street where, unexpectedly, Grace screamed. It was a release of tension and Marigold immediately joined in. Grace had faced the danger and stared it down, and like two madwomen, they whooped and shouted, not caring about the shocked glances from a passing couple. When they reached Belton Road, Marigold began to sing 'On the Street Where You Live'. Grace joined in, singing off-key in a silly voice on the understanding that it was a joke until Marigold said she was ruining it, and if she couldn't sing in tune she should shut up. Grace remembered how she'd sneered at her mother's fondness for Julie Andrews; how condescending she'd been. She was glad, then, that the street was dark, and that Marigold couldn't see her face.

'Sorry,' she whispered.

'Let's start again,' Marigold said, looping their arms together, 'from the top.'

They strode arm in arm, singing with gusto. Grace felt exhilarated. She was on the street where she lived and there was nowhere else on earth that she would rather be. And if (unlike the song) enchantment didn't quite pour out of every door, it didn't matter. She was singing with Marigold and life was glorious.

It was two o'clock in the morning. For hours she had tossed and turned, exhausted, her mind on an endless loop, going over and over the events of the evening. A jumble of thoughts and images that went from Marigold arguing with Ed in the pub, to the fight outside the flats, to singing on the way home and the feeling of being gloriously alive. How Marigold had said *you're mine*. It was a throwaway line, a joke, a way of side-tracking the conversation but Grace couldn't get it out of her head. And now, at two in the morning, the edifice of denial she'd constructed was crumbling. Like an unwanted, indestructible weed, the truth was pushing its way into the light.

She was in love with Marigold and had been for ages. It was hopeless because Marigold was straight, and even if Grace was not entirely straight, she was not a lesbian. But whether a lesbian or not, she was in love with a woman, and all she wanted was to be with

Marigold, to make love, whatever that meant between two women. Two women, but Marigold had said she was not gay.

That summer night when they'd been flâneuring, a few short weeks before the weather turned again. They'd walked for hours, coming home along Kings Road. Three women were standing outside a green door in a side street, smoking. At first, because of their suits, Grace had assumed they were men, until Marigold said they were not men, they were butches, and that the green door was the entrance to a famous lesbian club. She said she'd gone there with Shanti a few times because Shanti didn't want to go on her own. It was the first time Grace had heard that Shanti was a lesbian and was shocked at how off-hand Marigold was about it, like it wasn't a big deal. It had never occurred to her that Marigold too might be gay.

'I'm not gay,' Marigold said, as if she'd read her mind. 'A pity really, given how hopeless men are. We can go in if you want. It's very butch/femme, stuck in the fifties.'

'No thanks,' Grace replied. 'I'm not gay either.'

Marigold glanced at her.

'Oh, I have wondered.'

'Oh god no. I mean, it doesn't worry me. I just can't imagine … you know. I mean, I agree, men are pretty hopeless …'

'… but we're stuck with them.' Marigold finished the sentence for her and laughed. Grace joined in, hoping Marigold wouldn't notice how false it sounded.

They had almost reached the butches when she felt a change in the atmosphere, like the air preceding a thunderstorm. She could sense them watching and from the corner of her eye, took in their wide-legged, confident stance. The closest butch, one hand thrust in the pocket of her trousers, took a final drag on her cigarette before flicking away the butt. It flew into the air so that Grace had to swerve. The butch turned to her friends and laughed, a deep-throated sound that rumbled in the pit of Grace's stomach. She'd begun to walk faster then and had to stop herself from breaking into a run.

The image of the cigarette-smoking butch had stayed with her, no matter how much she had tried to forget it.

What torture it was to admit that she was in love, and that it was unrequited. Worse still, she was consumed with jealousy. All those times Marigold vanished for days to be with ugly old Ed. Grace was sure it was not a thing of the past and that she was still seeing him. And if not him, then it was some other guy. It was better to think it was Ed – she might have a chance against him. Hadn't Marigold said, *you're mine*? She'd been joking, but sometimes a joke was a way to hide the truth. Grace knew she was deluding herself. Marigold was not like her. She was not a coward. If she was a lesbian, she would say so.

As the hours passed, she began to convince herself that her love was not sexual or erotic. It was a love between friends – philia not eros, terms she dredged up from a lecture she'd attended in the first year of her arts degree, when she still turned up to such things. Philia, the love between friends, which Aristotle said was the highest form of love. A virtuous and loyal love. Wasn't this what she felt for Marigold? She was determined to think so, and holding onto it, she fell asleep at last.

11

T he afternoon mail had been delivered and Grace was slicing open the envelopes with a Venetian olivewood letter opener left behind by Elizabeth, the previous Girl Friday. The majority of the letters were mail order requests confirming, as Rita had revealed on the initial tour of inspection, that the business of Primo Press was not literary publishing but the selling of psychedelic art posters by mail order and in selected groovy shops. Grace was surprised how often the mail order letters contained actual cash rather than a cheque. Sometimes there were coins too, as if the senders had been saving their pocket money. Occasionally, she'd noticed a sweaty, adolescent boy smell mingling with the metallic odour of small change.

Given the boredom of her days and the lack of any meaningful work, the mail orders should have been a welcome distraction. Instead, she dreaded the task and was always procrastinating. More significant than her inability to remember the difference between an invoice and a receipt were the mistakes that crept in when counting the cash. On recounting, the final figures were subject to alarming variations. It was also her responsibility to consult the catalogue and make sure the order was matched with the correct code which, in theory, sounded simple. Sometimes, however, there was no such poster, and sometimes the code and poster didn't correspond. In desperation, there were times when she threw the order in the bin and used the money to pay Didier. There had been letters of complaint about missing orders, and she'd thrown them out too.

At the end of the week, everything was put in a canvas bag and taken across to the South London warehouse for the eventual attention of Basia who had rung her more than once about discrepancies. Grace worried that the bookkeeper suspected her of pilfering which, technically, was true. It was in a good cause (Didier) not that she could tell Basia.

She had almost finished opening the envelopes when the phone rang.

'Primo Press, Grace Manners. How can I help you?'

'Grace, how nice to hear your voice,' came the response. It was Max Meier, speaking in the same silky sonorous tones of his first call. Nevertheless, she was on guard, remembering the threats he'd uttered after she had failed to get Simon on the phone.

'I've had a letter from Simon, puss.'

She winced at the *puss* but let it pass.

'Unsatisfactory to say the least. I don't think he got my message, lovey.'

'Mr Meier, I'd prefer if—'

'Max. We're friends, aren't we?' He let the question hang for a second. 'You owe me a favour. Are you listening?'

'Yes.'

'Good girl. We should meet, Grace. I think we'd get on.'

She thought it was unlikely and didn't respond.

'Now, I want you to take dictation.'

'Don't you have a secretary ... or a Girl Friday?' she ventured.

'Puss,' he purred the word into her ear, 'there are circumstances of which it is best you remain ignorant. Listen to me, I'll make it worth your while.'

She was not seduced by Max's vague promise to make it worth her while. On the contrary, it sounded more like a threat, and yet she couldn't help a prickle of interest. What circumstances?

'Are you ready, Miss Manners?' Max cleared his throat. 'My dear Simon *comma*—'

She scrabbled for pen and paper, scrunching her head and shoulder together to hold the phone, knowing that she ought to hang up. *If he calls me puss or lovey one more time*, she said to herself, aware that this was nothing but a delaying tactic, curiosity having won out over scruples.

'I've reached the end of my patience *stop* I am prepared to take extreme measures that will bring down your house of cards *stop* Last chance you fat fucker *stop* Your faithful servant *comma* Max *stop*. Did you get that Grace?'

'Yes.'

'You're a treasure. You should come over to my side, I could use a treasure like you.'

It was obvious that he was already using her and that, in effect, she had already come over to his side, but she didn't say it. She had an urge to confess everything to Simon immediately. Another part of her was critical of him and believed he should be punished for not paying his creditors. She wasn't sure whose side she was on, despite Max's aggravating use of pet names.

'Type it up and sign on my behalf,' he instructed. 'My personal secretary, Jane Smith,' He laughed. 'I've promoted you, puss. Personal secretary.'

She said Jane Smith sounded like a fake name, but Max assured her that it was deliberate. He said nobody would make up a name like Jane Smith. He said she should trust him, they were in it together, which made her feel like changing her mind. It was too late because he had already put down the phone.

After typing up the letter, she followed the instructions Max had given her and signed on his behalf as his secretary, Jane Smith.

She addressed the letter to Simon and dropped it into the street pillar box with the rest of the mail on her way to buy the lunch provisions from Didier's. Not that she actually bought anything, it was still going on tick apart from the occasional contribution from the mail orders, which Didier said was a drop in the ocean. He was no longer giving her free *poires*. His patience was running out. She had discovered some time ago, that in English, the correct name of Didier's deli was The Prickly Pear after mentioning to Rita that she was going to The Barbarous Fig and did she want anything. Rita found it hilarious and enthusiastically adopted the new name, followed by Simon and Eric. The Barbarous Fig was destined to haunt her, a constant reminder of her colonial inadequacies.

The afternoon was interminable. She inserted a fresh piece of paper in the typewriter to distract herself from thinking about Max and what she'd done. Whenever it edged into her consciousness, she felt queasy. Nothing at Primo Press was turning out as expected. There was still no sign of the Scottish manuscript and her expertise on matters of a literary nature had never been called upon. Which in one way was good because she had none, having obtained the job under false pretences. She was a fake and was beginning to suspect that Simon was some kind of fake too.

She adjusted the paper and began to type, soothed by the gentle clacking of the machine and the magical appearance of crisp black letters. Seconds later, she came to an abrupt stop, her fingers sliding limply from the keys as she took in what she'd written. *Dear Mum and Dad, How are you?* Whatever she had intended to write, it was not this.

For weeks she'd put off going to the post restante office at Australia House where she knew there would be letters lying in wait from her mother. It had been ages since she'd scribbled a few lines on a postcard, telling her parents she was fine and not to worry. She was moving to a new flat and so best to stick to the Australia House address. It was tempting to reveal that the move was months ago, and that it wasn't a flat, it was a squat in the Free Republic of Beltonia, and her house mates were radical activists, astrologers and buskers who were creating a new kind of community. She imagined her parents' distress at the news and felt resentful. Why shouldn't she tell them the truth? Which, logically, meant sharing the news of her job at Primo Press too, a job that on the surface sounded reassuringly normal and was bound to please them. The thought of their approval was almost worse than imagining their distress. In the end, she had kept to the bare minimum, enough to let them know she was alive.

Betrayed by her fingers, her unconscious had spoken, unleashing a rush of guilt about her lack of communication, along with the sudden fear that uncollected letters from her mother might be returned to sender. Letters written to a version of herself that Grace had rejected and which she couldn't read without a sense of dread surging up; of feeling trapped by a web of associations to people and places from the past and of how she was perceived. The implied expectation that she would soon return, that she would fit in, become a teacher or take up some other respectable occupation, get a nice boyfriend, get married, have kids. It made her feel sick to think about it. The last thing she wanted was to be dragged into the past, that narrow world where everyone thought they knew her – her mother most of all. Who'd repeated more than once, *I know you better than you know yourself*. An infuriating assertion that Grace experienced as an unwanted invasion that might really be true.

But if reading her mother's letters filled her with dread, the consequences of them being returned were unpredictable and potentially worse. A missing persons poster with her face on it was too awful to contemplate.

The sun, a pale, sullen orb at the best of times, had already set when she left the office, bound for Australia House. Rita and Simon had gone out somewhere and were not expected back, and Eric said if

Grace wanted to go early, it was up to her. He didn't care one way or the other.

On the darkened street, she had an unexpected longing for blue skies and wide horizons. Skirting a tottering pile of uncollected rubbish – the bin men were on strike again – she spontaneously began to recite to herself the opening lines of a poem.

I love a sunburnt country,
A land of sweeping plains,
Of ragged mountain ranges,
Of droughts and flooding rains.

Tears welled up. She brushed them away with a vicious swipe, furious that her mind and emotions could betray her like this. She didn't want to long for Australia, and Dorothea Mackellar's famous poem, with its patriotic vision and romantic eulogising of the landscape was exactly the sort of thing she'd rejected. She knew every verse by heart and as much as she wanted to, could not un-remember it.

The tube station was in sight, and she sped up. The despised poem with its land of sweeping plains and droughts and flooding rains had made her think of William. He was somewhere in the vast Queensland outback, working as a jackaroo on a cattle station the size of Belgium. Since arriving in London, she'd dashed off the occasional postcard, to which he had not replied. Her brother was not a letter writer, and it brought a smile to her lips remembering his illegible scrawl – *the thumbnail dipped in tar* – like Clancy's shearing mate in the famous poem – not Dorothea's poem, but 'Clancy of the Overflow' by the bush balladeer, Banjo Paterson. It was William's favourite and as children, they had recited it to each other until it was indelibly imprinted. Another poem she was unable to forget. She imagined William somewhere out bush, on horseback, chasing scrub cattle at full gallop, whirling a stockwhip over his head. She saw him rolling out a swag and sleeping under the stars. He was two years younger than her. *My pigeon pair*, her mother called them. They had shared a childhood, a world. Now they inhabited separate universes.

She stood in the mail queue, eyes lowered, wincing at the sound of harsh Australian voices. Everyone carrying on about their latest travels, catching the Magic Bus across Europe to Greece and hanging out on the islands, living on the beaches, swimming naked every day and getting drunk on retsina. And from Greece, across to Turkey and Afghanistan and on to India. It seemed that the whole queue had arrived in London via India or was about to go there. Those who'd recently returned were easy to spot, looking half-frozen, their skinny, sun-browned bodies draped in flimsy, brightly coloured clothes, strands of beads around their necks and jangling bangles on their wrists. The two girls in front of her had jewelled studs in their noses and one had a faded red dot on her forehead. She couldn't help overhearing them going on about their gut parasites, and some weird fungal thing that had taken root in the pubic hair of the girl with the faded red dot. Apparently, it was worth the parasites and fungus because everything in India was so far out and so spiritual, even if there were beggars and dead bodies lying in the streets.

Grace had assumed they were friends, until she heard them exchange names. Janine with the red dot and the pubic hair fungus was from Brisbane. Cathy had grown up in Bendigo.

'At first it's awful seeing dead people but there's no such thing as death really,' Cathy said.

'Dharma, the wheel of life,' Janine responded, as if that explained why there was no such thing as death.

'The cosmic order,' Cathy added with a sage nod, just as Grace risked a sideways glance.

It was too late to look away. Janine was onto her immediately, introducing herself and wanting to know where Grace was from.

'London,' she replied.

'Yeah, but where in Australia?' Janine persisted.

'Melbourne,' Grace reluctantly admitted, adding, 'but I live here now,' determined to emphasise the huge gulf that separated her from them.

She had no desire for an extended conversation, but Janine and Cathy were so enthusiastic that she couldn't bring herself to freeze them out. They hung respectfully on her every word, deferring to her vast knowledge on everything to do with living in London. Before long she was telling them about the incredibly cool community of which she was a part. She boasted about breaking into empty houses to establish squats, and that she knew how to connect the electricity without paying a penny. Which wasn't strictly true, though Vanessa had offered to instruct her. The future was communal, they'd taken down all the back fences and had parties and bonfires and planned political actions like painting political graffiti in public places. In her descriptions, she was a leader although as she explained, they were against the concept of a single leader. 'We're all leaders now,' she said. There was no room for Primo Press in the world she described, and she didn't mention it. By the time they reached the head of the queue her life had become as thrilling as anything in a novel.

She waited as the mail sorter, an overweight woman with a fed-up look on her face, flicked through the letters in the M pigeonhole. Already, the bundle of letters from her mother was weighing her down, squeezing the life out of her. Why wouldn't her parents leave her alone? Couldn't they understand, she wasn't a child anymore? They were suffocating her. She was almost twenty-one and didn't need them. Her internal monologue was growing increasingly resentful when a single letter slid across the counter, cutting it short.

'Is that all?' she asked in disbelief.

The fed-up mail sorter ignored her and gestured for the next person to come forward. Grace was bustled out of the way, her surprise and shock at the lack of letters nothing compared to the next moment when, for the first time since leaving Australia, she saw her name written in her father's formal hand.

103

She turned from the counter to find Janine and Cathy waiting for her.

'I don't suppose ...' Janine said, looking hopeful. 'Just for six months, while I save enough money to go back to India.'

Cathy was looking hopeful too.

'We don't mind sharing,' she said, turning to Janine, who nodded her agreement.

One look at their pleading faces and Grace realised the folly of her boastful tales. The thought of them showing up at the squat and claiming her as a fellow Australian, of turning the house into a version of Earl's Court, was unbearable. In no time, the grapevine would go into action and there'd be dozens of Australians swarming down Belton Road wanting to have their London *living in a squat* experience before returning home to crow about it. Her situation was different – she was living there for real; she wasn't just dabbling in it.

'Sure,' she said, thankful that in her bragging, she hadn't said the name of the Free Republic, wondering what address she could give. All she could think of was Joel's, which not even her worst enemy deserved. Under pressure, she gave them the name of his street, and a house number chosen at random.

'I can't promise anything,' she said, desperate to be gone.

On the street, she shoved the unopened letter from her father to the bottom of her bag and hurried away, freaked out that Janine and Cathy might catch up with her. It was only when the tube doors closed and the train departed that she was able to relax, vaguely registering the recorded announcement that warned of unattended luggage and suspicious packages.

She hadn't always been so blasé. In the early weeks, new to London, the warnings had terrified her, every trip on the underground fraught with anxiety. She'd known nothing about the IRA. An Australian boy at the Earls Court Youth Hostel told her that the bombing campaign was part of their strategy to get rid of British rule in Northern Ireland and establish a united independent republic. There had been bombs at underground stations and places like Madame Tussaud's and Heathrow airport. People had been killed and no one could predict where it might happen next. That Londoners could live with such uncertainty and fear astounded her, until she discovered that her mind employed its own strategies – tuning out, turning down the volume so that the announcements and posters no longer registered.

She entered the house to the sound of a violin and knew that it must be Vincent. He had been absent for weeks which was not unusual. He was a drifter, coming and going at random, his identity and past shrouded in mystery. There were rumours that he'd taken too much acid, burnt out his brain and gone schizo, and that he'd been a child prodigy, destined for stardom in the world of classical music. Everything about him was a rumour. Had he trained at the Royal Academy of Music, or was it the Julliard in New York? Was he the son of a famous conductor, thrown out of home for taking drugs? A story circulated that his violin was a Stradivarius, only to be overtaken by other speculations. Nobody knew anything for sure, and Vincent's communications were rambling and disjointed. His violin spoke for him, and Grace, who knew nothing about classical music, was spellbound by his playing.

Sometimes she saw him in the street walking barefoot, his violin case strapped to his back, a tatterdemalion with ragged scarecrow clothes flapping, a thousand-yard stare in his eyes. She heard him speaking to himself: *you're guilty, you're guilty, you're a useless cunt.* If she'd been braver, she would have tried to tell him that he wasn't guilty or useless, but his madness scared her. She knew from Martin that he sometimes slept in the shattered remains of a house not far from Belton Road. It had been partly demolished years before the squatters arrived and was beyond saving. The roof was full of holes; there was no plumbing or power. Martin and Gerald had tried to persuade him to join one of the established squats, find a proper room, but Vincent wasn't interested. He couldn't live with other people. How could anyone be so alone in the world? Surely, somewhere, someone was looking for him.

The kitchen was filled with people. Vincent was standing on a chair, his eyes closed, body and violin like a single organism.

'Paganini,' Annie said as Grace squeezed in beside her. 'Caprice 24.'

'Is he okay?' she asked. 'He looks so thin.'

'Apparently, he can hear the vegetables screaming when he cuts them up so he can't eat them anymore. He's living on brown rice. Not sure what he's going to do if the rice starts to shriek.'

Before she could stifle it, Grace laughed. 'I'm sorry,' she said, 'it's not funny. Isn't there something we can do? I mean, isn't there somewhere ... a place—?'

'You mean a mental hospital?'

'I suppose.'

'It would kill him,' Annie said.

They watched as Vincent's playing grew more frenzied, turning into a wild Irish jig. Vanessa and a couple of the Orange People from the Rajneesh ashram house at the end of the street began to dance. Someone passed Grace a joint. She inhaled the smoke, taking deep, greedy drags trying to block out thoughts of poor Vincent and his screaming vegetables.

12

The letter from her father lay unread in the bottom of her bag. Its existence prompted her to scribble a note, this time revealing that she had a job – a boring office thing to pay the rent. She gave her Belton Road address, unable to face the prospect of returning to Australia House and the possibility of running into Janine and Cathy. She made no mention of the squat or The Free Republic of Beltonia. Arriving weeks later, her mother's enthusiastic reply ignored the paltry nature of Grace's letter. It was wonderful to hear from her and how marvellous that she had a job. What were the prospects? What kind of office? Perhaps she ought to ask for some more interesting things to do. She was too clever to be lumbered with dull work. But gosh, it was a start, which was wonderful. And please, could Grace tell her all about her new abode? Was she sharing with some other Aussies? What fun. How lucky she was. Reading it, Grace felt a surge of intense irritation. Her mother had no idea of anything. All that talk about the job, the new 'abode' and the idea of sharing with other Aussies. At the same time, there was no mention of any returned mail and Grace realised she'd been avoiding letters that didn't exist. The knowledge that her mother was not frantically trying to make contact ought to have been a relief, and she told herself that it was.

As for her father's letter, in the weeks that followed there were many times when she imagined throwing it away. Like the pea in the princess's bed, it was impossible to ignore. She thought about dropping it into the wastepaper basket at work or tossing it on one of the Beltonian bonfires to be consumed by the flames. The idea of reducing it to ashes was appealing and yet something held her back. She couldn't do it. But nor could she read it, sure that it contained a demand to return home. The letter in her bag was a lunging rein, tying her to him, giving him control. She was determined not to let him win and rejected his claim on her. Even if she couldn't forget its presence, she would not read it. She was not the daughter he wanted her to be, and he was not the right father, though it hadn't always been like that.

In earlier times she'd been his little offsider, tagging along with him as he went about the business of the farm. Bumping over tussocky paddocks in the truck and jumping out to open the gates, checking windmills and fences. Mustering sheep and riding through the swamp, where he taught her the names of the birds: the bald coots, black swans and water hens. Willy wagtails, swallows and swifts, and the corellas that flew in great squawking flocks overhead. The black cockatoos with their mournful cries. She remembered the hours they had spent together in companionable silence, for he was not much of a talker.

In time, she accompanied her father less often and her brother, Will, took over. One day, the farm would be his, and there was a purpose to teaching him the ropes. She came to understand that her role was to marry a farmer, not be one. Her life was changing, she was becoming a girl. Will replaced her, though she retained the things she'd learnt from her father – his knowledge and love of the land and its wildlife. Although the closeness of those early days had gone, it was only later that she came to see him as a hostile stranger, someone she wanted to escape from, even destroy.

Those first years at university, she'd brought home carloads of friends – city boys and girls who fell in love with her parents and the world of the farm. Hay carting and mustering on horseback, picking field mushrooms and catching yabbies in the dam, and on summer evenings, gathering on the verandah for gin and tonics. After dinner, they played charades and drank her father's whisky, about which he half-heartedly complained. 'Righto, I'm off to bed,' he'd say when the charades began. 'Don't drink me out of house and home.' He was the first to bed and the first to rise, while her mother stayed up with them, not wanting to miss a minute of it. Everyone loved her, she was so much fun. 'You can talk to her about anything,' Clara said, unlike her own mother, who was worn-out and bitter since Clara's artist father had run off with the daughter of a fellow artist, leaving her with debts and four kids. Grace never asked what her mother and her friend spoke of, and Clara never said.

In the final year of her Arts degree, she pleaded to leave the residential women's college. Clara had moved into the dilapidated Fitzroy mansion by then and there was room for Grace to join her. But her parents were adamant, she was too young, and without their financial support she was stuck. To spite them, she stopped bringing friends home. And anyway, those friends had begun to bore her – private schoolboys and girls who were destined to be lawyers and doctors. The only person to escape her condemnation was Clara, although they'd begun to drift apart. She had joined a student theatre group and no longer had time to hang out.

That year, Grace gave up attending classes. Like her former friends, the lecturers had become boring. Worse, they were sleazy, which had surprised her. She'd naively expected the professors to be noble intellectuals, god-like figures who had forsaken earthly desires for the life of the mind. Rather than going to lectures she stayed at the Fitzroy mansion, occasionally having sex with Sam, until she told him it was over. She couldn't go on pretending to be in love; pretending that the sex was great. 'I've got to study,' she told him, which he didn't believe. She didn't care what he thought; she was past caring. She got drunk to the point where she couldn't remember things. She felt out of control.

A period followed where she barely got out of bed, sleeping and smoking and eating packets of chocolate biscuits. After a few weeks, she roused herself from the lassitude that had overtaken her and went on an anti-Vietnam march. Anger galvanised her and made her feel alive again. She joined sit-ins and an occupation of the Student Union building and screamed abuse at the South African rugby team at an anti-Apartheid demonstration. In Canberra, some Aboriginal activists set up an Aboriginal Tent Embassy outside Parliament House, agitating for Aboriginal land rights, and for the first time in her life, Grace thought about where she'd grown up, the land over which she'd ridden, and to which she felt a connection. It was in her bones, she belonged to it and vice-versa.

On a reluctant trip home, she questioned her father. What did they do, the first settlers? Our ancestors. Had they killed the Aboriginal owners for this land? He said it was the way of things, that one race supplanted another, it was human nature, and the Scots, which were his people, her people, had been massacred by the English, their language and customs banned, driven from their land. It was the way of things, he repeated. It was how it was.

Her relationship with the land that she'd thought of as hers was now burdened with guilt, and yet what could she do about it? She didn't even know any Aboriginal people. She blamed her father and the love she'd had for him withered away and was replaced by a disgust of his views and values. Increasingly, a disgust of him. He was right-wing, racist, a Nazi in disguise, which she dared not say to him because he was a Rat of Tobruk. Accusing him of being a Nazi was too incendiary. She was filled with moral outrage and a sense of righteousness.

She began to dislike everything about her parents, seeing them through new eyes. Her mother was a phoney who'd pretended to be one of them, playing charades and sharing her cigarettes in an effort to ingratiate herself. It was all so cringeworthy. The idea of Clara and her mother having tête-à-têtes revolted her. How could Clara have been taken in? The scales had fallen from her eyes: her mother was a hypocrite and a snob, always nagging her about something – her hair and unflattering clothes. *You've got a lovely figure, you ought to show it off.* Comments to which Grace responded crudely, wanting to shock her, snarling that she wasn't interested in showing off her fucking figure. It wasn't the nineteen fucking fifties anymore. There were moments when she wished her mother would retaliate.

She dragged herself home for Christmas. University was over, she'd scraped through, with no idea of what to do next. The four-week typing course had filled a gap but it was over too and she had no intention of becoming a secretary. She felt two dimensional, flat, like the playing card characters in Alice in Wonderland, unable to scream or weep no matter how much she longed to. *What is wrong with you? What's the matter?* her mother asked. She didn't know, couldn't say, except that it was everything. The country she'd once loved, the paddocks, swamps and scrub, the trees she had climbed as a child, she hated it all. It stunk of death – death of the spirit.

In the evenings, she lay on the old leather couch in the living room, watching television to pass the time. Flicking between the two available channels, she saw a show about three girls sharing a London flat in the 1960s. *Come down to London town, see the people there,* went the chorus of the song over the opening credits. It was a siren song, and she was a sailor who had not plugged her ears with wax. A turning point had been reached. She wanted to smash herself on those London rocks, whatever the cost.

Back in Melbourne she moved into Clara's old room, as Clara had gone to Sydney to apply for the national drama school and was not returning. The lease on the house was nearing its end and any semblance of order had collapsed. People came and went, passing through to somewhere else. The TV was pinched, along with a leather jacket and some cash belonging to a girl who had travelled over from Perth. Grace pared her belongings down to the bone. She had nothing worth stealing. She was travelling light, preparing to leave.

She found a job in a bakery, selling boston buns and vanilla slices before getting sacked for giving them away to broke uni students and rough sleepers – the derros who came in, filthy and stinking, and for whom she felt sorry. Her plan to save money was already falling apart until a chance acquaintance told her there were jobs going at a big hotel in the centre of the city. She got work as a breakfast waitress, rising at five o'clock, cycling through the empty dawn streets while the city slept. The hotel was a favourite with interstate businessmen, predatory gropers who put the hard word on her. Some of the waitresses had a side-line going. 'We're not prostitutes,' they said, insisting it was a temporary thing and if she wanted to go overseas, she should do it too, but she couldn't. She told the girls who were not prostitutes, that she believed in love, and couldn't fuck someone for money, although when she thought about it, she'd never been in love with Sam. She convinced herself that it was different, and he had not paid her for sex.

She tried to forget about the girl who had kissed her at the Carlton party and almost rang Sam to ask if he wanted to go out sometime. But he had moved, she didn't have his telephone number and when she'd seen him last, they'd argued. He'd wanted her to go to the Law Ball and she'd told him it was elitist and full of private school shits of which he was one – she didn't exactly say he was one; it was implied. That she too had gone to a private school was not the point, she had rejected all of that. She couldn't help thinking about Sam during the hours she slaved away at the big hotel, serving the sleazy businessmen their bacon and eggs, thinking about how it might be different this time. He was kind and funny and not a shit. She thought about Clara too. There were loads of other people she knew, but she didn't want to see any of them. Just the same old thing, getting drunk and waking up the next day with a feeling of dread.

She had arrived home in a friend's car – forgetting to say to herself *my parents' place* rather than home, because it was not her home, that was the whole point. She'd come to tell them she was leaving for London, knowing they would try to stop her, predicting their arguments about her youth and inexperience, and how she ought to get a proper job and grow up. The prospect of confronting her father made her feel ill. She wished she could leave without telling them but couldn't bring herself to sever the ties between them like that. She had to make her stand. When her father lay down the law, would she really be able to defy him?

That afternoon, standing on the verandah with the sun slanting through the leaves of the grapevine, shadows dancing on their bodies, their greetings were only half said before the truth had burst out of her. She was leaving on Saturday and didn't know when she'd be back. (Never.)

It was worse than expected. Anger was her sole weapon and without it, she'd have collapsed. Her fury lit an answering spark in her father and his body trembled from the effort of holding himself in check. He was on the verge of violence, of shaking her until her bones rattled. She was not to go, he forbade it. He would cut her off without a penny. She forced herself to laugh in his face, to stare down his wrath. She didn't care about his clichéd threats. She didn't want anything from him and refused her mother's entreaties to stay the night, only wishing she hadn't looked in the rear vision mirror as she accelerated away. An image of them standing together, growing smaller. She drove back to Melbourne, convulsed by intermittent bouts of violent weeping.

13

Grace arrived at the Veritas Centre for the weekend encounter marathon that Vanessa had insisted she attend, to find a dozen people milling in the entry hall. Some were talking in a hectic fashion, their voices rising as they competed for attention, while others, like imminent roadkill caught in the headlights, seemed unable to move or utter a sound. Feeling that she was seconds away from joining this latter group, she forced herself to advance, searching for Vanessa.

She'd been about to leave for Veritas when Marigold once again tried to talk her out of it. Did she really want a bunch of sweaty loonies screaming their heads off at her? Grace almost capitulated, agreeing that it sounded horrible. But the day before, Vanessa had convinced her that encounter groups were life changing and would solve all her problems, brushing aside Grace's protests that she didn't have any problems.

'You're conflicted, and stuck. You need to let go of all that fixed energy,' Vanessa said. It was there in the chart and if it wasn't exactly the detailed psychological analysis Grace had hoped for when Vanessa had first drawn it up, nevertheless, it struck a chord. Somehow, letting go of her conflicts and fixed energy became the same thing as letting go of her attraction to women. Maybe Vanessa was right, and the encounter group really would be life changing. Not that she could tell Marigold. Instead, she said she wanted to be open to new experiences, aware that it sounded defensive and rather feeble. Marigold had rolled her eyes and wished her luck.

They were in the kitchen and Gerald had been listening to their conversation.

'You should get involved in something real,' he said. 'It's just a bunch of wankers going on about how their mummies and daddies never loved them.'

'How do you know if you haven't experienced it,' Grace replied, irritated by his criticism.

'I don't need to be in the train to know a train crash will be shit.'

She stifled the urge to respond and gave a nonchalant shrug. Since their failed sexual encounter, the tension between them had grown. She'd thought about saying something, but what? It was all too humiliating. She was left trying to pretend that it hadn't happened, and that there was nothing strained between them.

Her eyes flicked around the entry hall, still searching for Vanessa when she glimpsed a woman standing alone, separated by as much space as possible from the main group. Incredibly, it looked like Ingred. She craned her head to get a better view when someone tapped her on the shoulder.

'There you are.'

At the sound of Vanessa's voice, Grace turned.

'I think Ingred's here,' she exclaimed.

Instead of responding to this extraordinary revelation, Vanessa pointed to a man and woman who had just emerged from another room.

'That's them,' she said, sounding awestruck.

Like cattle, everyone had swung round to face the couple. The brittle, nervous chatter died away and a hush fell over the group, replaced by an electric feeling in the air, a hum of invisible, vibrating energy.

The woman was short, plump, and thirtyish, swathed in a simple purple robe that came down to her ankles. The man was a few years older, with shoulder-length blonde hair. He wore a white t-shirt and loose, white cotton pants tied at the waist with a drawstring. His feet were bare. The woman's feet were bare too. The way Vanessa had gone on about the group leaders and how amazing they were had led Grace to expect something quite different. Except for the purple robe, they looked ordinary.

'Welcome,' the woman said, 'my name is Paula, and this is Brian, and we are your group leaders this weekend. In a minute, we're going to enter the group room which will be your home for the next forty-eight hours. Before we go any further, is there anyone who wants to leave? If so, you must go now.'

At the conclusion of her announcement Paula remained still. Nobody said a word. And then there was a little flurry as people stepped aside and Ingred pushed her way towards the exit.

'Sorry,' she said, 'A mistake … I cannot stay.' Within seconds, she reached the door and was gone.

'Anyone else?' Paula asked. 'This is your last chance.'

Nobody moved. Nobody spoke. What had possessed Ingred to come in the first place? Grace wondered. It was so totally unlike her.

'Good,' Paula said, 'then let us begin,' and she led the way through the door from which she and Brian had recently emerged.

Grace stepped into a large room, empty apart from three wicker laundry baskets, a portable record player with a dozen LPs stacked beside it, a pile of cushions and, mysteriously, two plastic rounders bats. Looking around, she noticed the windows were covered with black-out cloth. This somewhat sinister detail provoked a quiver of anxiety and for a moment she wished she'd scuttled out with Ingred.

'Okay everyone, time to get your gear off,' Brian said, surprising Grace with his Australian accent. 'Put everything in the baskets. Clothes, jewellery, watches, and hats.'

A few nervous titters erupted at the mention of hats, of which there were none.

'You mean we're going to be naked?' a grey-haired woman asked in a tremulous voice.

Brian's only reply was a smile. 'Lock the door, Paula,' he said.

Paula turned the key in the door and Grace felt a corresponding stab of pain in her gut. Why did the door need to be locked?

People began to take off their clothes and she could smell the acrid tang of nervous sweat. Breasts wobbled and she caught sight of a dangling penis. Without their clothes, signifiers of status and style, the usual hierarchies were collapsing. Everyone was becoming more alike, differentiated only by the absence or presence of breasts and penises. Or, in the case of the tubby young Pakistani man, Sunil – whom she'd seen occasionally at the backyard bonfire nights in Beltonia – his brown skin. How vulnerable they all look, she thought, as Brian loomed into her field of view, so close she could feel his peppery breath on her face.

'You, what's your name?' To stop her from stepping away he hooked a finger into the neck of her jumper.

'Grace,' she said, in an unintended whisper.

He picked up her accent immediately. 'An Aussie. Where are you from, little Gracie Grace?'

'Melbourne.'

'Come on then Grace from Melbourne. Chop, chop.'

She hesitated, knowing that naked, any chance of escape would vanish.

'Want me to undress you? Is that it?' Brian said with a grin.

It was the spur she needed, and she ripped off her clothes. Everything was thrown into the baskets in the corner of the room and whisked away through another door which she hoped led to a bathroom. Already feeling a nervous need to pee, she was about to ask Brian if she could slip out to the loo, when Paula called for the group's attention. Everyone was to close their eyes. Grace glanced around. It was all happening too fast.

'I mean everyone,' Paula said in a stern voice, looking directly at Grace. Paula and Brian were the only ones still clothed.

'I'm not sure—' she began before Paula gently, firmly, pressed her thumbs against her eyelids.

'Trust me,' she said, 'it will be alright.'

Strangely enough, the experience of having her head held in this way, with thumbs gently pressed against her eyeballs and Paula's voice telling her that there was nothing to be afraid of, was instantaneously calming.

'That's right,' Paula said. She released her grip and Grace, keeping her eyes closed, felt her move away.

'Now, I want everyone to slowly circulate,' Brian said, 'and when you touch another person, stop and explore them. Keep your eyes closed. Use touch and smell and taste. Explore faces, chests, arms, legs, breasts, cocks. And remember, this exercise is not about sex. Get that straight. No fucking.'

Until Brian's directive, she hadn't imagined there would be any fucking. Now that it was banned, the exercise felt sexually loaded. She could feel people moving around, and then, someone touched her arm. Fingers began to trace a line down her spine, lips grazed her cheek and neck, a hand cupped her buttock, fingers ran through her hair, a tongue licked the back of her knee causing a rush of heat to her groin. Cautiously, she extended a hand, her fingertips connecting with soft hair and skin, the line of a chin, a beard. She began to explore, running a finger around the curve of an ear, the back of a neck. A floppy cock, the skin soft as an eyelid, awakened under her touch. She moved on, afraid that Brian would see, sure that he was prowling the room, ready to pounce on transgressors. Meanwhile, other hands and mouths roamed over her body, lingering on her breasts, a tongue licking her ear, a nose sniffing her armpit and fingers tracing patterns over her skin until she began to lose the sense of herself as separate, her body mingling with others in a sensual swirl.

'Stop,' Brian called. 'Open your eyes.'

She blinked, her eyes adjusting to soft candlelight flickering from the corners of the room. There was a moment of rearrangement as everyone returned to themselves and each person found their own little bit of physical space, and what had been a single organism became a group of individuals again. The unease she'd felt earlier had evaporated, her body buzzing from the sensual experience until she saw that the breasts she'd been touching (the word *fondling* flashed through her mind) belonged to Frances, the grey-headed woman who was older than her mother.

There was no time to think about it before Brian and Paula instructed the group to sit in a circle on the floor and introduce themselves.

'Say a little bit about yourself,' Paula said, 'why you're here and what you're hoping for.'

Sitting cross-legged in a circle, the fact of their nakedness impressed itself on Grace once more. Glimpses of scalloped pinky-brown labia; penises resting in nests of curly pubes; pert upright breasts, and pale, rounded orbs, lolling unrestrained.

Sunil was the first person to speak. Grace tried to focus on his face and not on his crotch. He revealed that he was lonely and wanted to connect with people. Next, Aidan, a skinny guy with John Lennon glasses and a haunted look, said he had relationship problems. As they went around the circle, she practiced what she would say. That she too had relationship problems, that she thought she might be … that sometimes she felt attracted to women. And men of course. She was attracted to men.

119

All too soon, she realised that nobody was speaking. They were waiting for her and as her eyes met Paula's, she knew she could not reveal the truth.

'I thought it might be interesting.'

Paula tilted her head. 'You thought it might be interesting.'

Grace tried to smile; sweat beading in her armpits.

Paula looked around the group as if inspecting them to see if they were interesting. 'We have an observer in the group,' she said, 'she thinks it might be interesting.'

Grace felt a subtle yet powerful sense of everyone uniting against her. She had to offer up a reason for being there, but what? She was sure that something terrible was about to happen.

'Who's next?' Paula said.

A reprieve, but for how long? She was stuck with the horrible feeling that worse was yet to come.

Once the introductions were over, Paula announced that it was time to work. Who was going to be first? Grace managed to remain on the fringes, watching on as, one by one, members of the group moved to the centre of the circle. It was all about feelings, which turned out to mean rage, followed by bouts of sobbing. What mattered was giving up the bullshit and getting to the truth, exposing the trauma and feeling it. As Marigold predicted, there was a lot of screaming and ranting, with the group urging and exhorting the person in the centre to *let it all out*, helped by bashing the cushions with a rounders bat in a frenzy of fury. If the performance was deemed authentic – the rage ferocious enough and the tears a *break-through* and not a *resistance* – the person working was welcomed into the arms of surrogate mothers and fathers to be cradled like a huge naked baby. Gerald was right; mummies and daddies, if not wholly to blame, were a major cause of everyone's troubles. Grace noticed how Brian and Paula choreographed the action, inciting the group to converge on one person after another, helping them to *break through*. She knew that sooner or later her turn was coming.

Day and night had become indistinguishable when Paula announced a break for dinner, handing out cotton robes to wear while they ate. Vanessa whispered to Grace that the robes were a new thing after a nasty scalding accident at a previous marathon. Brian brought in bowls of soup. Everyone was starving.

With the meal over, and the robes bundled away it was back to the business at hand.

At last, it was Grace's turn. She moved to the middle of the group, feeling as if she might throw up. Having seen the way it worked, the idea of revealing anything filled her with horror.

'So, Grace,' Paula said, 'perhaps you could start with how you're feeling.'

'Okay. Good.'

'Liar,' a male voice called out. 'You look freaked out to me.'

She was the target now, and there would be no mercy.

'Yeah, Grace, what are you doing here, because so far, you've watched everyone else like you're a fucking little princess,' spat weedy Aidan, suddenly emboldened after spending the rest of the marathon looking terrified.

She shot a glance of appeal to Brian, willing him to protect her. He smiled and her heart lifted.

'Great, Aidan, well done,' Brian said.

'I'm not a fucking little princess,' she said, dismayed by how weak and quavery her voice sounded.

'I'm not a fucking little princess,' Frances – old Frances who should have been curled up in a foetal ball because her life was almost over – repeated in a mocking tone.

And then others began to repeat it too, making a chorus of *I'm not a fucking little princess*. The chant grew louder and louder and everyone began to inch in towards her. Panic began to rise, her heart pounded, and she couldn't catch her breath. The whole group was moving towards her, squeezing the air from the room. She was surrounded by shouting voices. In addition to the chant, there were other words, other demands to speak, to tell them the truth, to stop acting like a fucking princess. *You're not Princess Grace. Who do you think you are? Princess Grace?*

Their leering faces, spittle spraying, and then, erupting from somewhere deep within, a voice, her voice, 'My mother never gave me her hand,' she screamed.

At a signal from Paula everyone stopped shouting and the room fell silent.

'That's good, Grace.' Paula said. 'Can you say a bit more?'

Grace could feel she was breathing too fast. She was holding a cushion, gripping it with both hands, clinging to a cliff edge. The others were waiting, she had seconds before it all began again. She had to say that bit more, whatever it was. What was the rest of the story?

'She never gave me her hand.'

'That's right, she never gave you her hand,' Paula repeated.

What else could she say? *It's the first line of a novel? Sorry, I'll start again?* But it was true, her mother wasn't one for holding hands.

'Come on Grace. She was distant and cold,' Paula said, leaning forward in an encouraging way.

She hesitated, transfixed by an image of her mother on the day of departure – the tender expression on her face, her whispered advice to take care – and then her mother faded, and she saw the faces surrounding her, intense and ferocious. She wanted to close her eyes. Instead, she continued to stare at Paula, knowing that she mustn't look away, that things would get worse if she tried to avoid Paula's penetrating gaze.

'Keep going,' Paula said, 'don't stop, pour it out Grace, let it out.'

'Go on, Grace,' one of the men called. And then others joined in, encouraging her, urging her on.

'Your mother never touched you,' Paula said, 'never held you by the hand.'

She wanted to cry out that it was all rubbish and that she was making things up, she wanted to go now. But the rules had been set, nobody could leave until the end. The door was locked, and they were naked. Escape was impossible. Everyone was shouting at her, telling her to keep going and free herself, get out her anger at her mother, who was a cold bitch, a monster.

In the face of her frozen silence, they began to attack her again – she was just like her mother, cold and withholding. An uptight bitch who thought she was better than the others.

Someone hit her with a cushion, followed by another blow and another, until they were raining down on her. And then she screamed. She heard herself screaming, as if she was separate from herself. She wanted to stop and couldn't, while around her the group was urging her on, louder, longer, more. The not wanting to scream part gave up and she let the other part take over, becoming the loony of Marigold's warning.

Brian thrust a bat into her hand.

'Go for it,' he commanded. 'Don't hold back.'

She raised the bat above her head and brought it down on the cushion in front of her. Again, and again. She was sweating from every pore, her body slick and glistening. The whole room stunk of sweaty, slippery bodies. She was caught up in the energy, surfing the wave until it crashed to shore, flinging her onto the beach like a clump of seaweed. She lay there while everyone crowded around and lifted her onto Paula's lap. They wrapped her in a soft blanket and laid gentle hands on her. In the background, Marvin Gaye was singing 'Mercy Mercy Me' and she began to weep.

Time passed and she was allowed to stay wrapped in the blanket and watch from the sidelines as others took their place at the centre of the circle. Paula smiled benignly at her and told her she was amazing. Apparently, she'd made a major breakthrough.

14

The next morning, Grace slept through her alarm, exhausted after forty-eight hours without sleep. By the time she woke it was already nine o'clock. Rita would be waiting impatiently for her morning coffee, ready with an acerbic putdown. It was too bad, let her wait. She closed her eyes. Later, she'd ring and make an excuse. A migraine. Or food poisoning.

Scenes from the marathon drifted through her mind to the accompaniment of a Marvin Gaye soundtrack. Marigold was right – a bunch of sweaty loonies screaming their heads off. Except that she was one of those loonies, screaming and bashing the cushions with the rounders bat, ranting about her mother, the cold-hearted bitch. It made her feel sick to think of how she'd betrayed her. How she'd let them believe it. She pulled the bedclothes tight, turned over one way, then back again, unable to get comfortable, her head filled with the memory of what she'd done. It wasn't her fault, she'd been desperate. But the excuses didn't change anything. And then, the memory of Paula's praise. At the end of the marathon, Paula had singled her out, telling her how much she'd achieved and how brave she'd been. Praise that she'd lapped up, enjoying the envious expressions on the faces of the others. Thrilled to be the favourite. She felt sick with shame, and the idea that the group would help make her straight now seemed absurd. One more thing to make her squirm.

Lying in bed any longer was impossible.

She crept up the stairs to her desk, hoping that Rita would be out. If not, she had decided on food poisoning, rehearsing her speech in a whispery, invalid's voice. It was a miracle she had made it to work at all.

Eric came out of his office and blocked her way. 'Where have you been?

'I'm not well. I've had food poisoning,' she said, forgetting to put on the invalid's voice.

'No, you haven't.'

'I have. I've been vomiting.'

'You've got a hangover.'

'I haven't. Where's Rita?'

'Shagging I suppose.'

'Come on, be serious.'

'I am. Don't tell me you haven't twigged?'

'Twigged what?'

'Rita and Simon.'

The instant he said it, she remembered their discussion about marriage and Marina. Eric's words: *Not that it stops him*. At the squat, everyone slept around, but that was different; they weren't married. Like the others, she didn't believe in marriage; it was an oppressive institution and one she had rejected years ago. The idea of parading down the church aisle in a white dress while her father gave her away was inconceivable. Nevertheless, in some unreconstructed part of her, she believed people who were married ought to be faithful to each other. Had it blinded her to the obvious?

'Bullshit,' she said, 'you're lying.'

'Think what you like. It's been going on for months.' If proof was needed, she should ring her predecessor, Elizabeth. 'Right, I'm

125

off,' he said. 'While the cats are away, and so on. Might be back later, I'll see.'

Watching Eric bound down the stairs, Grace recalled the times Rita had swished past, slamming Simon's door behind her. Sometimes she was in there for an hour or more, and once or twice, she'd emerged with her coiffed bob unusually tousled, a detail Grace had noticed without giving it a second thought. With Eric's revelation, it took on a new meaning. There was no need to ring Elizabeth.

The day passed slowly. Eric did not return and the single break in Grace's solitude came when Basia rang to discuss administrative details about the mail orders, a conversation that soon morphed into her fears of deportation and the awful fate that awaited her in Poland. It was a recurring theme. She was afraid of being dragged in front of the courts and thrown into prison for reasons Grace was never able to grasp. Sometimes her fears were less dramatic and more to do with the hard grind of daily life in Poland. There was so little of everything, and surviving was a battle.

'Is all grey, you understand Grace. Everything.'

According to Basia, corruption was everywhere. Grace listened, murmuring reassurances, wondering how much of what she said was based on fact. Knowing little about Poland, she was not in a position to judge. The reliability of Basia's information aside, it was hard to feel positive about Soviet-style communism given the respective fates of Hungary and Czechoslovakia. On the other hand, she couldn't support the capitalist system.

Basia had been going on for ages about the state apparatus.

'Sorry Basia, I've got another call coming through.' She put down the phone, intending to raid Simon's office for something new to read. Before she could implement her plan the sound of voices floated up the stairs, followed by the distinctive tap of Rita's high heels and the thump of Simon's heavy tread. A blank piece of paper was waiting in the typewriter for such a moment and by the time the lovers appeared, Grace's fingers were flying across the keys in imitation of an efficient Girl Friday. She offered a greeting smile, but engrossed in each other, they didn't respond, Simon's office door banging shut behind them.

She tossed the page of nonsense typing into the wastepaper basket when, unexpectedly, Rita emerged.

'He wants to see you,' she said, sailing past.

Grace hovered at the door until Simon looked up.

'Come in, sit,' he said.

Knowing that he and Rita had been off shagging, she found it difficult to look at him, convinced that her face would give her away. She crossed the room and perched on the edge of the chair.

'Why are you sitting like that?' he said.

'Like what?'

'About to bolt.'

She slid back a little and tried to relax.

'What do you want?' she said. 'I mean, Rita said you wanted to see me.'

'No need to make it sound like a crime.'

'Sorry.'

He waved away her apology. 'Are you feeling alright? You look a bit under the weather.'

'Tired, that's all.'

'Ah, the follies of youth.'

She couldn't think of a suitable reply and gave a weak smile.

'Right then,' he said, 'to business.' He opened the top drawer of his desk and peeled some bank notes from a thick wad. 'Weeks late, I know. Don't squander the lot at once.'

'Oh, thanks,' she said, too surprised by the fact that he had paid her in cash to say anything more.

Once out of his sight, she counted it. One hundred and twenty pounds. It seemed far too much and shoving it into her bag, she wondered if he had made a mistake.

Marigold was sitting up in bed wearing an ancient tartan dressing gown, typing on a portable typewriter when Grace, pretending that she was just passing, poked her head into the room.

'Sorry, I won't interrupt.'

Marigold stopped typing and set it aside. 'Boring translation thing. Come in. Tell me all about it. Was it ghastly?'

It took Grace a moment to realise that she was referring to the marathon.

'Ghastly,' she replied, mentally fending off a return of the guilt she'd managed to block out while at work, sure that if Marigold knew the truth – the way she had betrayed her mother and slurped up Paula's praise – she'd have been disgusted.

She wandered over to the window, navigating an obstacle course of clothing and bits of material littering the floor. Some women in overalls were carting furniture into the house across the road. 'Have new people moved in across the road?' she asked, keen to avoid any further discussion about the marathon.

'The men have gone. Gloria kicked them out and declared that from now on it's a separatist squat. Dykes and female *enfants* only.'

One of the women looked up at the window and Grace stepped back awkwardly, knocking the plant on the window ledge.

'Careful, that's my ironic aspidistra,' Marigold said.

Grace pushed it back into position, unsettled by the revelation that lesbians had moved in opposite. 'What's ironic about it?'

'You obviously haven't read Orwell.'

'I have.'

'Dear Grace, if you knew your Orwell, you'd know what I meant. For someone with a university education your ignorance often astounds me.'

'Why bother with me then?' She meant it to sound light-hearted, which it might have if the news about the separatist dyke house hadn't destabilised her.

'I bother because I think you're interesting,' Marigold said, 'and smart even if ignorant. Oh, and quite beautiful, which strictly speaking isn't a virtue. Still, it's pleasurable for the eye. And brave, although as you know, I think accosting that idiot was a stupid thing to do. Is that enough, or should I go on?'

Grace gave an awkward laugh, not expecting her petulant comment to elicit such praise. To hear that Marigold thought she was brave and beautiful kindled the flame she'd been trying so hard to dampen and she felt her commitment to the concept of philia begin to waver.

'Guess what?' she said, to create a diversion, 'Simon finally paid me. In cash too. Don't you think that's odd? He said not to squander it all at once.'

'Rubbish. You've got to squander it. Splurging your first pay is a rule. Think of something extravagant.'

The only thing she could think of was a meal at Parsons on Fulham Road. She'd heard about it from Vanessa because Pearl, the astrologer, recommended it. Marigold said Parsons was evidence of a lack of imagination and not nearly extravagant enough.

'I really should get on with finishing this,' she added, putting the typewriter back on her lap. 'You can stay if you like. Not hugely fascinating, I'm afraid.'

Grace understood it was a hint for her to leave. The initial shock of Marigold's praise had subsided, and she wished she hadn't been so quick to deflect it, feeling greedy for more. The moment had passed, it was too late. Before leaving, she glanced out of the window. The street was empty, the separatists nowhere to be seen. Marigold was hunched over the typewriter, banging away at the keys and did not look up as she slipped out of the room.

In the weeks that followed, she became less deferential to Simon. Knowing that he was unfaithful and a liar gave her a hidden edge and made her feel more of an equal. She lost interest in trying to

129

impress him with her Girl Friday skills – a relief, given that most of them were non-existent. She abandoned the charade of busyness with which she'd been obsessed and admitted there were things she didn't understand, discovering, to her surprise, that he didn't expect her to know everything and was happy to explain.

'I'm only the Girl Friday,' she said.

'With a first-class degree in English literature,' he added.

She was almost tempted to confess about the first-class degree.

Whether it was her new attitude or simply a coincidence was unclear, but he began to call her into his office more frequently. There were things to discuss. He was keen to get the publishing arm set up. They needed to develop a list.

'What sort of list?'

'Writers, Grace. We need writers. Up and comers like whats-hisname Amis.'

'Kingsley? Isn't he a bit old?'

'Not him. Amis the younger. And women writers too. Women read, ergo they buy books. Iris Murdoch. Marina reads her.'

It was the first time he had mentioned Marina to her.

'We need to lure them.'

'The women?'

'The writers.'

'How?'

'Filthy lucre. It's all writers want. Big fat advances. It's a matter of letting them know we've got deep pockets.'

'Have we,' she asked. 'I'm asking because—' She stopped, not wanting to bring up the subject of Max.

'Because?'

'Because how deep will they need to be?' she said, dodging the question.

'Leave it to me,' he said. 'You concentrate on the literary agents. Set up some meetings for us.'

It was when he began talking about actual things that she needed to do, like setting up meetings with literary agents – people she had no idea how to identify or contact – that she opted for changing the subject over revealing the extent of her ignorance. She couldn't help feeling that he was complicit with this, and that his vision of a publishing arm was more theoretical than real.

'Why not wait until the Scottish manuscript arrives,' she suggested, after they had been discussing the list again. It was due any day. She hoped they were not tempting fate by calling it the Scottish manuscript. She was thinking of the Scottish play and the curse attached to it.

They didn't always talk about work. Simon enjoyed regaling her with stories of his past. How he'd lived in a bohemian mansion in Ladbroke Grove and was friends with Syd Barrett before Syd freaked out, leaving Pink Floyd and disappearing from the scene altogether.

'Thought I was a writer in those days,' he said. My old friend, Larry, got me a part-time gig at IT. That was before I defected to Oz.

He rambled on about Oz and a trial of some sort while she tuned out, thinking about Marigold. She'd never heard of IT or Oz. Whatever he was talking about had happened in the sixties which was too long ago to be interesting.

'As a matter of fact, that's where I met Germaine.' He gave a suggestive chuckle and leaned back, waiting for her to respond and when she did not, wanted to know whether she'd listened to a word he'd said.

'Not really.'

'Germaine Greer. Don't tell me you haven't you heard of her?'

'If you think you're liberated, try tasting your menstrual blood,' she said with a grin. '*The Female Eunuch* – that's if you've ever heard of it.' The menstrual blood line was the one thing that had stuck in her mind, having flicked through Clara's copy without actually reading it. She and Clara had laughed, revolted and titillated by the idea of tasting their period blood.

'Hm, very funny.' He grimaced and told her she was a disrespect-ful trollop who owed him more respect. 'Don't forget, I'm your boss.'

'And I'm your Girl Friday,' she replied, suddenly aware of a vibe in the room and a recognition that she might be flirting. It wasn't serious; he was taken by at least two women already and anyway she wasn't attracted to him, but it made her feel more heterosexual.

She thought about Gerald and, for the millionth time, resolved to try again.

Although flirting with Simon made her feel better about herself, it was potentially dangerous. She didn't want Rita, who was spending more and more time in his office, to think she was a threat. Now that she knew they were unlikely to be discussing sales targets or print runs for the latest posters, their proximity made her tense. She imagined what they might be up to and found herself inventing scenarios. Simon's large furry body with Rita straddling him while he sat on his big leather office chair. Or the two of them on his desk, Rita on top, cushioned by his bulk. Simon standing, Rita with her legs gripping his girth. She began to worry that there was something perverted about her fantasies, like Martin and his public fucking.

To get away from them and distract herself, she diverted incoming calls to Eric's room and decamped there, lying on the leather couch while he introduced her to bands and songwriters from his extensive record collection. She had decided that he wasn't creepy, he was shy and that was what made him giggle and act a bit weird.

Listening to *Bryter Layter* was making her feel melancholy, especially since discovering that Nick Drake was dead. Eric said it was probably suicide and that he was only twenty-six. Side one finished and the needle lifted off the record. In the lull, the metal flap on the front door clanged, followed by the sound of the afternoon post hitting the floorboards. In the days that had followed the posting of the Jane Smith letter, her nerves had been on edge. She had to keep reminding herself that nobody, with the exception of Max, knew what she'd done. When the letter hadn't turned up, she convinced herself that she'd made an error with the address – a Freudian slip of the pen. Max hadn't rung again, and the entire episode had slipped from her mind. Or so it seemed, until the sound of the mail scattering on the floor triggered an uncanny feeling.

She sprang to her feet.

'Where are you going?' Eric called.

Outside Eric's room, she almost collided with Rita. 'Sorry, getting the mail,' she gabbled.

'Expecting a love letter, are we?' Rita said sardonically.

With an awkward laugh, Grace rushed on, relieved that Rita never bothered to collect the mail, even when she had to step over it on her way in. She skidded to a stop at the front door and scooped up the scattered letters, flicking through them until there it was – the handwriting of the treacherous Jane Smith. Glancing at it now, she could see a distinct similarity to her own handwriting, despite the care she'd taken to disguise such a link.

Returning to her desk, she was about to open the letter and decide its fate when Simon summonsed her. In a panic, she thrust it into her bag.

'Sit down,' he said, waving her in, fixing her with an intense gaze.

Convinced that he knew everything and was about to confront her with it, she tried to get in first.

'Max said ... I didn't want to—'

'A drink,' he said, drowning out her stuttered attempt. 'There are things to discuss.'

She was so fixated on the letter and her part in Max's plot to bring down the house of cards, that she interpreted the *things to discuss* as definitive proof that she'd been sprung.

'I can explain—'

'Good. The pub's around the corner, we can walk.'

'What for?'

'Because it's not far and we've got legs.'

'Don't you want to discuss Max?'

'Max? Why on earth would I want to discuss Max? We're going for a drink. Look, I'll throw in a bag of crisps if you like.'

The message got through at last, and she understood what he was proposing. 'I can't. It's my turn to cook.'

'Ah.'

'I would, but—' At which point, there was a knock on the door and Rita entered.

'No further explanation necessary,' he said with a casual wave.

'Oh, sorry,' Rita said, not sounding sorry. 'No explanation necessary about what?'

Grace stood up. 'Nothing,' she said.

She grabbed her coat and bag and left the office. Outside, she headed in the direction of a pyramid of uncollected rubbish that due to the ongoing dustmen's strike had been expanding for weeks. A putrid mountain of builders' rubble and household waste, old rolls of mouldy carpet and hundreds of black plastic bin-bags with rotting food scraps spilling like entrails and swarming with rats. Instead of crossing the road to avoid it, she stopped a short distance away, dug into her bag and withdrew the Jane Smith letter. Even if Primo Press was a house of cards, which was quite possible, she didn't want to be the one responsible for its collapse. She held her breath against the stench and ripped the letter to pieces, flinging it onto the pile, vowing never to think of it again.

15

Grace had told Simon the truth – it was her turn to cook dinner. She and Marigold were making ratatouille and brown rice. So far, Grace had done everything. She put the lid on the brown rice and turned the gas down to a simmer. Marigold was sitting at the kitchen table, chain smoking. She had gone out the previous night, returning an hour ago, wearing the same clothes – a black midi dress and her chunky work boots. She'd thrown her tartan cloak over the back of the chair.

After rambling on about work and how Rita and Simon were having an affair, Grace noticed that Marigold hadn't spoken for ages and asked if she was okay. She shrugged and went on jabbing an already dead cigarette butt into the ashtray saucer. It was obvious that something was wrong and after checking on the vegetables, Grace sat down beside her.

'It's out,' she said, extracting the butt from Marigold's grip. 'What's wrong? Is it Ed?'

Marigold had said the thing with Ed was over, and yet there had been other occasions where she'd intimated the opposite, implying she'd stayed overnight at his place in Brixton. There was no point asking for details and, in any case, Grace wanted to block Ed out, along with whoever else Marigold saw on the nights when she didn't return. Nights where Grace lay awake, listening for the sound of the front door, for footsteps on the stairs, consumed by feelings of jealousy to which she could not admit.

'Talk to me.' Up close, she could see the dark smudges under Marigold's eyes. 'You look tired.'

'I am,' she said, letting her head droop onto Grace's shoulder. 'But I was listening.'

She wanted to hear more about the goings on at the office – the affair, and Rita in particular. She was fascinated by Rita in a way that almost made Grace jealous.

'I'm not judging her,' Marigold said. 'Simon's the one cheating.'

Reluctantly, Grace agreed. She would rather have blamed Rita for leading him on. She couldn't understand what he saw in her, apart from sex.

'What's wrong with that?' Marigold said. 'It's probably what Rita wants too. And from her point of view there are other advantages.'

'Such as?'

'Expanding her world.'

'What do you mean?'

'Rich older man with money and power. Expensive restaurants, holidays abroad, introductions to interesting and successful people.'

'But he's cheating on his wife. You said it.'

'That's true. Maybe his wife knows and doesn't care. An afternoon affair, *cinq à sept* as the French say, can spice up a marriage.'

'What about love? Isn't that important?'

'You mean romantic love? What about pleasure, fun, sex? If you ask me, Epicurus was right. Love doesn't last and complicates everything. Much better without it.'

Hearing that Marigold had no time for romantic love should have bolstered her commitment to philia. Instead, Grace felt flattened.

'You could do with a lover too,' Marigold said. 'Forget about Gerald.'

Grace tried to laugh and said she had forgotten about him ages ago. She turned back to the stove in time to rescue the rice.

She was setting the table, a task that involved dumping a pile of cutlery, glasses and plates at one end, when Raymond came in bearing bottles of red wine. He was accompanied by his occasional French girlfriend Sylvie and her Italian friend Claudia, who had arrived from Milan and could have been a double for a young Sophia Loren, if the film star had ever worn a brown duffel coat and a pair of faded Levis and never bothered to brush her hair. Vanessa, Alan and Annie arrived next. They had no time to sit down or be introduced to Claudia when Gerald rushed in, throwing his coat in the corner.

'Did you hear there's been another bomb?' he said. 'A pub in Woolwich near the Royal Artillery Barracks. Two dead and dozens injured.'

'Has anyone claimed responsibility?' Marigold asked.

'IRA for sure. Targeting off-duty soldiers,' Alan said.

'A soldier is a soldier. Being off-duty makes no difference,' Marigold said. 'Anyway, I asked if anyone had claimed responsibility, not whether you had an opinion.'

'Haven't heard,' Gerald said. 'But Alan's right. Who else would it be?'

'Who else would what be?' asked Martin, entering through the back door.

'Weren't you going to an enlightenment intensive?' Vanessa said.

'Cancelled. Group leader broke his leg.'

Gerald raised an eyebrow and Grace expected him to make a sarcastic comment, but he said nothing. He sat down at the table and was soon followed by the others. Only Ingred was missing; she had gone to Hackney to visit friends. Raymond introduced Claudia, whose presence seemed to have motivated the male members of the house to sit straighter and look more alert. There was a sexual vibe in

137

the air, of which Claudia seemed oblivious. No doubt she was used to it, Grace thought.

Before long, a discussion about revolutionary politics became heated. Claudia was arguing in support of the Red Brigades, an Italian far-left group whose strategies included bank robberies, kidnappings, and executions. Alan, who never took part in political discussions, abandoned his usual reticence, his face mottled with emotion.

'How can you support them?' he demanded. 'They're drug traffickers and gun runners. And they're murderers.'

'So, we do nothing?' Claudia countered. 'Revolution is violent. Why should we care if fascist pigs from the MSI get it in the neck?'

'And innocent bystanders?'

'Whose side are you on?' Raymond asked. 'The corrupt imperialist state—'

'—or the Red Brigades?' Alan scoffed. 'Is that the only choice?'

'You don't understand,' Sylvie said. 'It's not just the BR. The Red Army Faction in Germany is fighting fascism too. The Nazis are still in power.'

'Gudrun Ensslin calls them the Auschwitz generation,' Marigold said, speaking for the first time in ages. 'She says you can't argue with the people who made Auschwitz because they have weapons and we don't, and that we must arm ourselves.'

'What are you on about, Marigold?' Alan turned to her. 'We won the war. We don't need to arm ourselves.'

'I was quoting Gudrun Ensslin.'

'Never heard of her.'

'She founded the Red Army Faction with Andreas Baader.'

'Oh, you mean the Baader-Meinhof Gang,' Alan said. The derision in his voice was palpable.

'We don't call it that,' Claudia responded. 'It is the right-wing press who want everyone to think it is a gang.'

'And by the way,' Marigold continued to address Alan, 'the Nazis didn't stop existing because we won the war. And winning the war hasn't stopped the British Government from being a ruthless imperialist power either. Look what's happening in Northern Ireland.'

'If you want Nazis, go to Argentina,' Martin said, but no one was listening to him.

'What? So now you're supporting the IRA?' Alan turned to the others, looking for support. 'They've just killed another two people and maimed dozens of others. They're fucking murderers—'

'Jesus, Alan,' Annie interrupted, 'calm down.'

Alan pushed back his chair and rose from the table. 'You're all talking shite.' He motioned to Annie. 'Let's go.'

Annie shook her head.

'Come on man, sit down,' Gerald said. 'Finish your meal.' He put his hand on Alan's arm only to be shrugged off.

'Let him go,' Marigold said. 'He'll calm down on his own.'

'What does he know,' Raymond said as Alan left the kitchen. 'You English and your British Empire. You're not the centre anymore.'

'Don't lump me in with the Empire,' Gerald responded. 'I'm fighting capitalism, it's a class war.'

'Oh, fuck war. Why do men always talk about war?' Vanessa cried. 'You're in love with it. We have to transform ourselves first, one by one,' she urged. 'That's the only way we can change society.'

'And don't lump me in with all men,' Martin said. 'Personal enlightenment will do more to change the world than anything else.'

He was drowned out by cries of dissent. Both he and Vanessa were spouting hippy rubbish as usual. Raymond, who was rather drunk, began to hold forth on the need to smash the nuclear family in order for the revolutionary power of desire to be liberated. Nobody could follow his Deleuze-inspired ravings, not even Sylvie. She demanded he shut up and open more wine, which he did. With glasses refilled, the mood changed, and politics were set aside. Martin rolled an enormous joint and the talk turned to music – whether Pink Floyd was a load of shite or brilliant, who was better, Hawkwind or the Pink Fairies, and was Glastonbury Festival ever going to return.

Marigold rose to gather the empty plates. Grace joined her and together they cleared the table and prepared to wash up, which, as the cooks for the night, was part of their job.

'I'll wash,' Marigold said. 'You can dry.'

They worked in companionable silence, while behind them the talk at the table grew rowdier with much laughter and teasing. Grace was still brooding on the earlier conversation.

'Do you think Claudia is really involved in the Red Brigades?' she said, as Annie joined them at the sink. 'She seemed to know a lot about them.'

Marigold shrugged. 'It's possible I suppose.'

'I don't agree with Alan, but executing people in cold blood—' Annie began, before Marigold interrupted her.

'It's just empty talk unless you're prepared to kill for your beliefs. That's the only question. Whether you have the courage to follow through. It's easy to mouth off about Nazis and fascists. Anyone can do that.'

'Yes, but you wouldn't, you know—' Annie left the rest of it unsaid. It was both a question and a statement, and Marigold turned to her, a look of contempt, or something like it, darting across her face. It was gone in a flash, and she laughed.

'Of course not. Are you going to help or just stand around?' she said.

Annie laughed too and grabbed a tea towel.

Once the washing up was done, Grace went up to her bedroom. The trippy sound of Tangerine Dream drifted through the house. She stood at the open window, smoking, feeling unsettled by the evening's discussion. She wondered if Annie had seen that strange hostile look on Marigold's face and what it meant. Or had she imagined it? A fleeting expression was easy to misinterpret, and Marigold liked Annie, she'd said as much to Grace.

She flicked the cigarette butt out of the window, watching the red tip spiral through the darkness, reliving the discussion that had taken place and how she hadn't said anything, because every time she'd been about to speak, she'd changed her mind, swayed first one way and then another. Violence was awful, but wasn't the violence of the state far greater than that of the revolutionaries? Wasn't the creation of a more equal society a goal worth fighting for? Revolution was necessary and hadn't Lenin said something about needing to break eggs to make an omelette? Or was it Gerald who'd said that?

Grace found the arguments for and against radical action equally convincing. But what she found more compelling, were the exploits of the Red Brigades and the Red Army Faction – exploits which gripped her with a desire for chaos that had nothing to do with equality or the creation of a socialist paradise. She was exhilarated by the idea of tearing everything down, of breaking the eggs and not giving a fuck about the law. It was only when Marigold said it was just empty talk unless you were prepared to kill for your beliefs that she'd felt a chill. The blunt brutality of it was a shock and her earlier exhilaration had evaporated. But surely Marigold was only talking theory, she wasn't a killer. Of course not, she'd said in response to Annie's question.

She wondered again about Claudia, and how far the Italian girl was prepared to go. Was she a member of the Red Brigades or just a sympathiser? It was a relief to realise that she, Grace, didn't possess the same political fervour and lacked the conviction needed to kill fascist industrialists and right-wing politicians. Or – an afterthought – bomb off-duty soldiers, drinking in a pub, which made her remember that Marigold had said soldiers were never off-duty.

Join the army, see the world, kill people, Grace and her friends had jeeringly chanted at anti-war demos. Naturally, they hated soldiers and cops, but that wasn't the same as bombing a soldiers' pub. She was sure Marigold would agree.

16

Whether or not Marigold agreed with Grace remained untested. The topic of the Red Brigades and revolutionary action never came up again and, if Grace thought about it now and then, it was only in passing, for after that night certain things changed. Marigold no longer disappeared for days on end and confided to Grace that the affair with Ed was over. She admitted she'd not told the whole truth. She had continued to see him, god knows why, but it was really over now. She said she wanted to rethink her life and as a result, had thrown in the translating job too. With enough money to survive for a few months, there was no point rushing into a new job and then regretting it. She was at a loose end, a good loose end she said, and one that meant they could resume their flâneuring, that is, if Grace wanted to. Which she did.

There were also films to see at The Gate and Electric cinemas and further afield, at the Ritzy and Screen on the Green. On weekends, when the weather was rotten or they felt too lazy, they lounged around in the communal room with the others, listening to music and smoking hash. Sometimes they cloistered themselves in Marigold's room, where Grace lay on the bed, reading to the intermittent stuttering of Marigold's sewing machine. Simon had instructed her to compile a list of young, up-to-the-minute authors he could lure to

Primo Press by means of his deep pockets. Her trips to the bookshops of Charing Cross Road were scouting expeditions where, inevitably, she became side-tracked in the labyrinth of Foyles, losing track of the task at hand, spending Simon's research money on things that caught her eye – novels such as George Orwell's *Keep the Aspidistra Flying*, in which she discovered that Orwell's aspidistra was a symbol of bourgeois respectability.

When Marigold grew tired of sewing, she demanded to be entertained, keen to hear the latest about Simon, Rita, Eric, and even Basia and Didier. Grace was happy to oblige, especially as it meant more time in Marigold's company. Lying together on the bed, regaling her with stories from work, it was almost as if they were lovers. It was an exquisite kind of agony to be so close, yet not to touch; the ever-present danger of losing control, of throwing herself on Marigold, kissing her, making desperate, ludicrous declarations of love. There were times when she almost convinced herself that Marigold felt the same way and that she was not completely straight. *I'm not gay*, Marigold had said that night when they'd seen the butches outside the lesbian club. Was it possible to be *not gay*, and still fall in love with a woman? Isn't that my situation too? Grace thought. She tried to turn the conversation to Shanti, hoping that it would lead to an opening, a way of saying something about her feelings. About not being gay, of being ... what? In love?

At the very least, she wanted Marigold to know that she wasn't interested in Gerald, declaring that he was a bore, always going on about the working class and squatters' rights. She felt guilty saying it because she didn't really think he was a bore. It was just that she wanted to make her position clear, at least in respect to Gerald, for in every other way it wasn't clear at all.

On Saturday afternoon, Grace was making pancakes when he wandered into the kitchen.

'What is it with you two,' he said. 'You're like Siamese twins these days. Anyone would think you're in love.'

144

Grace busied herself with the pancake batter, blood rushing to her cheeks.

'And if we were, would it turn you on?' Marigold asked, teasing.

'Maybe,' he said with a laugh.

Grace glanced around to see Marigold drizzling honey on a pancake, rolling it up. She popped it into Gerald's mouth before he could protest, using her fingers to wipe the honey that dripped from his chin. It was an intimate, flirtatious action, and Grace was pierced by a wave of jealousy so intense that she couldn't speak. For the second time, she turned to the stove, her heart skittering.

Gerald left soon afterwards. He was going round to the squat they'd broken into weeks ago to see how the West Indian family from Manchester was coping and whether they needed any help.

That evening, Grace and Marigold set out on foot to The Gate cinema. On the way, Marigold spoke about the film they were to see. The director was Jacques Rivette, an important member of the French New Wave who had begun his career as a film critic. She had high hopes for his new film.

'What's it called again?' Grace asked, distracted by a recurring memory of Marigold wiping honey from Gerald's chin and the piercing pain that went with it. She wished she'd kept her eyes on the stove and never turned around.

'*Celine and Julie Go Boating.* You've asked me that twice already. Sometimes I wonder what goes on in your head.'

If only I could tell you, Grace thought.

They entered the cinema and headed to their usual spot, near the front. As the house lights dimmed, someone whispered, and Marigold issued a warning shush. From the very first frame she demanded total silence.

Three hours later, they emerged from the cinema, into the winter night. For once, Grace didn't notice the cold, she was still in Paris where it was summertime, loitering on a bench in a sunlit square; dancing along dappled streets; climbing stone steps to the top of Montmartre. She was Celine and, because of her reddish hair, Marigold was Julie, inhabiting a world where fantasy and reality merged, and magic was real. Anything was possible. She whirled around a few times and grabbed Marigold by the arm, drawing her close as they hurried across the road to the nearby pub.

They found an empty table and sat down.

'I want to see it again,' Grace gushed. 'It's the best film we've seen in ages. Maybe ever.'

'Really?'

Marigold's response came as a shock. Grace had been so wrapped up in the world of the film and how much she adored it, that she'd assumed her friend felt the same way.

'Didn't you love it?'

'The French can be so self-indulgent,' Marigold replied. 'Honestly, I almost died of boredom. That interminable story within a story and the stupid play-acting and magic. Two silly girls and an even sillier plot.'

'I thought it was quite feminist,' Grace said in a stiff voice.

'Feminist? I didn't notice anyone fighting for women's rights. When did you become a feminist by the way? And all that repressed lesbian hoo-ha. Why not come out with it?'

Before Marigold revealed her contempt for the film, Grace had been about to say that Celine and Julie had reminded her of them. The intimacy between the characters, their telepathic communication and physical ease. Celine resting her head on Julie's shoulder and the tender way Julie removed the sweet from Celine's mouth – details she'd found secretly erotic. Hearing Marigold's scathing assessment, she felt winded, her delight evaporating. For three hours, she'd been in a dream world – Celine and Julie's Paris, but also a dream in which she and Marigold were lovers. Seated next to each other in the cinema, their arms had sometimes touched, and she'd become convinced that Marigold was experiencing the same urgent energy

146

pulsing between them. Cocooned in the dark, she'd forgotten her fears of being a lesbian, a dyke, a freak of nature. None of it mattered because it wasn't about that. It was about the two of them and they didn't need to call it anything. It was about being in love. How close she'd been to blurting it out.

Somewhere in the background she heard Marigold speaking.

'It's not a crime for us to disagree. If it makes you feel better, there were some things I liked. Montmartre. And the cats. And the allusions to Proust's madeleines and *Alice in Wonderland*. Honestly, Grace, if you're going to sulk, I'm leaving.'

'Go then,' she heard herself say. 'Don't let me stop you.'

'Oh, come on.'

She stared at her pint glass, refusing to look up.

'What's the matter? Because I didn't like the film? I don't understand why you're being so childish.'

Grace clenched her jaw to stop the gathering tears, determined not to cry. She couldn't speak without giving herself away.

'So, you're really going to sit here and say absolutely nothing?'

The answer was yes, conveyed through stony silence. Grace wanted her to feel the same pain, the same agony that was engulfing her. It was out of proportion, yet in another way, it was not. It had been building for a long time.

'This is ridiculous. I'm going.' Marigold stood up.

Grace could feel her waiting for a response.

'I'll see you at home then,' Marigold said at last. She threw her cloak over her shoulders and left. And still, Grace did not look up.

There was a bitter satisfaction to getting drunk. The thought of stumbling home on her own and something bad happening. Then you'll be sorry. She knew how childish it was. Marigold had already accused her of the same thing. *Why are you being so childish?* She swallowed another mouthful of beer, consumed by fantasies of hurting her, of making her suffer the way she was suffering. It was all mixed up with self-loathing. The stupidity of over-reacting like this but she couldn't stop. She hated Marigold, hated everyone, including herself. She drained the rest of her drink. One more and she'd be really drunk. Why not?

Just as she was about to get up and go to the bar, she caught sight of a man crossing the room with two glasses of red wine and saw that it was Simon. She couldn't bear for him to see her like this. With nowhere to hide she tried to make herself inconspicuous, watching from the corner of her eye as he made his way to a table near the back of the room. He didn't look in her direction and sat down opposite a woman. Rita!

Instinct took over and she ducked under the table, pretending to search for something. As she scrabbled around on her fake search, it struck her that she couldn't go on like this. She was not the one having a clandestine affair; there was no reason for her to hide. She sat up and began to gather her things. It was time to leave.

It was impossible not to look in their direction and she risked a glance, shocked by the unexpected sight of Rita crying. Simon leaned across the table, extending his hand to her in a conciliatory gesture, but Rita batted him away, knocking over her glass of red wine. She jumped up, and Simon rose too. Grace could see that he was trying to calm her down. Around them, others had begun to take notice. Rita was shouting that he'd ruined her life; she'd given up everything for him. Then she grabbed her bag and swung it around, hitting him on the back of the head.

On her way towards the exit, she passed Grace's table and stumbled. Their eyes met, and Grace had the strange sensation that it was happening in slow motion. Rita gave no sign of recognition, her face a crumpled mask of misery. The pub door banged shut behind her and time resumed its normal pace.

Grace left soon after. She hoped Simon hadn't seen her and felt embarrassed for him. Her feelings for Rita were more complex. To see her suffering should have been gratifying, even enjoyable.

An enemy laid low. But in that strange, elongated moment when their eyes had met, she'd had an urge to reach out and comfort her.

Outside, Rita was nowhere to be seen and as the pub receded so did the scene she'd witnessed. What had taken place with Marigold was far more important.

Turning into Belton Road, she met Vanessa who had been visiting the Orange People house.

'I haven't seen you for ages,' Vanessa said.

'I know,' she replied. 'We should do something together, I've missed you.'

It was a white lie, told to distract Vanessa in case she mentioned Marigold. Everyone knew they'd gone to see a film together. She couldn't face making something up, pretending everything was fine.

'I'd like that,' Vanessa said. 'There's another marathon in a fortnight. Why don't you come? Paula's been asking about you.'

Grace made affirmative noises, knowing that later, she would invent an excuse. Hell would have to freeze over before she joined another encounter group.

As they arrived home, Vanessa was explaining the importance of Saturn in the natal chart and Grace was pretending to listen. She was in a heightened state, thinking about Marigold, the moment of seeing her and how to act. Whether to gloss over what had happened and admit that she had gone a bit mad. Make a joke of it.

'Sorry Vanessa,' she said, interrupting the astrological analysis, 'I'm going to bed.'

She lay awake for a long time, wishing that Marigold would appear, imagining a scene between them where Marigold apologised and put everything right between them. A scene where they got into bed together and went to sleep, wrapped in each other's arms.

17

Grace put the kettle on the hob. She was up early to catch Marigold whose habit it was to make a cup of tea before returning to drink it in bed. Her plan was to play it cool and act as if nothing had happened at the pub, or nothing that mattered. The genie of her passionate feelings had burst from the bottle and she couldn't find a way to stuff them back in. Revealing them was equally out of the question. They were friends, not lovers, and to carry on with the disagreement in the pub was too weird, too out of proportion. She had to drop it. Except that secretly and by some twist of logic, she believed Marigold was responsible for fixing things. She was the one who needed to apologise for walking out. It was up to her to put things right.

Soon enough, she came down to the kitchen.

'If you're making a pot, I'd love a cup,' she said, tying the cord of her tatty tartan dressing gown, though not before a glimpse of pearly flesh.

Grace responded to the request with a grunt, wanting to make it plain that something else was required and that she wasn't interested in small talk. She was caught in a trap of her own making, having to convey that something was wrong without appearing to care one way or the other.

'Off to work?' Marigold said. 'You'd better take a brolly. I think it's going to rain.'

Grace grunted again. She poured the tea in silence, a heavy, smouldering silence, hoping that Marigold would ask if anything was the matter. That would be something, and she could respond, *no, why?* meaning the opposite. She would force her to acknowledge that something was wrong, even if it didn't lead to a rapprochement and, instead, caused an argument. A connection, whether positive or negative, was better than nothing.

Marigold yawned and leaned against the bench. She didn't say anything more, and Grace felt a tic start up in her cheek. Marigold was about to swan back upstairs with her tea as if everything was normal. She wasn't going to apologise or ask what was wrong. It was obvious that the disagreement in the pub meant nothing to her. She had brushed it off. The silence grew, and with it, Grace's desire to hurt her, to leave a mark, a wound. To make her suffer the way she was suffering. Her hand shook as she put the mug of tea on the table.

'Careful, you're spilling it,' Marigold said. She picked it up and, with a vague smile, padded away.

Dragging herself to work, Grace discovered that Rita had not come in. Nor did she appear the next day.

'No idea,' Eric said, when Grace asked if he'd heard anything.

If Simon knew, he chose not to reveal it. He was holed up in his office where she could hear him roaming around, growling into the phone, banging things. She was sure his mood and Rita's absence were connected. Remembering the tragic look on Rita's face as she stumbled past in the pub, Grace hoped that she was okay. She thought about ringing to check and told herself she would do it tomorrow, until tomorrow turned into Friday.

She was lounging at her desk when the downstairs front door slammed, and she heard Rita call a greeting to Eric. Moments later, she appeared.

'Coffee, my office,' she barked.

Grace placed the cup of coffee on the desk, intending to scuttle off at once.

'Stay for a minute,' Rita said, her black eyes gleaming like the Greek olives at Didier's deli.

'I would, but I should get back to work, things to do.'

'I doubt it. Sit down.'

Rita's invitation had turned into an order, and she gave in, perching on the edge of the chair. To avoid eye contact she stared at Rita's red boucle jacket, which had been buttoned in the wrong holes, making it lopsided. It was a peculiar lapse and Grace was on the verge of pointing it out when she realised her folly. Rita would definitely not thank her for it.

'You're feeling better?' she said, smiling in what she hoped was a sympathetic way. The genuine sympathy she'd felt a few days ago had evaporated.

'How was your weekend?' Rita said.

'Weekend?' Grace repeated the word, momentarily confused because it was Friday and the weekend seemed ages ago.

'Yes, the weekend, Grace. Did you do anything interesting?'

'Not much,' she replied. She could feel Rita staring at her and began to prattle. 'Although I did see a film. A French film about two women who meet because one of them drops her scarf and then the other one, Julie, follows her, sort of like the white rabbit in Alice in Wonderland and they become friends and move into Julie's flat and then things start to get weird when they enter an imaginary world. I mean, it's not a world, it's just a house—'

'For god's sake, I don't need the whole plot.'

'Anyway, the French can be quite pretentious. The story within a story—'

'Enough. I don't want to hear any more about some stupid film,' Rita snapped.

'Sorry. I was trying … you asked did I do anything.'

'I was making conversation. I wasn't expecting a monologue.'

'Oh. Sorry. What about you?'

'Me?'

'Did you do anything interesting?'

'I'm not here to answer personal questions.'

Grace wanted to protest that this was not fair, and that she wasn't there to answer personal questions either. Had they ever been asking each other personal questions?

'You do realise you're the Girl Friday? You can be replaced like this.'

Rita clicked her fingers in a demonstration of how instantly it could happen, and Grace understood then that the reason she'd been invited to *stay for a minute* was so that Rita could issue a warning. She wasn't even sure she cared about being replaced and yet the unfairness of it rankled. To be discarded in such a cavalier fashion. She wished she could think of a withering retort, but her mind had gone blank.

'Given you're so desperate to know, I spent the week in the country,' Rita said.

Grace was about to say that she wasn't desperate to know when Rita continued.

'The Cotswolds. You've heard of the Cotswolds? I drove up after work last Friday. I'm only telling you because you asked,' Rita said in such a furious tone that, this time, Grace felt compelled to defend herself.

'I didn't ask—'

'Rodney and Marian.'

'Who?'

'My friends. In the Cotswolds. Who else would I be talking about?'

It was on the tip of Grace's tongue to say 'Simon', just to see what would happen, but skewered by Rita's unblinking black-eyed gaze, she suffered a failure of nerve. The message was unambiguous: Rita had never been at the pub with Simon, she was in the Cotswolds with Rodney and Marian, she had not seen Grace and Grace had not seen her and the whole thing in the pub was never to be mentioned. How could it be when it had never taken place?

'I've decided,' Rita said, 'I'm going to be honest with you.'

'Okay,' Grace replied, with a familiar feeling of dread.

'He's going to use you and the next thing you know you'll be on the scrap heap. He can't help himself, it's a compulsion. You're the latest in a long line. I give it two months at the most before he's back knocking at my door.' She leaned forward with an intimidating stare. 'Well?' she demanded.

'I don't know what you're talking about,' Grace lied.

'He's leaving his wife,' Rita shouted. 'He's leaving her for me.'

'But you've broken up. I mean, isn't that what—'

Rita sprang to her feet. 'That's a fucking lie,' she said in a furious voice.

Grace glanced towards the door, wishing she had the courage to walk out. She didn't want to inflame Rita any further and lowered her eyes. After a while, Rita blew her nose, and Grace looked up to see that she had been crying.

'Are you okay?'

Rita glared at her. 'I'm thirty-three. I'm the first person in my family to get my A levels and work in an office. An office! Do you know what that means? To have a job where you're not on your feet all day and actually get to sit down. It took me years to get rid of my accent. Do you have any idea what it's like to hear the snide comments, the sniggering?'

'I'm sorry—'

'Stick your stupid sympathy. Did I ask for it?' Mascara was running down her cheeks. 'He promised me,' she shouted. 'I've worked like a slave. I've lied for him. You don't know what I've done for him.' She banged her fist on the desk. 'I forbid you, Grace. Do you hear me?'

She returned Rita's stare, unable to think of anything to say, only that she had to hold her ground. They faced each other, Rita breathing heavily and Grace scarcely breathing at all. The seconds ticked by with no further outburst, and she wondered if it was safe to leave. Rita gave no sign, except that her eyes had taken on a glassy, unfocused appearance. It was possible she'd gone into some sort of fugue state. Grace had begun to experience a disconcerting out of body thing, looking down on the two of them from a point near the ceiling. From that vantage point, she and Rita looked like actors who had forgotten their dialogue and no longer knew what play they were in or what the plot demanded of them. They were both stuck and might have stayed that way if Eric hadn't poked his head in the doorway.

'Mind if I interrupt,' he said, sauntering in, puffing on a cigarette.

With a jolt, Grace returned to her body, and Rita blinked for the first time in ages. Eric propped on the edge of the desk and continued to smoke. He looked from one to the other.

'What's wrong? I heard someone shouting.'

'Nothing,' Rita replied. 'Get your skinny arse off my desk.'

Grace seized the opportunity and leapt up, declaring that she had things to do, waving away Eric's protest. As she turned to leave, she caught Rita's eye, which no longer looked like a glossy black olive, but murky and dangerous.

She had almost reached her desk when Simon, who had been out all morning, leapt up the stairs. He grabbed her by the arm.

'Need you,' he said.

They reached the front door and were on the street before she had a chance to catch her breath or ask him for an explanation. He took her arm again and hustled her along the footpath.

'Where are we going?'

'I'll explain in the car,' he replied.

They pulled out into the flow of the traffic.

'Sorry,' he said. 'All a bit of a rush. Thanks for helping.'

155

'With what?'

'Old friend, Guy Aubrey. He's going to smell pretty awful.'

'Why? What's happened?'

'It's a bit complicated. Don't be scared, he's as gentle as a lamb.'

Up to that point, being scared hadn't occurred to her. She was about to seek more information when he swerved, accelerating past a van, almost colliding with an oncoming car.

'Bloody idiots,' he yelled. 'The main thing is to get him off the street for a few days. Clean him up, get some food into him.'

'He's on the street?'

Simon did not reply. They were approaching Barons Court tube station and he swung across to the left and pulled up, ignoring the no standing sign.

'I'll be as quick as I can. Drive round the block if you have to.'

He leapt out of the car and ran towards the station entrance, leaving the car keys dangling in the ignition.

Grace waited, watching the people coming and going from the station, feeling anxious that at any moment a policeman or a traffic officer would appear and tell her to move on. She had not driven a car since arriving in London and manoeuvring Simon's Mercedes into the traffic and around a busy city block was a far cry from driving Clara's old Beetle to the farm. That she had a driver's licence in the first place was due to the lax approach of the local policeman, Mr Dixon, who'd allowed her to drive along a deserted road for a few miles, during which time she hadn't seen another vehicle. There was no need for three-point turns or reverse parking, Mr Dixon said. And no need to bother with the question-and-answer part of the test either, as he was in a bit of a hurry to get to the races and more importantly, he knew her father.

Five sweaty minutes passed when Simon returned, accompanied by Guy, rail-thin in a filthy mac that came down to his ankles. She caught a glimpse of an aquiline nose, a smear of blood on his cheek and a black eye as he folded himself into the back seat, the stench of unwashed clothes and flesh filling the car. Simon was already turning on the ignition, motioning with a discreet hand movement to open her window as he made hasty introductions.

'Hi,' Grace said. She almost said *Hi Guy*, stopping herself at the last moment because the rhyme made it sound odd and flippant which, given the state of him, seemed inappropriate. Guy remained silent.

Cold air from the open front windows blasted them all the way to Battersea, where they pulled up outside an imposing red brick mansion block. Simon led them into the building and an old-fashioned cage lift, which took them up to the top floor. Grace knew that Simon and Marina and various children (a horde of brats according to Eric) lived in something called a mansion flat. In Melbourne, everyone she knew lived in houses, and the sum total of her knowledge of flats and their spinster inhabitants had been gleaned from English novels. She was expecting something dingy that smelled of boiled cabbage, whereas the voluminous entrance hall alone was almost as large as the entire ground floor of the squat.

Simon guided them down a long wide passage, passing doors on each side.

'Right,' he said, coming to a stop. 'Bathroom. I'll get Guy organised. Why don't you make a pot of tea? Straight on, turn left at the end.'

She was glad to find herself alone in the kitchen, remembering Eric's description of Marina as dangerous. The confrontation with Rita was more than enough. She made the tea and waited for Simon. As the minutes ticked by, Rita's words came back to her. How she was the first person in her family to get A levels and work in an office. How it had taken her years to get rid of her accent, a fact that Grace couldn't help noticing was a link between them. She wondered what sort of accent Rita had erased. For the first time, she thought of Rita as a person with a history. Someone with her own hopes and dreams and who, behind her intimidating façade, had feelings. Rita hated her, but did it have to be that way? If only she'd been able to explain that she wasn't interested in Simon.

The tea had grown cold when he appeared.

'All good,' he said. 'I've told him, half an hour's soak at least.'

'What happened to him?'

'Sleeping rough. Woke up with two young thugs going through his pockets. Bashed the hell out of him.'

'Shouldn't we take him to hospital?'

Simon shook his head. 'He won't go. Believe it or not, I've seen him in worse shape. He'll be alright.'

Grace boiled the kettle again. They sat at the kitchen table which was French oak and had been salvaged from a monastery. Apparently, Marina was keen on old French things. 'She doesn't mind about Guy?' Grace asked.

'Not up to her. He was my best friend at school. Still my best friend.'

His voice wobbled a bit as he said it. He lit a cigarette and puffed on it. She waited, unused to seeing him like this.

'He hears voices that tell him he's got to save the world by living on the streets and starving himself. Vow of poverty and God's chosen messenger. That sort of thing. Then there are times he knows it's a delusion. You'd think he'd be happy about that, but sometimes it's worse.'

'Why?'

'Because he understands what he's lost. A normal life. A job, a house, a wife and kids. He was a brilliant student, dux of the school. And kind. He'd give you the shirt off his back.'

She grimaced, remembering the stench in the car, and Simon laughed.

'Alright, not such a good idea.'

'What will he do now?'

158

'He'll stay here for a night or two, get his strength back and off he'll go.'

'Onto the street? Why can't you—'

'It's not up to me,' he said, interrupting her. 'He knows he can stay here for as long as he likes, I've told him many times. But he won't.'

'Why not?'

'Ah well, he's a free spirit.'

'I know someone like him,' Grace said, thinking of Vincent. 'Although I don't think he has a fairy godfather.'

'Hmm, fairy godfather, am I? Thought I was more of a big, bad wolf.'

He gave her a wolfish grin and a look that seemed preparatory to eating her up, which made her giggle nervously. Then he laughed and thanked her for helping him. He told her she ought to go home and walked her to the front door. She was about to step into the lift when he called out for her to wait.

'Here,' he said and took a ten-pound note from his wallet. 'For the taxi.'

'I'll give you the change tomorrow,' she said.

'Don't be an idiot,' he replied. 'Now off you go.'

18

Grace was late for the house meeting. She entered the kitchen and sat down in the only available chair, ignoring Marigold. 'Shall we start?' Ingred said.

Someone began banging on the front door.

'It's probably Vincent,' Annie said. 'I saw him in the street earlier. He'll give up in a minute.'

There was general agreement not to answer the door; they knew that Vincent would disrupt the meeting. When the banging continued, Gerald was forced to go and deal with it.

'Wasn't Vincent,' he said on his return. 'A bloke looking for someone called Stella. I told him to try opposite.'

'The dykes?' Martin asked.

Ingred gave him a sharp look. The correct term was lesbian separatists. It was not his place to call them dykes.

'It's probably one of the sannyasins,' Vanessa said. 'Remember when Pratima's dad came looking for Angela and no one knew who Angela was.'

'All I know is, he was bloody rude,' Gerald said. 'Can we get on with the meeting?'

He began to summarise the issues for discussion. Grace fixed her gaze on him, pretending to listen, while her whole being was tuned to

Marigold. They were no longer speaking, and Grace had convinced herself that Marigold was to blame. It was a reversal of the truth, which in certain moments she knew and refused to admit. In her confused emotional logic, Marigold had to pay for the crime of not loving her. To the rest of the world, she made a point of acting as if everything was fine.

Gerald's mouth was still moving when she heard Marigold rise and, for a fraction of a second, their eyes met. Grace registered how pale she looked; her lips pressed together in a tense line.

'Sorry,' she said, 'I can't stay.'

She left the kitchen, ignoring the protests that erupted around the table. That she hadn't even bothered to give an excuse made it worse, though not to Grace, who interpreted her departure as a sign that she couldn't cope with sitting opposite her. It was a sign that they were still connected. That Grace had had an effect on her. It was a negative one, but negative was better than nothing.

In the middle of the night, she woke to the sound of a muffled boom and a tremor that rippled through the room. The window rattled and the wardrobe door swung open and then shut with a bang. She sat up, heart pounding. The bomb warnings on the under-ground, suspicious packages, the IRA, all flashed through her mind. Or could it be the National Front, finally making good on their threats? She waited, caught between the desire to leap out of bed and get dressed in readiness for what lay ahead, and an equally strong urge to cower in her bed. She hadn't decided when Ingred appeared in the open doorway.

'Grace? Are you awake?'

'Yes.'

'Can I come in?'

'Sure.' She leaned across and switched on the bedside lamp. 'What's happened? I heard a bang.'

Ingred was wearing her usual shaggy brown coat and black boots, an old huntsman's bag slung across her body. Her coat and hair were flecked with white specks. Far from her usual composure, she looked freaked out.

'Oh, it's snowing,' Grace said.

Ingred shook her head. 'My ceiling fell in. Can I sit down?' She crossed the room and sat down on the bed. 'I just got home. A few seconds later ...' She trailed off with a shudder and Grace realised that the white specks were not snowflakes but tiny bits of plaster. 'I am unharmed, as you can see,' Ingred continued. 'Can I ask you? Is it okay if I sleep here tonight?'

'Of course.'

Grace was surprised that in her hour of need Ingred had chosen her. They were not friends and she'd always found her distant and inclined to be superior. To look at, Ingred reminded her of Ingrid Thulin in *Cries and Whispers*, a film directed by Ingmar Bergman that Marigold had insisted was essential viewing.

Ingred undressed down to her underpants and slipped into bed, positioning herself on the edge of the mattress.

'Turn out the light,' she said, peremptorily.

Though separated by a space, Grace felt the heat radiating from Ingred's body. She hoped Ingred would speak and when she did not, tried to think of something suitably intelligent to say. But Ingred's self-possession, that regal, superior air, was too daunting. She gave up and closed her eyes, only to find sleep elusive.

'I saw you at the encounter marathon,' she said, unable to hold out any longer.

'Mm.'

'You didn't stay.'

'No.'

Grace stared at the ceiling, wishing Ingred would say something more. A scene from *Cries and Whispers* came to her in which the sisters, Maria and Karin, frantically caressed each other's faces.

162

She tried to blank it out, feeling agitated. Then, when she'd given up expecting it, Ingred spoke.

'My father was a Nazi,' she said. 'He was a member of the Danish Nazi party. When I was eighteen, I found a photograph of him in an SS uniform. He never spoke about the war. I believed he was like a lot of Danes, who went on with their lives. A lot of them resisted the Germans in small ways. They were not heroes, but they were not Nazis. They were not fucking traitors and Jew haters.'

She spoke in a quiet, flat voice, as if telling Grace something ordinary and not very important. Even when she said *fucking traitors and Jew haters*, she didn't sound angry. The revelation was so unexpected and shocking that Grace couldn't think of anything to say.

'After I found out, I left home. I didn't want to live in the same house.'

'Did you ask him why?' Grace asked, having found her voice again.

'*Blut und Boden*,' Ingred said. 'Blood and soil. They were farmers, him and his parents, my grandparents. They believed all the Nazi shit about the pure race and the homeland. The ideal of the rural life. I think it made them feel important.'

'You grew up on a farm?'

'Mm.'

'Me too.'

'With a Nazi papa?'

Grace laughed briefly, remembering the accusations she'd wanted to hurl at him – that he was a Nazi in disguise. It was not something she wanted to tell Ingred. 'No. But he is right-wing.' Then, having damned him, she was overcome by a protective urge. 'He fought against the Germans in the Middle East. He was a Rat of Tobruk.'

'A rat?'

'The Germans called them rats as an insult and because they were besieged, living in fox holes and dug outs. In the end, they beat

163

the Germans and turned the name into a badge of honour. The Rats of Tobruk.'

'So, there are good rats and bad rats. I got the bad rat.'

'I'm sorry.'

'There's nothing to be sorry about. Good night, Grace,' she said, turning away to face the opposite wall.

Ingred's breathing soon deepened, each exhalation becoming a little longer and slower, until it seemed she had fallen asleep. Grace wished she could sleep too. Instead, her mind swirled with questions. Was Ingred's father still a Nazi? Was he alive? Was he the reason she'd gone to the encounter group in the first place? She tried to imagine Ingred thrashing the pillows with a rounders bat, screaming abuse at him, and was glad that she'd made the decision to leave. She didn't want to see Ingred lose control. She didn't want to witness her shame. Not that she had anything to be ashamed of; it wasn't her fault that her father was a Nazi. Except that shame didn't work like that, it wasn't logical.

Her thoughts drifted away from Ingred, and she began to think about her own father, the Rat of Tobruk, the 'good rat' as Ingred had called him. An image came to her of his hands on the steering wheel of the old land rover, the way he drummed his fingers on the wheel, his sun-browned fingers tapping out a rhythm that only he heard. Her father never talked about his past, everything she knew came from her mother. It was just before the war, and he'd passed his final exams. For some reason, he returned to boarding school for an extra year. She couldn't remember why; all she knew was that he spent the year perfecting his Fred Astaire tap dancing and that he'd even dreamed of becoming a professional tap dancer. Sometimes she wondered if her mother really had told her this, or whether she'd dreamt it, because the idea of her father as an aspiring tap dancer was utterly strange and unlikely. She'd never seen him dance, not tap nor anything else. He was a farmer, a Rat of Tobruk. A good rat, except that he was also racist. He wasn't simply one thing, and it made her think how impossible it was to truly know another human being and especially her father.

Before she could block it out, she had a vision of his letter, lying unopened in the bottom of her bag. She hadn't thought about it for ages, and as the weeks had gone by, the decision not to read it, which she'd only ever imagined as temporary, had hardened into a more permanent resolve. She was convinced it would be full of orders and instructions. A demand to come home.

In the morning, Grace woke to find that Ingred had already gone. It wasn't a surprise; Ingred was notorious for rising at some unthinkably early hour. She'd been as silent as a cat, and the bedclothes on her side were pulled up neatly so that it looked as if she'd never been there. Grace hadn't heard a thing.

By the time she got home from work, Raymond and Vanessa had helped clean up the fallen ceiling. Gerald was arranging things with a friend who had access to some plasterboard from a renovation job in Knightsbridge. The owners were filthy rich; it was only fair they should contribute, albeit unwittingly. Ingred had to buy a new mattress too as the old one was contaminated with plaster dust and giving her asthma.

'Are you sure you don't mind if I stay for another night,' she asked. 'I could sleep in the front room, on the couch.'

'I don't mind,' Grace replied, surprised to find that it was true.

In the past, she'd accepted that Ingred wasn't interested in getting to know her, retaliating by declaring (to herself) that she wasn't interested in Ingred either. All of that changed with the unexpected story about her Nazi father. She'd revealed a more vulnerable side and Grace wanted to hear more. It was important not to sound too keen, knowing it was the sort of thing that might put her off.

In keeping with the not-too-keen approach, she waited for an hour before following Ingred to bed, where she found her sitting up, flicking through *The Prime of Miss Jean Brodie*. It was a second-hand copy from Foyles, and one of the purchases she'd made with Simon's research money. Muriel Spark's novel had caught her eye because of the front cover photograph of Maggie Smith who had played the title role in the film version. Before things had gone wrong between them, Marigold said she was sure Grace would find it interesting. *You'll see*, she said, when Grace asked why. Reading about the charismatic Miss Brodie and her students, the crème de la crème girls who were in love with her, those words returned. She couldn't get rid of the idea that Marigold had been sending her a message. A coded way of saying she hadn't believed her that night outside the lesbian club. There was no point worrying about it; they were no longer speaking.

Justifying her first-class literature degree and role as literary scout, Grace had mentioned Muriel Spark to Simon, who was dismissive. He was interested in the zeitgeist and not characters like Miss Jean Brodie. Recently he'd become obsessed with *The Dice Man*, a novel about a bored psychiatrist who, in a quest for freedom, begins to make decisions based on the roll of the dice.

'You see, Grace,' Simon explained, 'he gives himself options, for example, whether to rape his neighbour, and if the dice say yes, then that's what he does.'

'Oh, great idea,' she said.

'Alright, it sounds bad, but the neighbour fancied him, so it wasn't really rape. The idea is to let chance take over and trust in fate. Look, the point is, the book has sold millions.' Simon was convinced it was the kind of thing they needed to put them on the map.

She undressed quickly, pulling on a ragged t-shirt and a pair of long johns. She didn't own any proper pyjamas and preferred to sleep naked until the freezing London winter had forced her to improvise. She slipped into her side of the bed. Ingred was wearing striped pyjamas and, because she was sitting up, Grace felt she had to sit up too.

'Do you want to keep reading?' she asked.

'Not really. It's quite boring.'

'Oh?'

'What is this prime of Miss Brodie? No, don't tell me.' She dropped the book beside the bed.

Her blunt judgement made Grace think of Celine and Julie and Marigold's negative opinion; how it had been the beginning of their rift.

'You can turn off the light,' Ingred said, 'Goodnight.'

An hour later, Grace was wide awake. The lack of conversation had been disappointing. She felt restless, constrained by not wanting to disturb Ingred, yet the longer she remained still, the more uncomfortable she became. And then, at the point when she managed to turn off her brain and was falling asleep, she was wrenched awake by a series of rhythmic cries. They went on and on, until the woman came to orgasm. In the quiet that followed, she wondered who it was. The sounds had come from downstairs, where the bedrooms belonged to Martin and Gerald. She felt a pang at the thought of Gerald fucking someone, but it was momentary. She was over him.

It was no use. She was more awake than ever. She slipped out of bed, pausing to check that Ingred was still asleep before tiptoeing from the room.

A candle flickered on the kitchen table as she entered, alerting her to the fact that she was not alone. Marigold turned at the kitchen bench, a mug in each hand, naked except for an unbuttoned shirt. Gerald's shirt.

'Oh, hello,' she said as she began to pad barefoot towards the door. 'There's more tea in the pot if you want it.'

She moved past, smiling as if nothing was wrong and there was no reason for any animosity. No reason, because they were just friends, a final shattering of illusion that Grace could not bear. She swung out her arm, a reckless blow that caught Marigold on the shoulder, causing her to cry out as the mug flew from her grip, splashing hot tea across her naked body.

Horrified by what she'd done, Grace fled.

19

For two days Grace tried to hide, creeping in and out of the house, timing her visits to the kitchen at odd hours to avoid everyone, especially Marigold. That she'd caused her physical harm was unbearable. She was desperate to apologise, to plead for forgiveness, and yet the fear of Marigold's scathing response held her back. The rejection that was sure to come. She half hoped that they might run into each other, a chance meeting that would change things for the better.

But their paths didn't cross and, with each passing hour, the idea of seeking her out became more and more impossible.

It was early evening, and she was pretending to read in her room. If there had been a door to lock, she would never have let Martin in, but as it was, he refused to take no for an answer and dragged her off to play Monopoly.

She was on the verge of snapping up Mayfair when Gerald came leaping up the stairs with the news that the Pewsey Street squatters were about to be evicted. Supporters were needed to man the barricades and he insisted they answer the call.

After the panic Grace had experienced in the middle of the surging throng of Pewsey Street supporters, she reached the wall of the nearest squat and sank down beside it. Fumbling in the pocket of her jacket, she found a cigarette and sucked greedily. Smoke flooded her lungs and she grew calmer, already feeling foolish for that frantic flight through the crowd. She took a last puff and ground the cigarette out on the pavement. A door to her left opened and seconds later, Marigold rushed past, hurrying away in her black and green cloak.

Impulsively, Grace leapt up, the fear of rejection eclipsed by an overwhelming desire to speak to her no matter what. She called out, but Marigold was already some way ahead and did not respond. Afraid of losing her, she threw herself back into the fray, pushing her way through, until she was close enough to grab hold of the cloak. Marigold spun around with a savage look.

'It's me,' Grace blurted.

'What are you doing here?'

'We're all here. I didn't think you were.'

'Well, I am.' Her hostile response was a confirmation of Grace's worst fears.

'I'm sorry, so sorry. I didn't mean to … I know you must hate me. I hate myself—' She began to cry. Ugly, wrenching sobs. 'I don't blame you for hating me.'

Marigold took her by the arm, shaking it in a comforting and slightly impatient gesture. 'Stop it, Grace. There's no need.'

'So stupid—'

'It's alright.'

'No, it's not. I wanted that tea to burn you. I wanted to hurt you. I was jealous … of you and Gerald. Not because of Gerald. You. Do you understand?'

'Stop crying, come on,' she said, jiggling Grace's arm.

But Grace could not stop.

'Listen to me,' Marigold said, 'we never splurged your first pay. What do you say we go to Paris for a weekend? It's perfect for splurging. Paris, in a fortnight. Are you listening?'

170

Ignoring Grace's tears, she quickly outlined a plan involving the Night Ferry from Victoria station to the Gare du Nord, declaring that she would arrange everything. 'You'll love Paris. How's your French?'

'I can't really—' she began.

'Don't worry,' Marigold interrupted, 'it's one of my second languages. Honestly, stop crying, you're making me want to cry too.'

'Sorry, trying,' she said, wiping her eyes. They were sore and gritty from weeping.

'If you like, we can stay in Montmartre. You can sit on a park bench reading a book and I'll walk past and drop my scarf.' She put her arm around Grace's shoulder, squeezing her. 'What do you say?'

'You hated that film,' Grace said, managing, at last, a weak smile.

'I did. But who knows, maybe we'll find a haunted mansion and be whisked into another dimension, never to return, and all our troubles will be over.'

She removed her arm from Grace's shoulder and looked around, scanning the crowd. Throughout their conversation, she had emanated a tension, a sense of urgency that now grew stronger.

'Listen, I need you to do something for me,' she said.

'Of course.'

'Swap coats with me. And give me your hat.'

Before Grace had a chance to offer her black woolly hat, Marigold snatched it, stuffing her distinctive russet curls inside so that they were not visible. They swapped coats, and she tugged the hood of the cloak over Grace's head. 'Keep the hood on,' she said.

'Why? What's going on?'

'Now, go. And if anyone stops you, because they think you're me, you don't know me.'

'But it's your cloak.'

'You found it.'

'Where?'

'Come on, Grace, can't you think of something? Lying on the ground or something. And you were cold, so you picked it up.'

'Who's going to stop me? Is it Ed?'

'No. I mean, yes, it's Ed.'

'You said it was over.'

'It is over. I can't explain now, there's no time.'

'Are you in danger?'

Marigold laughed. 'Yes, mortal danger. They're out to get me,' she whispered in an exaggeratedly melodramatic voice. 'I'll leave that sort of thing to Gerald. But not a word to the others. Promise me.'

'Can't you tell me?'

'No,' she barked. And then, more gently, 'Trust me. Please, just trust me.'

An unguarded, vulnerable expression flitted across her face, and Grace wanted more than anything to say that she was in love with her and would do anything for her.

'I promise, not a word,' she said.

'And Paris, in a fortnight.' She placed her hand against Grace's cheek in a tender gesture. 'Take care of yourself,' she whispered, slipping away through a gap in the crowd. There was no time to say goodbye. A glimpse of the black woolly hat and then nothing. She was gone.

Grace wove her way through the crowd in the opposite direction. She felt embarrassed and more than a little ridiculous for her *Are you in danger?* question. Marigold was avoiding Ed; there was nothing more to it. Persistent Ed, who had turned out to be a pest. If he accosted her, she'd tell him to back off. She began to imagine a confrontation with Ed in which she told him he wasn't wanted. She would puncture his masculine confidence, his arrogant assumption that he was desirable, and that Marigold should submit to him.

'Grace. We've been looking for you.'

She had come face to face with Annie. Alan and Vanessa were a step behind.

'We thought you must have gone home,' Alan said.

Vanessa peered at her. 'You're wearing Marigold's cloak.'

Marigold's desire for secrecy won out and Grace said nothing about the true situation, only that Marigold had lent it to her because she was cold. It didn't make any sense because she'd given Marigold her Afghan coat which was warmer than toast, but Vanessa didn't seem to notice.

'Oh.' She shrugged. 'Did you know, Gerald's been arrested.'

'They've evicted everyone,' Annie said. 'They've won, it's over.'

Looking around, Grace noticed that the crowd had begun to disperse. Defeat was in the air and the earlier joyful defiance had subsided into dejection. Even the newly homeless Pewsey Street squatters had lost the will to fight and were more concerned with the immediate task of finding some kind of roof over their heads.

Annie and Alan went off to leave a note on the windscreen of the van, telling the others that Gerald had been arrested and everyone would need to make their own way home.

'We may as well go too,' Vanessa said.

Grace wondered if she ought to stay longer, to lure Ed out of the shadows.

'Yes, let's go home,' she said. The thought of a warm kitchen and food was too enticing.

20

Gerald arrived home the next morning just as they were about to go down to the police station to find out what had happened to him.

'Fuckers stuck the boot in,' he said, showing them the bruises on his torso.

Having doled out rough justice, the police had decided not to charge him, and he was let go with a warning. Now he was off to see a solicitor who was sympathetic to the squatters' cause. There were others who were still in the lock up and needed help.

Marigold hadn't come home and Gerald said she wasn't among those who'd been arrested. Her absence was nothing unusual and Grace ignored a flicker of anxiety, triggered by the unresolved question of why she'd needed to hide from Ed. Grace had asked her whether she was in danger, and she'd laughed it off. But was that the truth? Maybe she'd just gone off somewhere without bothering to let any of them know. It was the most likely scenario, in which case there was no need to feel worried. All that mattered was that Marigold had forgiven her.

Drifting through the following days, she remained confident that Marigold would return in time for their Paris weekend. She thought of her often and wondered if she'd understood the true meaning of her confession of jealousy. That she was in love with her. She imagined saying it outright and had fantasies of them wandering the streets of Paris like genuine flâneurs, following in Celine and Julie's footsteps, drinking pastis in bars where the locals hung out, returning to their attic atelier in the early hours of the morning to sleep entwined in a big feather bed.

Meanwhile, at work, Rita was behaving erratically, veering from manic cheerfulness to outbursts of unprovoked anger. Eric told her that Rita had confided in him about the split-up and that she was the one who'd ended things, which he didn't believe. She was far too devastated. He was sure Marina had got wind of things and forced Simon's hand. Grace kept quiet about what she'd seen and, apart from taking Rita her morning coffee, tried to avoid her. She tried to avoid Simon too, knowing Rita noticed everything, not wanting to inflame her any further.

Simon was treating Rita like a bomb about to explode, instructing Grace to keep the door to his office open at all times. He said it was so that he could call her in for dictation, a lame excuse as he could buzz her on the phone, or simply yell out through the closed door the way he'd always done. She was sure it was to prevent Rita from cornering him and pretended not to know anything about what was going on.

The weekend came and there was still no sign of Marigold.

'Aren't you meant to be going to Paris with her?' Annie asked.

'Next weekend,' Grace said, adding, 'she'll be here by then,' annoyed by Annie's sceptical expression. 'I don't know why you're looking like that.'

'I don't want you to get hurt. We all know how you feel about her.'

'There's no need to worry about me,' she replied. 'I don't give a stuff whether she comes back or not.' She couldn't bear the idea that the others had discussed their friendship, and ended the conversation, pretending she had to meet a friend from work.

But the seeds of doubt had been sown, and her belief that Marigold would return in time for Paris began to waver. How could she disappear without a word? Didn't their friendship mean anything? She was determined that when Marigold finally turned up, she'd have it out with her and rehearsed furious speeches in her head. Beneath the fury lay an aching bereavement and she ricocheted between hating Marigold and hating herself, remembering her abject behaviour at the eviction – her tears, and how clingy she'd been.

The second week wore on and the date for Paris loomed. A new phase began in which she convinced herself that Marigold would appear, armed with a story that explained everything. In response, she would be stern, prepared to forgive, though not before a genuine apology. Sometimes she imagined rejecting those apologies, no matter how heartfelt and sincere. *It's too late*, she'd say, *I'm not interested in your excuses anymore*, putting Marigold in the place of the beseecher, revelling in her power to do so.

The day they were due to leave on the Night Ferry, she couldn't concentrate. The train left Victoria Station at nine p.m. and they needed to arrive early to buy tickets. Her lack of concentration wasn't important, there was nothing much to do. But the effect of her anxiety was to make the day drag interminably. In desperation, she rang Basia, hoping for distraction.

'We are checking the stockpile, Grace. I can't talk,' Basia said.

On the dot of five o'clock she abandoned her desk and sprinted to the tube station. At the usual stop she leapt off and ran the last leg, invoking a vision of Marigold sitting in the kitchen, smoking a cigarette as if she'd never been away. They were going to Paris together; Marigold would not let her down.

The vision proved illusory and, as the time to leave approached, Grace knew she was on her own. Thinking of their last encounter at the Pewsey Street eviction, she wondered if Paris had been a ploy to calm her down, a way for Marigold to escape without a scene. How could she blame her? She saw herself through Marigold's eyes – hysterical, weeping, begging for forgiveness and, worse, for love, like a needy child. It made her feel like throwing up. She was pathetic, and her Celine and Julie fantasies were humiliating and shameful.

The clothes she'd hastily stuffed in her backpack were thrown back in the bottom of the wardrobe. If only she had the courage to go on her own; to prove to herself that she didn't care, and that she was independent and bold. But the thought of arriving at the Gare du Nord alone, not speaking the language was too intimidating. How could she cope with the Parisians' arrogance, their meanness and refusal to speak English, about which even Raymond agreed? There was nothing to be done; she was a timid country mouse.

She lay on her bed, feeling miserable, until the smell of Friday night curry, and the boredom of self-imposed isolation drove her downstairs. The kitchen was buzzing with Beltonians, including Sunil and his friend, Melbon, from number forty-five and two orange-clad girls from the Rajneesh squat. Rice and dhal were heaped onto platters in the centre of the table. Alan had cooked a vegetable curry and was ladling it into bowls.

'I knew you wouldn't go on your own,' Annie said before Grace had a chance to declare that she'd changed her mind; that she'd never wanted to visit Paris in the first place, the Parisians were far too up themselves.

Two more weeks went by. Grace began to feel afraid that something awful had happened. Paris was irrelevant now; it was in the past. What mattered was Marigold's safety.

'I've triple-checked her room,' she told Vanessa. 'All her clothes are there. As far as I can see, she didn't take anything.'

They were working in the garden, ripping out weeds. Nearby, Gerald and Alan were putting up a trellis on the south wall for runner beans. Along the extended communal garden, groups of Beltonians were at work preparing beds and digging in compost. The weather was still wintry and cold, but spring was around the corner. It was almost time to plant vegetables and the marijuana seedlings that Martin had nurtured in a home-made hothouse he'd constructed with bits of timber and plastic sheeting.

'Don't you think that's strange? I think we should do something.'

'What can we do?' Vanessa said with a shrug.

'Go to the police. Report her missing. We should have done it straight away.'

'We can't do that. She'll freak out.'

'We don't have a choice.'

'Yes, we do. She'll be furious. If something awful has happened to her, we'd know.'

'How?'

'If she's been in an accident, or had to go to hospital, she'd give her address so that someone could get in touch. And if she hasn't told them, then she doesn't want us to know. That's what she's like, Grace. She's always come and gone, it's the way she is.'

'What if she's unconscious? Or lost her memory.'

Alan had stopped work and was listening. 'Come on,' he said. 'Why would she lose her memory?'

'I'm just saying, anything could have happened.' She couldn't get their last meeting out of her head. Marigold's nervousness, the way she kept glancing around and her demand to swap coats. At first, she'd denied it had to do with Ed before changing her mind. Grace no longer knew what to believe, except that Marigold had been afraid of someone or something. But she had sworn her to secrecy, a pact that she couldn't break.

'If anything like that had happened, which it hasn't, it would be in the newspapers, or on TV,' Vanessa said. 'They'd try to identify her and ask the public for information. We can't go to the pigs. We can't have them sniffing around Beltonia.'

Even Alan agreed. There was no way they could get the police involved.

Up to that point, Gerald had said nothing. 'Face it, she's gone,' he said. 'Someone else should take her room, it's not right to leave it empty.'

'How can you say that?' Grace cried. 'All her things are here.' She appealed to Vanessa and Alan. 'We can't give up on her.'

'We could wait another week,' Vanessa offered.

'A week? That's not long enough. It's not fair.' She turned to Gerald, about to launch into a furious tirade – that he didn't like Marigold and wanted to get rid of her because she challenged him, she knew he was a sexist shit – before remembering that whether they disliked each other was no longer clear.

'I get it,' he said, 'you're her friend, you want to support her. But when we came here, we made an agreement. There are people desperate for somewhere to live, and we've got an empty room. If you ask me, she's gone for good. She never really needed to be here. You know that.'

His reasoned tone took the wind out of her sails and remembering the dreadful night when she had attacked Marigold in the kitchen, she felt in no position to oppose him. The way in which he'd acknowledged her position made it even more impossible.

'What about her things,' she protested. 'She wouldn't leave without them.'

As the words left her mouth, she knew she was on shaky ground. Everyone knew Marigold didn't care about *things*. It fitted neatly into Gerald's theory: she was a rich girl slumming it and didn't need a room in a squat. At first, there was no response to her plea, and Grace sensed the others were thinking the same thing.

'We should discuss it at the house meeting,' Vanessa said at last.

That night, the household gathered in the upstairs room for the meeting. Grace had given up the idea of going to the police; it had been overtaken by the need to save Marigold's room. Gerald was not around when, earlier, she'd sounded out the others to see who would support her. While sympathetic, nobody was prepared to wait indefinitely. A date had to be set. She had decided, therefore, to propose a month's delay. If Marigold hadn't returned by then, the room could be given to someone else. She expected Gerald to disagree, to argue for immediate action but, once again, he surprised her. It was over within minutes. One month. It was unanimous.

21

Except for Gerald, everyone was sure that Marigold would return. Grace wanted to believe they were right and used their confidence to bolster her own. In the meantime, she tried not to think about her, only to discover that it wasn't possible. Marigold was always in the back of her mind. Was she safe? Where was she? How could she leave like this? She tried to convince herself that Marigold was selfish and uncaring and there was no point worrying about her. It made no difference. She was in love with her. It was a relief to go to work where, for a while, she was distracted by other things.

'Grace,' Simon shouted. 'Need you.'

Sticking to her new policy of keeping a distance, of not settling in for one of their *things to discuss* meetings, she stopped at the door to his office and waited.

'Come in,' he said.

She took a step into the room.

'I'm not shouting at you over there. Come and sit down.'

She did as he asked, glancing at the brown paper parcel positioned prominently on the desk.

'As you can see, it's arrived,' he said.

'The manuscript?'

181

'The very same.'

That it existed at all, unexpectedly came as a shock. She had become used to it as something that would arrive in the future – a future that was endlessly deferred and thus always anticipated without the bother of having to deal with it. The presence of the manuscript raised the prospect that the publishing venture might really get off the ground, disrupting the comfortable rut into which she had fallen.

'I'm promoting you to editorial assistant,' he said, beaming at her with magnanimity. 'Read it and provide an assessment on whether we should publish.'

'Whether we should publish,' she echoed.

'I'll need a report. Outline of the story, strengths and weaknesses. That sort of thing.'

He poked the parcel, pushing it a few inches in her direction. 'You could look a bit more enthusiastic. I'm offering you a step up, an opportunity.'

Somehow, without Grace noticing, Rita had entered the room.

'What opportunity?' she said in a belligerent tone.

'Ah, Rita, come in,' Simon said.

'I am in. What's going on?'

'Nothing,' they replied in unison.

Rita jabbed a painted nail at the parcel. 'What's that?'

'Calm down,' he said. 'It's the manuscript. Grace is going to give us an opinion.'

'You can't give it to her, she's the Girl Friday,' she squawked.

'I've got a degree in English literature,' Grace said, irritated by Rita's response. 'That's why you gave me the job.'

'No, it wasn't.'

From the corner of her eye, Grace glimpsed Rita moving forward and, realising that the manuscript was at stake, she lunged across the desk and grabbed it, forgetting that moments earlier she hadn't even been sure she wanted it. Rita was determined not to give in and

182

tried to yank it from her grip. The whole thing was so undignified that Grace was about to let go when Rita yelled, 'Give it to me, you stupid Australian.'

As much as she hated her country and had worked to disguise her origins, the fact of Rita throwing it in her face as the ultimate insult was too much to bear. A surge of outrage gave her the strength to break Rita's hold just as Simon stepped around the desk and inserted himself between them.

'Enough,' he said, separating them like the umpire of a boxing match. 'Grace, take it and leave. Rita, stay. And Grace, close the door on your way out.'

Outside Simon's office, Grace felt wobbly. Spurred into action by the awful prospect of another round with Rita, she collected her jacket, stuffed the manuscript into her bag and hurried down the stairs. Eric came out to investigate and wanted to know where she was going. She explained what had happened, and that she was going home early.

'I can't face her again today. She's deranged.'

'She's lashing out because of the break-up,' Eric said.

'Maybe, but it's not my fault.'

'She's a good person when you get to know her.'

Grace said he was now sounding deranged too and that she couldn't think of anyone less deserving of the description. Anyway, she wasn't going to hang around.

'If Simon asks, tell him I've gone home to read it,' she called on her way out.

On the way home, she gazed out of the train window at the graffiti flashing past. *Same thing day after day – tube – work – dinner – work – tube – armchair – TV – sleep – tube – work – how much more can you take – one in ten go mad – one in five cracks up.* The last bit had never made sense to her. One in ten go mad, one in five crack up. Wasn't going mad and cracking up the same thing? Not long after arriving in Beltonia, she'd boasted to a smartly dressed female passenger that she and her friends had painted it. The woman looked shocked, which Grace had found hugely gratifying. Pissing off a member of the bourgeoisie made her feel like a real Beltonian. Thinking of that fictitious claim, she was consumed with embarrassment. How desperate she'd been to place herself in the thick of everything. She'd seen the graffiti dozens of times without it occurring to her that she was now one of those people –a drone going to work, day after day. It was a shock to think of herself like that. Was it really what she wanted? She had to remind herself that she wasn't a sleepwalking drone, she had prospects. A career. Marigold had said it first – a career in publishing.

She emerged from the tube station and began the fifteen-minute walk home. Her earlier ambivalence had vanished, and she was glad she hadn't given in; that she'd fought Rita for the manuscript. She wondered what sort of novel awaited her and how to tackle the report about its strengths and weaknesses. It was the sort of thing Marigold would know. Where, oh where was she? Encouraged by the serendipity of their original meeting, Grace began to feel a sense of optimism, even certainty, that she had returned. How could she not, when it was all because of her that she had the job? She needed Marigold now, more than ever. Fate had brought them together; surely fate would play its part again. She sped up, feeling more and more certain that Marigold was waiting for her, forgetting, or at least ignoring, that she'd felt this way before and been disappointed.

She turned into Belton Road and raised a hand in greeting as Vincent ran past, bare feet slapping the footpath, muttering to himself. The air churned and she caught a whiff of him, the smell of poverty and madness. She couldn't help an involuntary shudder and rushed on, soon reaching the front door.

'Hello,' she called, 'Marigold?'

At this time of the afternoon there was almost always someone around and it was a surprise to find the kitchen empty. The table bore signs of recent activity – a scattering of cups, a cooling teapot and a solitary piece of chocolate cake with a handwritten sign beside it that said *Eat me*. She opened the back door and called out again. The fantasy that Marigold had returned was already fading. Returning through the kitchen, she grabbed the slice of chocolate cake and took a bite. By the time she reached the stairs, she had devoured it.

Upstairs, the front room was deserted. So too was Marigold's bedroom. The usual sounds of activity – of music and voices and Gerald either demolishing or building things – were missing and, in the silence, she experienced the same uneasy feeling she'd had when Vincent ran past. The house felt abandoned. She told herself sternly to stop imagining things, that it was a blessing in disguise; there was no one to disturb her, and she could get on with reading the manuscript.

Entering her bedroom, she pulled it from her bag and dropped it beside the bed before taking off her boots and burrowing under Shanti's moulting eiderdown to warm up. Her eyes closed. A few minutes was all she needed.

On opening her eyes, she couldn't tell if she had fallen asleep, or how much time had passed. Only, that something wasn't right. Her body seemed to have dwindled away to nothing, leaving her with an enormous head. She tried to stand but the process involved complicated movements and the coordination of too many parts so that she soon gave in and sank back, watching as the room began to glow and then pulsate. The window was rippling like a belly dancer; the walls bulging and retracting as if alive. And yet, in spite of it all, she felt calm. Everything was connected and cosmic consciousness suddenly made sense. Where were the others? She wanted to tell them and made another effort to rise, distracted by the sight of her left hand which had become translucent. Blood streamed through veins, a kaleidoscope of rushing psychedelic cells. Staring at her

185

hand, she recalled the note beside the slice of chocolate cake: *Eat me*. The same message, spelled out in currants on the little cake that Alice had eaten after falling down the rabbit hole.

In Beltonia, dropping acid or doing mushrooms was no big deal. Tripping was almost de rigueur. Nearly everyone had dropped a few tabs, and in the early days, Grace let the others think she had too. Her desire to appear cool, an insider who knew the ropes about everything, had led to quite a few lies, including that she'd dropped acid heaps of times. The *heaps of times* had slipped out without thinking, which she'd since regretted, everyone concluding that she was an expert. Alan, for example, had come to her for advice about what to do if things went wrong. Too late to admit that her experience with psychedelic drugs was non-existent and that she was scared of having a bad trip and going mad, she'd put on a confident air, telling him he'd be safe as long as he was accompanied by a friend.

With the dawning realisation that there had been something in the chocolate cake, her heart began to race. She could feel it leaping, trying to escape the confines of her chest. The perception of cosmic oneness vanished. Her room, with its breathing walls, was no longer part of a benign universe. It had transformed into a malevolent mausoleum where time had stopped. Inside her head, she heard someone from the recent encounter group exhorting her to *be in the now* which struck her as a hellish prescription. Time had ceased to exist and *the now* was forever. Everywhere she looked, strange shapes ballooned and spread like inkblots. Nothing was stable, half-formed thoughts became hallucinations. Inside the gaping wardrobe a shadowy shape transformed into a sinister Rumpelstiltskin, angrily stamping his feet before dissolving into a blob on the floor. She was terrified of catching sight of her reflection and not recognising herself. Of seeing an image that she didn't want to see – she didn't know what. She began to feel claustrophobic. It wasn't the room she had to escape, it was her own body. She was trapped inside herself and couldn't get out. A feeling of dread metastasised; something awful was happening.

Curling into a foetal position under the bedclothes, she tried desperately to think of calming things. Flowers. Her mother's garden with its clumps of Japanese iris and gladioli, the pink rambling roses on the trellis, and blue delphiniums. The smell of the lemon-scented gumtree in summer and willy wagtails fluttering on the lawn.

'A thing of beauty is a joy forever,' she muttered, 'its loveliness increases … something, something … nothingness.' She got caught up on the word nothingness, the idea of it expanding, engulfing her. She tried to focus on the thing of beauty, repeating the phrase over and over like a mantra until she no longer felt scared. Experimentally, she poked her head out and glanced around to discover that every object in the room – the brick and plank bookcase, the upturned tea-chest she used as a side table, even the heap of dirty clothes on the floor – was emanating a radiant energy. A life-force full of beauty and harmony. She laughed, delighted to have discovered the secret: that it was all about thinking the right thoughts. But the problem, as she quickly discovered, was controlling those thoughts. The more she tried not to think of dark and scary things, the more they proliferated. How could she banish the thought of turning into a giant cockroach without thinking it in the first place, therefore bringing it instantly into being?

She was plunging into the bad trip again when a shape shimmered across the room and knelt beside her. She couldn't remember the right words to explain things.

'Eat me,' she mumbled to the shape. It was all that emerged of a long sentence about Alice, the cake, and what was happening to her. She closed her eyes.

Coming to in the dark, her head felt as fragile as a wren's egg; her limbs laid out like a body on a slab. Slowly, her eyes adjusted, the darkness dissolving to a pale city glow from the curtainless window.

A few random images appeared and floated away before she had time to grab hold of them, connect one to the other. Gradually, things came back to her. She'd come home, the house was empty, she'd eaten the slice of chocolate cake. Oh, god, she wasn't still tripping?

On the verge of a freak-out, she sat up expecting the worst, only to find that everything looked normal: the bookcase, the wardrobe, the tea-chest side table. The adrenalin of a moment ago ebbed like a receding tide and she was about to lie down again when Vanessa burst into the room, followed by Annie, Raymond, Martin, and Gerald.

'Grace, you're here,' Vanessa cried. She kicked off her boots and slid under the bedclothes, pressing her icy hands against Grace's cheeks. 'It's freezing outside.'

'Where have you been?' Raymond said. 'We missed you.'

'Been to London to visit the Queen,' Annie chanted. 'Lucy in the sky with diamonds,' she sang and kissed Grace on the forehead.

'Mushrooms,' Martin said. 'Where were you? We saved you some cake.'

More boots were discarded as they surged onto the bed, except for Gerald, who leant against the wardrobe, watching.

'Getting off with a secret lover,' Vanessa said. 'C'mon, Grace, we know you're a dark horse.'

The others joined in, teasing, demanding to know what she'd been up to. Who was she with? In the middle of her denials, she had a vision of the shimmering shape that had knelt beside the bed. The image was fleeting, she couldn't tell if it was a real memory or an hallucination.

'Marigold?' she croaked.

'Now there's a dark horse,' Martin said. He began to roll a joint.

Vanessa rested her head on Grace's shoulder. 'You should have come,' she said.

'Yeah, amazing trip,' Annie murmured, snuggling in on the other side.

'How could I?' she said, 'I didn't know where you'd gone?'

'Course you did,' Vanessa objected. 'Gerald, you left her a note, didn't you?'

He did not reply and when Grace looked across, she saw that he was no longer there.

22

Martin and Raymond had gone, and Vanessa and Annie had fallen asleep in her bed when Grace looked at her watch and saw that she was already late for work. Not wanting to wake her friends, she flung on her clothes in the half-dark, grabbed her bag and ran to the tube station. Halfway there, she remembered the manuscript and realised she had left it behind.

On the train, she felt fragile, as if the magic mushrooms had sloughed off a layer of protective skin. It made the spectre of Rita more daunting than ever and recalling their undignified struggle for control of the Scottish author's novel, she wondered if it was worth it. Why not let Rita take over?

Arriving at work, the impulse had already waned, replaced by a determination to make a start on the manuscript that evening. And, as luck would have it, Rita had gone to a meeting with the printers, thus delaying any threat of a further confrontation. It meant she could relax and get back to reading *The Drought*, one of the Ballard novels she'd begun ages ago. She had only just found her place when the phone began to ring.

'Grace?' Basia said.

'What?'

'It's proper to say your name, Grace, otherwise it could be anyone. Where is the mail order? If I lose my job, they will send me back to Poland.'

A week ago, she'd promised to do the outstanding orders and had been procrastinating ever since. She tried to convince Basia that another day or two would not matter, and that she wouldn't lose her job, she hadn't done anything wrong, and there was no chance of being sent back to Poland, or of being imprisoned for life – the fate Basia insisted awaited her. The bookkeeper, however, was not placated and grew more and more agitated.

Grace knew from previous conversations that there were a lot of Poles like Basia who lived in fear of being forced to return to Poland. They had overstayed their visas and were working without the right documents. Their best hope was to marry a British citizen which had led to a thriving black market of arranged marriages. It was a route to permanent residency and a handful of Beltonians had already benefited from the one hundred pounds that such arrangements were worth. Basia, though desperate, was both romantic and religious and had resisted the temptation to seek a fake husband. She lived on a knife edge of anxiety, and Grace's reassurances that she had nothing to fear, fell on deaf ears. The mail orders had to be dealt with today, and Grace had no alternative. She had to swear she'd get onto them immediately.

She worked her way through the backlog of orders, suspecting that Basia would find multiple errors. The pile had grown marginally smaller when Simon shouted from his office.

'Close the door,' he said. 'And no need for that,' he added, indicating her shorthand pad. 'Want to have a chat about how things are going. So, how are things going?'

'Good.'

'You've made a start on the manuscript?'

'Mm.'

'First impressions?'

191

'Interesting.'

'And—?'

Feeling it was too late to say she hadn't exactly started, she tried instead to think of encouraging yet vague pronouncements and remembered a blurb on a novel she'd flicked through at Compendium. She'd been waiting for Vanessa who had gone in search of the latest book by Pearl, the famous astrologer.

'So far, an innovative new voice.'

Simon's eyes lit up.

'Can't say anything more yet,' she added hastily.

'Understood. More soon, I hope.'

'Definitely,' she replied. She stood up, assuming that the chat was over.

Simon leapt up too and came around to her side, where he took her by the arm. 'Wait a moment,' he said. 'There's something I—'

The door opened and a woman entered. She was tall and blonde. The word glacial sprang to Grace's mind.

'Oh,' the woman said, staring at the two of them.

Simon let go of Grace's arm. 'Ah, Marina,' he said. 'I don't think you've met Grace. We've been discussing a manuscript.'

Marina stepped forward, extending a slim, cold hand.

'Nice to meet you,' Grace said, wishing her own hand was not clammy.

Marina's lips stretched into an approximation of a smile, withdrawing her limp paw almost immediately.

'Right then, Grace,' Simon said in a hearty tone. 'A report by the end of the week. You'd better get cracking.'

As she closed the door behind her, Eric's warning came back to her. *Don't get on the wrong side of Marina.* She wished Simon hadn't been holding her by the arm.

She slid into her chair and tried to focus on the mail orders. It soon became apparent that Simon and Marina were in the throes of an argument, making it impossible to concentrate. Marina's voice grew louder.

'What is wrong with you?' she shouted. 'Tell me the truth for once in your life.'

Simon's voice was pitched too low for Grace to make out his response. She thought of Rita and the scene in the pub. Whatever he said did not placate Marina. The door to his office flew open, and she rushed past, disappearing down the stairs.

'Marina, come back here,' Simon yelled. He reached the doorway and seemed about to go after her, before changing his mind and retreating.

It was almost lunch time when he re-emerged with a twenty-pound note and asked her to go to Didier's.

'Get a bit extra,' he said. 'We might have a visitor.'

'Marina?' Grace asked.

'Marina? No,' he replied sharply. 'Why would you think that?'

'I thought—'

'Thought what?'

'That it might have been.'

'Well, it's not,' he said. 'Off you go.'

She stuffed the money in the pocket of her jeans and put on her denim jacket. Ever since Marigold had taken her Afghan coat, she had shivered her way to work. She was sick of being cold, but couldn't bring herself to wear Marigold's cloak, seeing it as an admission that she was never going to return and that her things were becoming common property.

At the Prickly Pear, Didier took the twenty-pound note and refused to give her any change.

On her way back to the office she wondered if the visitor might be Roger, the Scottish author. Perhaps he'd come down to London yesterday to deliver the manuscript by hand and had decided to stay on for a few days. She tried unsuccessfully to remember if the parcel had been stamped and how it had been addressed. The idea that Roger would deliver his precious manuscript in person made sense, although Rita had mentioned that he was a recluse. She sped up, excited at the prospect of meeting a real writer, even a reclusive one, wishing she'd at least begun reading his novel and thus able to offer insightful opinions. From never giving the author much thought she had a sudden desire to impress him.

She had finished laying out the lunch things on the meeting room table when the sound of Simon's familiar laugh was followed by the appearance of his burly bear-like frame in the doorway.

'Aha, the very person we wanted to see,' he said, wrapping an arm around a male shoulder as they entered the room. The author! He was tall and lean, dressed in green velvet flares, a tight cerise shirt with over-long lapels visible beneath a brown leather coat. His appearance was nothing like the shabby hermit she'd been imagining.

'Grace,' Simon called, 'come and meet Max.'

By the time she had partly recovered from the shock of hearing the name Max and the realisation that he was not the Scottish author, Max had detached himself from Simon and was rapidly approaching, his hand outstretched.

'Grace Manners, we meet at last,' he said in his velvety voice, taking her hand in both of his, pulling her closer.

'Well done,' he said, sotto voce, into her right ear. 'Hit the mark, puss. All sorted.'

Her first confused thought was to do with the manuscript which made no sense.

'I'm in your debt, Miss Smith.'

The letter! 'I didn't—'

'Our little secret, puss. Didn't I say we worked well together?'

'I said meet her, not eat her.' Simon had joined them and once again threw his arm around Max, steering him away. There was a hint of steel behind his jovial façade. 'Shouldn't you be helping—' he said, addressing Grace, motioning with his head that she should make herself scarce. She had the impression he was regretting his enthusiastic introduction of her as he propelled Max away.

Eric and Rita entered and began picking at the food.

'Looks like Max has taken a fancy to you,' Eric said.

'Don't be stupid,' she replied, bristling. And then, feeling she had over-reacted, and that Eric was the one person in the room to whom she could safely talk and didn't want him to desert her, she tried to change tack. 'Sorry. A bit shocked. No one told me he was coming.'

'Typical of Simon,' Rita said. 'He never bothers to communicate. You don't have a plate, Grace. Aren't you hungry?'

Rita's plate held two small slices of smoked salmon. 'We were just talking about you. Weren't we Eric?'

'You were talking about her,' Eric said.

'I thought you were at the printer's,' Grace said, hoping to distract Rita from elaborating on whatever she had been saying, sure that it was something negative. They were standing either side of her, making her feel trapped.

'I was, and now I'm here,' Rita replied. 'Incredible isn't it.'

Grace forced herself to laugh. She glanced around and caught Max looking at her over Simon's shoulder. The intensity of his gaze further unnerved her. Was he sending her a signal of some kind? The last thing she wanted was Max drawing her into his nefarious schemes. She grabbed a laden charcuterie platter from the table.

'Replenishment,' she muttered, 'back in a minute.'

In the kitchen, she abandoned the platter to the bench. She had no intention of returning. If Simon asked tomorrow, she'd say she had period pains. Men never wanted to hear about that sort of thing.

Grace stared in bewilderment at the spot beside the bed where she remembered tossing the manuscript. It was not there. She sat down on the mattress and scanned the room, her mind churning. Had she, for some mysterious reason hidden it while she'd been tripping? She sprang up and began to turn everything upside down, scattering clothes, pulling books from the plank and brick bookcase, ripping the bedclothes off the bed, and tipping up the mattress to check underneath. It was to no avail; the manuscript was not in her room.

Nor was it in the kitchen or the communal room. Nobody remembered seeing a brown paper parcel.

'What am I going to do?' Grace directed her question at Vanessa, who was drawing up Martin's chart at the kitchen table. She was vaguely aware that for Vanessa to be drawing up his chart suggested there was something going on between them, but she was too distracted by the missing manuscript to find out. It wasn't even that she expected her to have a solution; only that she had to talk to someone. Vanessa shrugged.

'It's bound to turn up. Have you asked everyone?'

'Of course I have,' she replied.

Except that she hadn't. The shimmering shape by the bed. Could it possibly have been Ingred?

She gave a tentative knock on the darkroom door and was almost turning away when the door opened.

'Quick, come in,' Ingred said.

Grace squeezed past and into the dim womb-like interior, lit by a red safe-light. Trays filled with chemicals were lined up on a bench, and the sour, vinegary smell caught her in the back of the throat. Pegged on a cord strung across the small enclosure, a row of photographs dangled like clothes on a washing line.

There was barely room for the two of them. Her arm brushed against one of the hanging prints.

'Careful,' Ingred warned, 'they're not dry yet. She removed a print from the third tray with a pair of tongs. 'What do you want?'

'Sorry. I've lost a parcel. A brown paper parcel. A manuscript from work. I put it beside my bed and it's gone. I wondered if you'd seen it.'

'No.'

'I thought—'

Ingred hung the print on the clothesline and turned to her. 'Yes?'

'Last night. You might have seen it.'

'How could I have seen it?'

'I thought you might have come in … last night. Into my room.'

Crammed in the tiny space, their bodies were almost touching and combined with the photographic chemicals it was making Grace feel overheated and woozy. Ingred shook her head.

'What do you think?' she asked, gesturing at the drying prints.

Feeling on the verge of a flashback, Grace tried to focus on the black and white photographs. The first was a group shot of the Orange People from the ashram-squat doing their crazy meditation. The camera had caught them mid-jump, arms raised, hair and malas flying. The next print was of two pale naked bodies entwined on a mattress; their faces obscured by long hair and the angle of the shot. It could have been two men, two women or one of each, she couldn't tell. She inched along the row, peering at each image. Sunil leaning on a garden fork in the communal garden. A naked pregnant woman sitting on a chair in an otherwise empty room. Tina and Dave, the junkies who lived next door, preparing a fix. Vincent standing on the kitchen table of their squat, playing the violin. The second last photograph was a shot of a crowd, a homemade barricade with a precariously balanced bathtub visible in the background. She recognised it immediately from the Pewsey Street eviction protest. A stifled gasp escaped her – there, in the middle of the crowd, was her black woolly hat.

'What is it?' Ingred asked.

The wearer of the hat was hidden from view behind a press of bodies. Nevertheless, Grace was sure it was Marigold, and that she was looking at the last known sighting of her friend. She wanted to speak, to reveal the fears she held for her, but the words jammed in her throat.

'Nothing. Nothing,' she repeated, and transferred her gaze to the next and final photograph. It looked like an abstract landscape until, belatedly, she realised it was her own face. An extreme close-up with her mouth slightly ajar, her eyes closed in sleep.

'You don't mind?' Ingred said.

'No,' she replied, an automatic response, her head still filled with thoughts of Marigold. As she continued to look at the photograph, she began to wonder when it had been taken. Could it have been last night? Or was it on the earlier occasions when Ingred had stayed in her room? That Ingred had photographed her while sleeping made her feel uncomfortable. She didn't know why. It wasn't like her soul had been captured by the camera.

'Is that all you wanted?' Ingred asked. 'Because I must keep going.' She moved to the row of trays and went on with her work. 'Make sure you shut the door,' she said.

Grace returned to her bedroom which was in chaos. After stuffing things into the bottom of the wardrobe and piling books onto the shelves, she picked up the cloak from the floor where it had lain ever since she had taken it off, weeks ago. She took it back to Marigold's bedroom and threw it on the nearest pile of clothes, at which point a small white object flew out of the pocket and came to rest at her feet. A compacted lump of paper that had been folded repeatedly and that, once smoothed out, revealed an address in Kentish Town, scrawled in Marigold's distinctive handwriting. She was about to screw it up when it hit her. Somebody outside of Beltonia knew Marigold.

23

The doors were closing as Grace jumped aboard a Northern line train at Tottenham Court Road. The carriage was packed, and she became wedged in the centre aisle, behind the dandruff flecked coat of the man in front. With so many people crammed together, she was trapped, unable to move. At each station, passengers poured on and off, pushing past her in their desperation to grab a spare seat. She never got a chance to sit down and soon lost track of where they were until the crowd began to thin. Too late, she realised her mistake. She was travelling on the wrong line, towards Edgware and not High Barnet. The next stop was Hampstead.

Outside Hampstead station, she opened her A to Z. Rather than backtrack to the correct branch of the Northern line, she decided to walk to Kentish Town, calculating that it would take her less than an hour. The Tube was no longer the novelty it had been in her early London days, and she'd discovered that real Londoners considered it a form of travel to be endured, not enjoyed.

She set off along the street, skirting around a group of American tourists gathered outside a patisserie, the women in synthetic pant suits and the men wearing baseball caps. Glancing into shop windows with fashionably dressed mannequins and expensive shoe displays, it was as if she'd arrived in a different city where the air smelled fresh, and the traffic slid past quietly – a far cry from Beltonia's grit and the roar of trucks on the Westway.

The shops petered out and the road began to slope downhill. She was the only person on the street. The sounds of the city were muffled, no more than a distant hum in the sharp evening air. In Beltonia it still felt like winter; here there was a promise of spring. Tiny green buds were beginning to unfurl on the street trees, and she caught sight of a sprinkling of pearly-pink blossom in a front garden. Set behind stone walls and high hedges, she glimpsed large, prosperous looking houses and wondered who lived there, who the people were and what their lives were like.

Rather than hurrying, she began to slow down. The mystery of Marigold's whereabouts was on the verge of being solved. She wanted to savour the anticipation of a joyful reunion, forgetting her anger and anguish, the feelings of abandonment and the things she'd been determined to say.

Dusk was falling when she turned into Lady Somerset Road where the affluence of Hampstead was replaced by rows of shabby Victorian terraces. Though taller and more imposing than those of Belton Road, many of them were in a run-down condition. Houses that looked like squats, with hand-painted rainbows and peace signs on the front doors. Further along, scaffolding indicated that a process of renovation or demolition was underway. A man and woman were shouting at each other on the footpath, and she crossed the street to avoid them. Lady Somerset Road was not what she'd expected, having made the unthinking assumption that, like her parents, Marigold's friends would be loaded.

She stopped at a house with a red door and checked the number written on the scrap of paper. It was the right one. The excited anticipation of earlier drained away, leaving her with an uneasy feeling. Rather than delay the moment, she leapt up the steps, grabbed the lion's head knocker on the front door and banged twice.

After waiting, she knocked again, noticing that the bay window was shuttered from the inside. Minutes ticked by until she was forced to accept that there was nobody home.

An hour passed with no sign of anyone. Sitting on the top step, her bottom had grown numb and worse still, she was desperate to pee. She rummaged in her bag and found a stub of pencil and a piece of paper. On one side was an old list for the Prickly Pear. It was all she had and would have to make do. The message was brief – her name and address and the telephone number at Primo Press, with an explanation that she was a friend of Marigold's. Would they please ring her as soon as possible? She poked the note through the slot in the front door and set off for Tufnell Park station, desperate to find a public toilet.

By the time she reached the end of the street and was about to cross Fortress Road, all she could think of was not wetting her pants. When it finally sank in that someone was calling her name, she looked around, sure that it couldn't be directed at her, and that there must have been another Grace nearby. A girl from the other side of the road was waving at her.

'Grace, Grace,' the girl yelled, darting around the traffic. 'I thought it was you,' she announced on arrival.

Grace smiled, pretending to recognise her.

'It's me, Janine. We met at Australia House.'

'Janine. How are you? How great to see you,' she replied, overdoing her enthusiasm in an attempt to deflect from the awkwardness of the situation, having never expected they would meet again after she'd fobbed them off – Janine and the friend whose name she had forgotten – by deliberately giving them the wrong address.

'Far out,' Janine said. 'It's great to see you too.'

After this Grace couldn't think of anything more to say, trapped by a guilty conscience that prevented her from uttering the usual kind of lies about meeting someone and needing to rush off because

201

she was already late. She felt obliged to go on with her act, that she was thrilled to see Janine and what an amazing coincidence it was to meet her like this. When Janine suggested they have a drink at the pub on the corner to celebrate, she had no choice but to agree. There was nothing she wanted to do more. Which, it suddenly occurred to her, was true because the pub would have a toilet.

She returned to the bar where Janine was waiting for her.

'My shout,' Grace said. 'What would you like?'

'I'm really into Guinness,' Janine replied.

'Me too,' she lied, trying to deflect her guilty conscience by being agreeable.

They found a table in the corner and sat down.

'Cheers, eh.' Janine raised her glass.

'Cheers.'

No longer at the mercy of her bladder, she was already wishing she'd given Janine the brush off. Instead, she was stuck drinking Guinness, making dull small talk.

'How's your friend? I've forgotten her name.'

'Cathy. We went to that address you gave us. They'd never heard of you. It wasn't a squat either.'

'Oh? That's weird? Are you sure you went to the right house? I wondered why you never came. I assumed you must have found somewhere else.' She was babbling and knew it. Worse, Janine's friendly, open face had taken on a baleful cast.

'Yeah,' she said, 'I knew you gave us the wrong address. I told Cathy after you left. She didn't believe me, otherwise I wouldn't have bothered to go. But Cathy's got a heart of gold, she said I was too cynical.'

Grace could feel herself blushing. 'That's not true. You must have written it down wrongly.'

'Come on, there's no need to bullshit me. You couldn't wait to get away. It was pretty obvious.' Janine picked up her pint and drank, her eyes fixed on Grace. She wiped her mouth with the back of her hand. 'We weren't good enough for you.'

'No, not at all,' she managed to stutter.

'Just because that's what you thought, doesn't mean we agreed,' Janine went on, ignoring Grace's denial. 'I suppose you're wondering why I called out to you?'

Feeling that she had already dug herself into a hole, she did not answer, but Janine was having none of it.

'Well?'

'Yes. I suppose I am.'

'I never expected to see you again and when I did, I wanted you to know that I thought it was a shitty thing to do. That's all.' Having said her piece, Janine stopped talking and drank the rest of her Guinness. She finished and stood up. 'I'm glad I bumped into you,' she said. 'I feel better about it now.' And slinging her bag over her shoulder, she was off.

'Wait,' Grace called. 'There might be a room coming up. My friend Marigold ... we're not sure, but I could let you know.'

'It's okay.' Janine shook her head. 'We don't need it. See you then.' At the door she turned and gave a final wave.

At first Grace tried to brush the incident aside, relieved that Janine had gone and that she could forget about her again. Except that she couldn't. Far from feeling superior, she found herself admiring Janine's honesty and courage, her guts in saying exactly what she thought. She sat in the pub for a long time, filled with remorse at her shameful behaviour, slowly sipping her pint of Guinness, determined to drink it to the last drop.

The encounter with Janine had shaken her up and as a further self-punishment she set out on foot along Kentish Town Road for the long trek home. Her denim jacket was no protection against the cold. To help warm herself up she strode along, passing kebab shops and shoe repairers, shopfronts filled with tired displays of dry goods,

203

and charity outlets selling bric-a-brac and second-hand clothes. There was a neglected air to the street and the people she passed seemed similarly down at heel, the women prematurely stooped in bulky, shapeless coats, and the lined, ashy faces of the men. A group of teenage boys approached, jostling, mock fighting, forcing her to shrink back against a dusty shop window. The leader stepped forward, thrusting his face into hers. 'Boo,' he said, dancing away to an outbreak of raucous laughter. She didn't protest, feeling it was no less than she deserved.

Almost two hours later, she trudged upstairs to the sound of Joni singing about a free man in Paris. Two hours of self-castigation had gradually and inexorably transformed into a series of justifications. What else could she have done? Janine and Cathy were too uncool, too eager, too Australian, too naïve and enthusiastic. They were not her kind of people, that was all there was to it. Having convinced herself that she'd done the right thing, she heard her mother's voice. *What a little conformist you are.* She had said it in an off-hand way about something which Grace could no longer remember. What remained was her furious denial, a response re-ignited now, because she was not a conformist, and what did her mother know. Hadn't she gone off to London on her own? Wasn't she striking out to live her own life? What was conformist about that? She railed against her mother's judgement, while trying to block out scenes from the past that rose up in support of it. Tantrums that continued into her teenage years, because she was too skinny, her body was all wrong and her clothes were awful. She would never be accepted by the right girls and would be stuck with the rejects and odd bods. Her fear of that deformed fate, the half-life lived in the shadows, was all part of the same thing. She reached the open doorway to the communal room and could not go in. Her mother was right. She was a conformist, and the knowledge of her inadequacy was too raw.

In the middle of the night, she was woken by someone shouting on the street. At first, she thought it was part of a dream in which she was being pursued by a group of young men like the boys on Kentish Town Road. She turned on the lamp and saw that it was two o'clock. A woman was screaming for help.

Ingred was already at the front door, buttoning a coat over her pyjamas.

'What's happening?'

'Dave and Tina. I think this time it is Dave,' Ingred replied.

Grace knew that Dave and Tina were always trying to get off the junk, but it was too hard. They were not the evil drug fiends, preying on innocent lives that were portrayed in the press. The only lives being destroyed were their own, even if they were no longer innocent. It was a harsh existence with non-existent career prospects and the probability of an early death.

Martin ran across the street towards them. 'We're taking Dave to casualty in Gerald's van. Tina's coming with us.' He sprinted away, calling for them to check the upstairs fireplace.

Ingred went back to fetch her torch because Dave and Tina had never got their act together to get the power connected. On her return, they approached the house and found the front door open. Dave and Tina did not encourage visitors and Grace had never been inside. Ingred shone the torch down a hallway cluttered with junk. The stink of mould and general rot mingled with an acrid smoky smell.

They made their way upstairs to the front room where a fire smouldered in the grate of a Victorian fireplace. A mattress lay on the floor with clothes and bedding scattered around. A ragged blanket hung over the broken glass in the window, sucking in and out with the wind. It reminded her of the squat where she'd slept the night next to Martin, and then Marigold. How cold and bleak it was. But it had been vacant for years, it wasn't someone's home.

'Nobody should—' She wanted to say, nobody should have to live like this. The words stuck in her throat.

'Nobody,' Ingred echoed, as she shone the torch around, alighting for a moment on a teddy bear and a doll, sitting side by side on a broken armchair like abandoned children. Grace's throat tightened further, she wondered if Dave and Tina had kids somewhere and hoped not, for all their sakes. She wanted to say something, anything, to dispel the gloomy atmosphere. Nothing came. Ingred was silent too. And then the blanket flapped at the window as a gust of wind swirled into the room and smoke billowed from the grate.

She crouched at the fireplace where the last embers emitted a feeble glow. The hearth was littered with ash and half burnt bits of timber that had fallen out of the grate, along with a few singed pieces of paper, one of which she picked up. Ingred moved next to her, directing the beam of torchlight onto the paper. Grace's eyes skittered over the typed words without taking them in, as an awful thought forced itself upon her.

'Oh no,' she muttered.

'What is it?' Ingred asked.

'Give me the torch.' She grabbed it from Ingred and flashed it around the room.

'What are you doing? What are you looking for?'

'There.' Grace leapt forward to where a crumpled piece of brown paper and some string lay on the floor near the armchair. She knelt down, smoothing out the brown paper. 'Oh no. See, it's addressed to Primo Press.' She looked up at Ingred, despairingly.

'Here,' Ingred said, 'let me.' She took back the torch and worked her way across the room. Finding no further pages, she returned and squatted at the grate, shining the beam of light onto the dying fire.

'Come, look,' she said, beckoning to Grace. At her touch, a sheaf of tissue thin pages like mushroom gills, disintegrated into ash. 'Your manuscript.'

Incredible as it seemed, the evidence of the brown paper wrapping, the singed pages and the mushroom gill ashes, was overwhelming.

Grace remembered it now. How she'd opened the back door to the garden, hoping to find someone at home. She'd gone upstairs without locking the door. It was obvious. The shimmering shape that had knelt by her bed was either Dave or Tina.

'I suppose they must have thought it was something they could sell. Instead, it was only good for the fire.' Ingred got to her feet. 'We should go.'

After making sure the fire was out and that the squat was not going to burn down, they returned home. The fate of the manuscript was sealed, it no longer existed. Tomorrow she would have to tell Simon.

At the top of the stairs, she said goodnight to Ingred, who lived in the other half of the squat, on the other side of the hole in the dividing wall. But instead of heading down the passage, Ingred followed her into the bedroom.

'Oh, do you want something?' Grace asked, feeling flustered because Ingred was standing so close to her.

'Yes,' she said. 'You.'

Which didn't make sense until Ingred took her by the hand and gently pulled her down onto the bed. Before she could question what was happening their lips met and all thought evaporated, obliterated by the electric connection of tongues. Soon their clothes disappeared too, and she felt Ingred's long Danish body covering hers, stomach against stomach, breast against breast, and Ingred's leg between her legs and the feeling of Ingred's thigh pressing against her swollen vulva. They went on kissing until Ingred pulled away, whispering mysterious Danish words in her ear, before sliding down, mouth to her breasts, then her belly, gently pushing her legs apart. She tried to sit up, only to be pushed back. She gave in and allowed her legs to be parted further. The touch of Ingred's tongue, slipping and sliding over her clitoris. She felt herself opening, like a bud unfurling into flower. Her body arched, she couldn't hold back, orgasming in a great, rippling wave, dissolving in a flood of pleasure so intense that time seemed to stop.

When she returned to the world, they kissed again, and she tasted herself, salty and faintly sweet, on Ingred's lips. 'Touch me,' she whispered, taking Grace's hand, guiding it down. 'Fuck me,' she commanded. Which Grace did, thinking of Sister George and Childie and their terrifying relationship only once and, even then, it was only in passing.

Afterwards, they lay curled together. She could hardly tell where she ended and where Ingred began.

24

Grace woke up alone and for a second everything was normal. Then she remembered: Ingred. They had fucked and it was incredible. She'd never had sex like that. It was a revelation. She lay in bed, wanting to savour the memory, but the longer she lay there, the more the whole experience began to take on a different aspect. Was this it? Did it mean she was a lesbian after all? She hoped Ingred would keep it to herself and not tell the others. Maybe Ingred wasn't really gay either and it was just something that had happened, a one-off thing, and they didn't need to talk about it or tell anyone. She wasn't in love with her. She'd been seduced and what happened did not define her. It didn't mean anything.

Even if it didn't mean anything, once she was at work, Grace fell into an erotic revery, remembering the way Ingred's fingers had slipped into her. She felt her cunt swelling, becoming wet. Rushing to the bathroom, a single touch brought her to a shuddering climax. To stop fantasising about sex, she made herself focus on boring things – the mail orders, receipts and invoices and reconciling the figures.

On the way home, she felt increasingly jittery. What would they say to each other? She didn't want to say anything and hoped Ingred would be locked in her darkroom and that she could avoid her.

'Did you hear about Ingred?' Annie asked, catching her in the hallway before she could sidle upstairs.

Her stomach twisted and she felt a rush of blood to her face.

'Her mother's sick. She's gone to Denmark to see her.'

Grace was so relieved that she let out a strangled sort of laugh. 'That's awful. Is she coming back?'

'Yes. A week, she thought.' Annie was looking at her strangely.

'Okay,' she said, as if the news wasn't important. There was no need to hide in her room and she went off to the kitchen, already convincing herself that by the time Ingred returned they would both pretend nothing had happened.

Almost a week had passed and Grace was about to visit Eric and bot a cigarette when Rita stopped beside her desk.

'Have you finished it yet?'

'What?' she said, playing for time. At first, the thing with Ingred had pushed the fate of the manuscript into the background. But with each passing day, she had grown more on edge, expecting Simon to ask the same question, saved only by the fact that he'd hardly been in. His occasional appearances were rushed; he looked agitated, and she had decided, conveniently, not to bother him. She was avoiding the inevitable and knew that soon, very soon, she would have to come clean. *It's not lost, just misplaced,* she imagined saying. *It's bound to turn up.*

'The manuscript,' Rita said.

'Oh, good, great.'

'I haven't seen you working on it.'

'I took it home. There are too many distractions here.'

'Good idea,' Rita said, propping her bottom on the edge of the desk while Grace fiddled with a couple of pencils and a half-eaten stale Marathon bar in a pretence of work-related activity.

'I'm sorry, I've got a lot to do.'

'Haven't we all,' Rita agreed in a falsely sympathetic way.

'Seriously, I should get on with some work.' Did she have to scream at her to leave?

'So, have you read it yet?'

'Yes. I mean, no, not all of it.'

'Well, don't take too long. Simon wants me to read it too.'

'Oh, he didn't mention it.'

'No?' Rita gave one of her smiles, the kind that did not extend beyond her mouth.

They had reached a stalemate until Grace had a sudden brain wave.

'Why don't you get the author to send another copy? That way we could both read it.'

'Another copy?' Rita cocked her head to the side observing her like a crow about to peck out the eyes of a newborn lamb. 'You do realise you've got the only extant copy?'

'Extant?' She heard her voice rise to a squeak.

'Yes. Extant, Grace. The only one in existence.'

'Simon didn't say. I'm sure he would have told me if—'

'I'm not lying,' Rita interrupted. 'Ask him if you don't believe me.'

Grace tried to shrug as if it was neither here nor there, unable to meet Rita's eye.

'You haven't lost it, have you?'

'Of course not. How would I lose it?'

'I was merely asking. All I'm saying, is hurry up.'

She slid her bottom off the desk and departed, leaving Grace to contemplate the demise of her fledgling publishing career. Simon would be furious. The only extant copy reduced to ashes. How long could she hold out before telling him? Not the truth, but a version of it, leaving out details about junkies and overdoses, which made her life sound sordid.

The telephone began to ring.

'Grace, is perfect you rang,' Basia exclaimed.

211

'I didn't. You rang me,' she replied in an expressionless voice.

'Same. I need advice from a proper English friend.'

Basia had never grasped the fact that Grace was not English, a misconception she'd failed to correct. Except for the brief period when Ingred had believed she was South African, Basia was the only person deceived by her 'English' accent.

'I met a man, Grace. He's Anglik.'

'What's Anglik?'

'From England. He's not Polish. I must know – is he good?'

'What do you mean by good?'

'Can I trust him?' Basia replied.

Him, as she related, was a man called Barry. She'd met him on a bus when he stood up to give her his seat. After the person beside her left, Barry sat down and started a conversation. He was a bus driver on his day off and liked to travel as a passenger to see it from the other side. He took notes about the quality of the driving and gave his own private rating system for each driver, a detail that put Grace off, although it didn't seem to be an indication of untrustworthiness.

'He wrote down my telephone to ask me out. He could be after my money,' Basia said. 'I need a second opinion.'

From everything Grace knew about Basia, she wasn't exactly loaded. In addition, her concerns were premature as she and Barry had yet to go on a date.

'That's what I'm asking, Grace. Can I go out with him?'

'Trust your intuition.'

It was what Basia needed to hear, and she announced that she had to get off the phone straight away in case Barry was trying to call. She had given him the warehouse telephone number. 'We can't chitter all day.'

'You mean chatter,' she replied, but Basia had already hung up, leaving her worried that the Polish bookkeeper had been too keen to accept her advice, and that intuition was not necessarily a reliable guide to detecting untrustworthy men.

At five o'clock she was putting on her jacket to leave when Simon came out of his office.

'Come on,' he said. 'I don't care if you're going to see a film with your friend Buttercup, there's a new wine bar on the corner. We're going for a drink.'

'Her name's Marigold, she's not a cow. And I can't.'

'Yes, you can. I'm ordering you.' He took her arm and marched her down the stairs.

They arrived at the wine bar, where he ordered a bottle of Beaujolais and some olives.

'Cheers.' He raised his glass to her. 'Anything wrong? You seem flat.'

'No.'

'Right. Are you sure you're not coming down with a bug?'

'No. I mean, yes, I'm sure.' She gulped down a few mouthfuls of Beaujolais, preparing to tell him the truth – or at least, a version of it.

'Good. And no shop talk,' he said, topping up her glass. 'We're here to relax.'

By the third glass of Beaujolais she'd almost forgotten that the manuscript had ever existed. Simon was charming and funny, and it was encouraging how much she was enjoying his company. True, he was a bit on the fat side, but better fat than a bag of bones. His size was reassuring; he wouldn't get blown away in a storm and could shield her from the slings and arrows. The wine was making her think in clichéd metaphors. Anyway, nothing was going to happen. It was theoretical, to see if she could feel attracted to him. Theoretically, she decided she could.

They were onto the second bottle when he reached across and took her hand. He raised it to his lips and kissed it.

'Dear Grace,' he said, 'I can't wait any longer.'

Before she could stutter out an excuse – that she was flattered by him propositioning her, but as his employee she didn't think it was right *and* he was married – he went on.

'The manuscript.'

'Oh,' she said, still in the middle of mentally constructing an excuse that wouldn't hurt his feelings.

'Very, very keen to hear your opinion.' He let go of her hand and raised his glass with an encouraging smile, which, if she had read it might have encouraged her. A few hours ago, she'd contemplated telling him the truth.

'I'm sorry to be the one to tell you, it's terrible.'

He stared at her intensely and, for the first time, she noticed his eyes, though an attractive shade of blue, were on the small side.

'Definitely not publishable,' she added.

'The last time we spoke about it, you said it was interesting,' he said, accusingly.

'Interesting because it's so bad. That's what I meant.'

'What about the innovative new voice?'

'I was wrong.'

'And what? You don't think we should publish?'

'A disaster.'

'Well, that's one opinion. I think Rita should—'

'Sure, Rita, Eric. Might as well ask Basia too. Anyone who can read. I mean, why believe the one person who's qualified to give an opinion? Who studied literature and got a first-class degree.'

'Okay, enough. I get your point. Put it on my desk first thing tomorrow with your report.'

'What for?'

'What for? Because I need to read it, that's why. Because if we're not going to publish it, Roger's going to be bloody furious, and I need to make bloody sure I agree with you.' He grabbed his wine glass and drained it, his small blue eyes glinting dangerously.

'Well, you can't.'

'With all due respect Grace, I bloody well can.'

'I've sent it back. With a letter of rejection.' Mimicking his earlier action, she grabbed her glass of wine and gulped it down, knowing

214

she'd gone too far into what could only be described as a cul-de-sac. There was no way to change her story without sounding like a complete lunatic.

'What the hell did you do that for?' he burst out.

'Because you hate dealing with angry people,' she flung back, suddenly invigorated. 'I'm the one who has to make up the excuses and listen to them raving on about you not paying your bills. I assumed you'd want me to deal with it, so I did.' And then after a pause, she added, 'as usual,' in an attempt to make him feel guilty.

'You should have checked with me first.'

Rather than the fury she expected, he sounded almost sulky. She interpreted it as a capitulation.

'I know, but I wanted to save you the trouble.'

'I should sack you,' he said. 'You know that.'

'Yes,' she responded meekly.

'You're bloody lucky I haven't.'

'I know.'

He went on for a while, telling her that anyone else would have sacked her on the spot and he was a fool and that she had better prove him wrong (about being a fool) and so on. She could see that he needed to berate her and that the best thing to do was to go along with it, while trying to suppress the growing fear that she had dug herself into a hole. She heard her mother saying *in for a penny, in for a pound.*

They were the last to leave the wine bar, the proprietor herding them out into the night. They were alone on the street except for passing cars.

'I'll get the tube,' she said, trying not to teeter.

'No, you won't. It's too late. Trains have retired for the night.' He waved at an approaching black cab. 'What's say we adjourn to the free love commune?'

'We can't,' she said.

215

He took hold of her jacket and tugged her towards him until his lips brushed her forehead. 'Give me one good reason.'

'You're married.' Not that she really cared about Marina. She was hoping that a reminder of his wife would bring him to his senses, although the affair with Rita tended to suggest otherwise.

'I am,' he said. 'Things are not ... never mind,' he sighed. 'I don't want to burden you with that.'

His earnest expression, the frank, unblinking gaze of his small blue eyes, was making her feel dizzy.

'You know how I feel about you, Grace.'

For one mad moment, she had an urge to let go and fall into his arms. To let him take over. Let him be the answer. She was on the edge of a cliff and jumping was almost irresistible. She could feel her grip on the situation slipping.

'You right guv'nor?' the cabbie spoke through the open window.

It was enough to break the spell, and she pulled away from him.

'You're not coming. Don't even try. I'm serious.'

He held up his hands in a gesture of surrender and let her get into the cab alone, thrusting some bank notes into her hand for the fare. Then he spoke to the driver, telling him to make sure she got home safely.

The cab swung out into the traffic. 'Where to, my lovely?' the cabby said, glancing at her in the rear vision mirror.

Once she told him the address, his friendly demeanour evaporated. He wasn't going to be mugged by junkies and hippies who lived like animals. As far as he was concerned, the whole street should be torn down. Not even the fact that she had money swayed him. He refused to drive down Belton Road and let her off near the tube station.

She stumbled out of the cab and began the fifteen-minute walk to the squat, wishing she hadn't drunk so much wine and that she'd told Simon the truth. The invented story was a time bomb that had already begun to tick. She'd almost reached Belton Road when a figure ran past, veering across the street and into a derelict house that Martin had pointed out to her months ago as the house where Vincent dossed. It must have been him, poor crazy thing. She continued on, until an afterimage jolted her to a stop. The cloak, flapping behind him like an enormous bat. Marigold's cloak.

Outside the ruined house, a vein pulsed at her temple. She didn't want to go in, knowing it would be choked with rubbish and possibly worse. Stories of places where dossers camped, of rooms filled with human shit. The fact that Vincent sometimes slept there wasn't reassuring, and she almost turned away. But she couldn't leave without knowing.

Groping her way along the hall, broken glass crunched underfoot. 'Hello. Anyone there?'

She reached an open door and entered, accidentally kicking an empty bottle, spinning it across the floor. An explosion of dark, whirring shapes hurtled upwards. A wing brushed her face, and she cried out, stumbling against the door jamb. In the silence that followed, all she could hear was her own ragged breathing. The pigeons had flown off and as she grew accustomed to the dark, she became aware of moonlight falling from above. A large section of the ceiling and first floor had collapsed, revealing the skeletal remains of the roof. Rubbish covered the floor – empty bottles and tins, scraps of clothing, broken bits of furniture and a blackened fireplace filled with ashes and half burnt bits of wood. On the wall above the fireplace, someone, Vincent, she supposed, had painted the word love, repeating it three times in a rainbow arc. 'All You Need Is Love' began to play in her head, a mocking counterpoint to the desolation.

She continued through the house, but there was no sign of life. What had she really seen? It was dark, she was drunk, it could have been anyone. Yet no matter how much she tried to get rid of it, an image of Marigold's billowing cloak persisted.

25

At the entrance to Marigold's bedroom, Grace felt a drop in the temperature. Without the vibrancy of her presence, the room was lifeless; the objects that had created an exotic atmosphere now seemed like tawdry trinkets. The air was still, and a layer of dust had settled over everything. Infected by the dismal atmosphere, Grace urged herself to move, to stop standing in the doorway like the dressmaker's dummy she'd once been. She stepped towards the mound of clothes where a week earlier she'd thrown the cloak. How long ago it seemed. A single glance was enough to reveal that it was not there. Though she'd anticipated as much, it still came as a shock, and she began to rifle through the pile, not stopping until it had been turned upside down.

The cloak was gone, but who had taken it? The evidence pointed to Vincent. He was the one living in the ruined house, not Marigold. He was also a frequent visitor to the squat, and it was easy to imagine him poking around. Like everyone else, he knew that Marigold had not come home for weeks and, from his point of view, her cloak would have been fair game.

Mulling it over, Grace let her gaze wander to the window. She wasn't looking for anything in particular and had already begun to step towards the door when she registered that something was wrong with the brick plinth. The aspidistra was missing. Crossing the room, she found it lying on the floor with its roots exposed, the pot in pieces. For weeks, she'd been watering it, determined to keep it alive for Marigold's return. *Be careful, that's my ironic aspidistra*, she'd said, criticising Grace for not understanding the reference to Orwell. She remembered how hurt she'd felt, and how Marigold had responded by telling her she was interesting and smart and quite beautiful. And brave. Thinking of those extraordinary words, Grace felt an intense longing for her, followed by a familiar surge of anger. Why hadn't she cared enough to leave a message? Instead, she'd disappeared without a trace, leaving her to carry the burden of worrying. She blinked away an image of her parents as they waved goodbye, annoyed that it had come into her mind. She was not the one who'd disappeared without a trace, her situation was completely different.

She knelt down and began to scrape the soil into a heap, noticing that it was still moist. It was hard to believe that Marigold would have knocked over her ironic aspidistra. On the other hand, it was easy to imagine Vincent checking at the window to see if anyone was coming, turning in a hurry, and accidentally bumping it off the plinth. Yes, she was sure now. It was Vincent who'd run across the street. Knowing this, she realised how much she'd wanted it to be Marigold, to reassure herself that her friend was alive because, lately, she had begun to fear the worst.

She stood up to look for a temporary container in which to put the soil. Outside, drizzly rain had begun to fall. There was a light on in the upstairs window of the separatist dyke house and a few people hurrying past on the street. She thought about how Marigold had saved her from Joel's and without her help, she might still be stuck there, and how she couldn't give up on her. She had to go back to Kentish Town, even if it meant waiting all day.

The front door of the separatist house opened, a woman emerged, followed by another. Ignoring the rain, they stood on the doorstep and kissed. As the kiss turned into a prolonged pash, Grace began to get turned on. When the lovers finally separated, she saw that the taller woman was Ingred.

Winded by a wave of unexpected jealousy and afraid that Ingred might look across and see her, she bobbed below the sill. For a week she'd dreaded Ingred's return, practicing what she was going to say. *No offence but it just isn't for me, I'm not really into women.* She'd imagined that Ingred was in love with her and would be upset. Instead, she was getting off with one of the separatist women. How humiliating to discover that Ingred wasn't interested, and that she'd misread the whole thing.

Her legs began to ache from crouching, and she slid down onto the floor, her cheek resting on the pile of dirt. Whatever happened, she couldn't let Ingred know that she'd misinterpreted things, or that she gave a damn. She had to act cool, remembering how her mother often said that her face was an open book. *You must learn to conceal your emotions; you don't want everyone to know what you think.* At the time, she'd retorted sulkily that she couldn't see why not. Why shouldn't she be an open book?

Too late, she heard footsteps and looked up to see Ingred in the doorway.

'Grace?'

She sat up, grabbed a broken piece of pot and began to fill it with soil.

'Here,' Ingred said, arriving to kneel beside her. 'You've got dirt on your cheek.'

'Leave me,' Grace cried, immediately regretting how hysterical she sounded. 'It's fine, it's nothing.' She went on filling the broken pot, knowing it made her look weird because the soil kept spilling out.

'What's wrong?'

'Nothing's wrong.'

'You're angry.'

'I'm not.'

'Okay, you're not.' Ingred stood up. 'You want me to go, so I'll go.'

'I didn't say that.' Once Ingred said she would leave, Grace had to challenge it. She didn't know why.

'I saw you across the road,' she said.

'I saw you too,' Ingred replied, 'at the window.'

'It's nothing to do with me because I'm not—'

'Not what?'

'I'm not interested. Okay?'

Nothing was coming out the right way. Why had she said she wasn't interested? It sounded childish. She stood up, unable to look Ingred in the eye. She wanted to meet her gaze and force her to look away. She couldn't do it and felt furious with herself. Furious with Ingred too.

'I think you're not telling the truth,' Ingred said. 'You're angry because you saw me kissing Thea.'

'You're wrong, I couldn't care less. I'm angry because someone knocked over Marigold's plant which is precious to her. I don't suppose you care about that.'

She risked a glance at Ingred and saw the incredulous look on her face. It was the moment to laugh and say she didn't know what she was talking about. She was an idiot. Or, failing that, to walk out while holding onto some shred of dignity. Instead, she dropped the broken pot and ran out of the room.

Back in her own bedroom, she couldn't relax. Without a door to close she felt exposed. She didn't trust Ingred not to follow her and demand an explanation.

She entered the kitchen to find Gerald, Martin, Vanessa and Annie, sitting in silence. At first, she was sure they had been talking about

221

her and that everyone had suddenly stopped because she'd come in. That they knew about her and Ingred.

'Grace, sit down,' Annie said. 'Something's happened.'

She registered Annie's sombre tone and snapped out of it. 'Marigold?'

'No.' This time it was Gerald who spoke. 'Vincent is dead.'

'Dead? He can't be. I saw him tonight.'

Gerald shook his head. 'He died this afternoon. Annie and I went to the hospital.'

'His sister was there too,' Annie said.

She explained that the sister was arranging everything, taking his body to Cornwall where his mother still lived, and where he would be buried. Someone had found him beside the overground railway track near Gospel Oak. He'd been hit by a train. Nobody knew if it was an accident or whether he'd tried to kill himself, or why he'd gone all the way to north London. Annie said he'd been estranged from his family. The sister, whose name was Jennifer, said they'd tried to stay in touch. Vincent pushed them away, he was always difficult, even when they were children. His mother was heartbroken. Grace listened as Annie continued to talk, occasionally someone else spoke, remembering Vincent and the times he'd come to the squat, his music, such divine music, and whether they should have done more. Grace was remembering how she'd heard him muttering that he was guilty, a useless cunt and she hadn't done anything. She saw the words above the fireplace: *love, love, love,* and tears welled up and spilled down her cheeks – for Vincent, and for knowing that she had made a fool of herself in front of Ingred, and for crying about that when Vincent was dead which was final and tragic and how could she even put the two things together on the same plane. She didn't want to cry but the tears took no notice. Hands reached out to comfort her and Vanessa put an arm around her shoulder. It was awful, they all felt the same.

222

26

Vincent was dead. Two years ago, her grandfather had died of a heart attack, but he was old. No matter how much Grace repeated to herself, *Vincent is dead*, it didn't feel real. He would never again dash past her on the street, or leap onto the kitchen table to play his violin. He was gone, irrevocably gone. She wanted to hold onto him, keep him alive in her mind and not let the onrushing flow of her thoughts condemn him to oblivion.

But before long, all she could think about was Marigold and that it must have been her she'd seen disappearing into the derelict house because Vincent was already dead by then. To come back for her cloak and then disappear again didn't seem to make sense and Grace felt sure there must have been some other reason for her return. Could it have been the address written on the pellet of paper that she'd found in the cloak pocket? Perhaps Marigold had come back to get it, believing it was still there, grabbing her cloak without checking first. It was a flimsy theory and Grace knew she was clutching at straws and that it was all a mystery, just like Marigold's disappearance in the first place.

Vincent's death was a mystery too. And then her thoughts turned to Ingred, not because she was a mystery, although she was, but because of what had happened. That mortifying exchange in

Marigold's room. And Simon at the wine bar – her stupid lies about the manuscript, destined to be revealed as soon as the author got in touch. And Rita, who hated her, no matter what she did. Her mind flicked like a firefly from one thing to another, searching in vain for a safe harbour.

It was time to get up, and yet she couldn't face the prospect of going to work. Better to ring from the phone box near the tube station and say she'd caught a bug. Or perhaps she wouldn't even ring up, and go in tomorrow, say she'd been too sick. It wasn't hard to convince herself that she didn't feel well. Huddled under the bedclothes, she willed herself back to sleep, to the realm of dreams which, however disturbing, was preferable to the torture of consciousness.

She woke up with the day half gone. It was already afternoon and she felt disorientated, cut off from everything, as if she was sick after all. Lying on the floor, where weeks earlier Ingred had dropped it, was *The Prime of Miss Jean Brodie*. She reached across and picked it up.

If she hadn't been under the spell of the book, she might have heard Raymond shout from downstairs that there was someone to see her, alerting her to an unexpected arrival. People were always coming and going, finding their way upstairs or into the squat next door via the hole in the adjoining wall, without the need for an introduction. As it was, she was propped up in bed, wearing a holey t-shirt, while Miss Brodie was transforming her girls into the crème de la crème, when a discreet, warning cough made her look up.

'Oh, shit,' she exclaimed. 'What are you doing here?'

'I could ask you the same thing,' Simon replied with a grin.

She grabbed the eiderdown and pulled it up to cover herself.

'Can I?' He indicated the end of the mattress.

'No,' she responded, her tone sharp enough to stop him halfway.

He straightened up, thrusting his hands in the pockets of his corduroy trousers, apparently unruffled by her refusal. 'You weren't at work. I was worried something might be wrong.'

224

'Well, there's not. I mean, I've got some kind of bug.' She emitted an unconvincing cough. 'I'm feeling a bit better.'

'Good. Glad to hear it. What are you reading?'

'Nothing. Muriel Spark. What do you want?'

'As I said, I was worried. And someone rang for you, I thought you'd want to know. For a person named Grace you're not very gracious.'

She had been about to demand he leave her room. 'Who? Who rang?'

'Ed somebody. Must say he was rather rude. To tell the truth, he rang a few days ago.'

'A few days ago? She was almost screeching. 'Why didn't you tell me?'

'I'm not the Girl Friday, Grace. If you weren't always sneaking off early, you would have spoken to him yourself.' Simon moved to the window and looked out.

'What did he say?' she demanded, ignoring his critical comment, overshadowed as it was by the momentous news that Ed had rung. That it was Ed who lived at Lady Somerset Road. Suddenly, Marigold was within reach.

'Not a boyfriend I hope?'

'No, a friend.'

'Good. It's freezing in here Grace, no wonder you're sick.'

'I'm not sick. I mean, I was. I don't feel the cold,' she lied.

He began to roam the room like a landlord inspecting for damage. Grace wished she wasn't half naked. It made getting up impossible and yet bed felt far too intimate given what had happened outside the bar – his revelation that he was mad about her. She needed to be on guard.

'Did he leave a number?'

'You can't live in a squalid dump like this. You'll end up with pneumonia.' He tore off a long strip of wallpaper that had been dangling for some time, releasing a burst of mould spores.

'It's not squalid. Anyway, we're fixing it up.' She didn't want to admit she'd had similar thoughts.

He approached the mattress again, and this time, sank to his knees. She clutched the eiderdown to her chin.

'Let me set you up in a nice comfy flat. Chelsea. Elm Park Gardens. No strings, I promise.'

She stared at him, dumb struck.

'I'm serious Grace. Let me take care of you.'

'I don't need taking care of.'

'Yes, you do. You most definitely do.'

He tried to reach for her, and she fended him off with her elbow.

'You'll love it there. Bohemian but classy. Joyce Grenfell's got the flat upstairs.'

In some far recess of her mind, she registered the name Joyce Grenfell. Wasn't she an ancient comedian?

'I want you to leave.'

'You don't. Not really.'

'If you don't leave, I'm going to scream.'

'You wouldn't.'

She drew in a breath, exaggerating it to let him see that she was serious. She was about to shriek when he raised his hands in a motion of surrender.

'Alright, you've made your point.' He stood up, smiling down at her. 'Don't think I'm giving up.'

He retreated, stopping beside the brick and plank bookshelf where he extracted his wallet from the inside pocket of his leather jacket and took out a wad of bank notes.

'What are you doing?'

'Buy yourself some warm pyjamas. And a decent coat,' he said, casually tossing the wad on the shelf.

'I don't want your money. I don't need anything. I'm not taking it.' She wrapped herself in the eiderdown and tried to shuffle towards him.

'Think of it as a bonus. You've earned it.'

'I don't want it.'

'Don't worry about seeing me out.' With a smile, he blew a kiss at her and left the room.

'I'll throw it away,' she shouted.

Pulling on some clothes, she stuffed the money in the pocket of her jacket and raced down the stairs in time to see Simon's black Mercedes disappearing around the corner.

On the tube, she kept her hand in her pocket, fingers gripping the wad of cash which she'd had no time to transfer to her bag. There had been warnings about gangs of pickpockets who worked the underground and though it was irrational, the money made her feel like a target. As the train picked up speed, she thought of the waitresses at the hotel in Melbourne, how they were always talking about sugar daddies, hoping that one of the sleazy businessmen would turn out to want more than a fuck. As far as she knew, it had never happened. Sugar daddies only existed in fantasy. Whereas Simon was real. He wasn't like those businessmen; he was often funny and sometimes kind – she was thinking of his friendship with Guy. She remembered the crazy moment outside the wine bar when she'd almost fallen into his arms. The desire to let him take over and be the answer to her problems. And Marigold had said there were advantages – expensive restaurants, holidays abroad, introductions to interesting and successful people. She'd been talking about Rita, but it was all the same.

Walking from the tube station to Primo Press, Grace argued with herself. Why was she even contemplating Simon's offer? She wasn't in love with him. He was trying to buy her. She didn't care about expensive restaurants and meeting successful people. He was a hopeless womaniser who would never change his ways. There was only one thing on the other side of the argument: could he change her? Was he, in spite of everything, the right man to do it?

She arrived at work knowing that whatever happened, she didn't want to be in his debt. Simon, however, was not in his office. She considered leaving the money on his desk, only for it to feel wrong. She needed to do it in person. While waiting for him, she would look for Ed's phone number and settled herself in his chair, feeling sure that he would have jotted it down on whatever was to hand.

His desk was the usual jumble of books, newspapers, correspondence, and unpaid bills. Amongst the rubble she glimpsed a half empty packet of Gauloise Bleu cigarettes and the pair of dice that had appeared when he'd first begun raving on about *The Dice Man*. Her eye snagged on a piece of paper covered with hastily scrawled figures. Closer inspection revealed a series of additions and calculations, none of which looked like a telephone number. She began to search in earnest, confident of finding it somewhere in the chaos.

After a fruitless half hour she gave up and went downstairs to ask Eric if he knew when Simon would be back. Eric was lying on the leather couch, and she called out to him before realising he was not alone. Four legs were entwined on the sofa, two of which were female.

Hearing his name, Eric leapt up, flapping his hands at her.

'Out,' he cried, trying to shield the woman from view while shepherding Grace towards the door. 'Busy, come back later.'

'Oh, let her stay,' came a familiar voice. 'She's seen us now.'

Grace stepped around Eric to see Rita, sitting on the couch, buttoning her blouse.

'Rita?' she exclaimed, unable to disguise her shock.

Rita lit a cigarette. 'Yes, Grace, it is I. You look surprised.'

'No, not at all,' she lied. 'I didn't mean to interrupt you.'

'Too late, you have. What do you want?'

'I was hoping you might know where Simon is.'

'Didn't he tell you? Gosh, secrets already,' Rita mocked.

'Oh, get fucked,' Grace cried. 'Stop being such a bitch.' It wasn't what she planned to say but Rita's mockery was the last straw.

'Listen, why don't we adjourn to the pub,' Eric said in an attempt to soothe the waters. 'We can talk there.'

Eric returned from the bar with three pints of bitter. Grace sipped her pint while Rita and Eric sat together, snuggling on the other side of the table, ignoring her. She was sure Rita was doing it deliberately, to make her feel uncomfortable. It was annoying but no more than that. To her amazement, Rita's intimidatory hold had evaporated like a wisp of steam the moment she'd told her to get fucked. It was extraordinary and liberating to realise that Rita's power was an illusion she herself had fostered. But no longer.

She finished her pint and went to the bar, ordering another round for the three of them, paying with Simon's money, assuring herself that she would top it up later before giving it back to him. The wad of notes, now transferred to her bag, seemed more at home than it had a few hours ago. On her return, Rita and Eric were taking a breather.

'Cheers,' Rita said, raising her glass. 'I owe you a thank you.'

'No need, it was my shout,' she replied.

'Not that. I mean you did me a favour.' She turned to Eric and gave him a peck on the lips, then back to Grace. 'If you hadn't thrown yourself at Simon—'

'I did not throw myself—'

'I mean it Grace, I'm truly grateful. The funny thing is that I gave you the job because I was sure you were gay and wouldn't pose a threat. It was that awful haircut. I took you for a proper little dyke.'

'Shows you can't always tell a book by its cover,' Eric said.

'And speaking of books,' Rita added, 'you wanted to know where he is. Apparently, he's taken Roger to lunch.'

'Probably signing the contract,' Eric said. 'And getting badgered on French champagne.'

229

Then Rita began to talk about Grace's manuscript report and that it must have done the trick and she had underestimated her, and that they ought to join forces, become a team and together achieve great things.

'What do you say? Hello …' Rita waved her hand in front of Grace's face. 'Anyone home?'

'She's gone into shock,' Eric said.

Rita laughed and the two of them began to smooch again, giving Grace the opportunity to recover. She was in shock, as Eric had correctly surmised. Not, as it happened, from Rita's suggestion that they become allies, she'd stopped listening by then. It was not even the revelation that Rita thought she was a proper little dyke (although that was horrible and shocking, and she would need to clear it up later). It was the news about Roger and the fact that Simon would know by now that she'd never sent the manuscript.

She left the lovers at the pub and returned to the office to continue her search for Ed's phone number, hoping to find it before Simon returned. She didn't feel up to facing him now, even if it was only delaying the inevitable.

Rifling through his papers, she heard the front door open. A familiar voice began to belt out 'Stairway to Heaven' in the wrong key. Moments later, Simon swung into the office, still singing with gusto. Halfway across the room he caught sight of her and stopped.

'You,' he said. His face was flushed, and he was grinning in a gormless sort of way.

'I'm sorry about Roger's manuscript, I should have told you.' After all the agonising about what to tell him, it was the first thing to spring from her lips.

'Don't worry about Roger the Dodger,' he said, with an airy wave, flopping into a chair beside the coffee table. 'Turns out you were right.'

Grace caught a pungent whiff of alcohol.

'What do mean?'

'Unpublishable.'

'But—'

'Rog said so himself. Relieved we weren't going ahead. Must say he was a bit confused. Says he never received the manuscript you sent back.'

'I know. I wanted to tell you—'

'All a waste of time,' he went on. 'No money in it. Decided to get out and go into potboilers. Turns out the Dodger is on a roll.' He laughed. 'Very productive lunch. Drank too much French fizz. Thanks to Max.'

'Max was at lunch too?' Grace was struggling to keep up. Rita hadn't said anything about Max.

Simon was slumped in the chair, legs splayed, his face a dangerous shade of beetroot. He was beginning to slur his words. 'Not at lunch. Anyway, agreed to terms, cut the old poof loose.'

'I thought you were friends?'

'Come here.' He patted his knee. 'Got a proposition.'

Then he blathered on about potboilers and how there was a fortune in quickie crime and whodunits. Opportunities galore for expansion, and for her too. Brilliant prospects for her. His long-winded rambling gave her time to adapt to the new situation – that Roger the Scottish author was now writing whodunits and she no longer needed to confess about the manuscript. And whatever had gone on between Simon and Max, the old poof had been cut loose.

'Bugger literary publishing, Grace,' Simon declared. 'Full of upper-class cunts.'

'Pricks,' she said, automatically.

'Pricks,' he repeated. He got to his feet, unsteadily, and with a glint in his eye wobbled a few steps in her direction. 'C'mon, Grace. Lemme set you up—'

'Stop. Sit down,' she ordered, mimicking the tone he so often took with her.

231

He hesitated, a puzzled look passing across his face. He stepped back and sank into the chair.

'I've told you I don't want to be set up.'

'I need you.'

'No, you don't.'

'Can convince you.'

'You can't. You only want me because I'm saying no.'

'Not true. Been mad about you from the start.'

'You're drunk. And you're married.'

'Don't worry about that. Got an understanding.'

'Listen to me. I need that telephone number.'

'What number?'

'Ed, the guy who rang. You spoke to him.'

'Ed?'

'You can't have forgotten. He rang a few days ago.'

'No number.'

'What do you mean? He must have left a number.'

She had moved from the desk and was standing in front of him when he grabbed her by the jacket and pulled her onto his lap.

'That's better,' he said, wrapping his arms around her.

'What are you doing? Let me up. Let go of me.' She tried unsuccessfully to push him away.

'Kiss first.'

His hands were all over her, pinching and squeezing. Slobbery lips trailed saliva across her cheek.

'Stop, Simon. Please,' she begged.

'Just a little kiss. Sexy minx.'

In desperation, she grabbed his hair, and wrenched his head back as hard as she could. He gave a pained yelp and his grip on her loosened. It was all she needed. With a twist, she slid from his lap.

'Why the hell did you do that?' he yelled, lunging for her.

She scrambled away, scattering books and poster tubes that lay in her path.

'Come back here,' he shouted.

She heard him crash into the coffee table as she made it to the door. She didn't look back and leapt down the stairs, taking them two at a time. As she reached the bottom, the front door opened. She hurtled past Rita and Eric without stopping.

27

The following day, Grace did not go to work, unable to face Simon, even though she convinced herself that what had happened was nothing, really. She had overreacted and felt guilty because of the times she'd flirted with him. It was her own fault; she'd led him on.

On the third day, when she still hadn't returned, she knew it was over. She was never going back and told the others she'd left her job.

'Are you sure?' Annie asked. 'You seem a bit depressed.'

'I'm not depressed. I'm tired, that's all.' She didn't want to admit to feeling low, even to herself.

Later, sitting in the kitchen with Raymond and Martin, there was a knock on the front door. As they bickered amongst themselves about who should answer it, the knocking grew louder and more insistent.

'Grace, are you there? Grace?' called Simon.

She jumped up from the table and moved to the back door, heart thumping.

'I don't want to see him. Please, can one of you get rid of him? Tell him I've moved out.'

'Why? I thought you liked him,' Martin said.

'Please Raymond. Say you don't know where I've gone.'

Simon was thumping on the door. Raymond closed the French newspaper he was reading. 'Yes, I know. You are not here. You have disappeared.'

Grace slipped out into the back garden and hurried away, worried that Simon might barge past Raymond and come looking for her. At the end of the row, Indian music floated from an open upstairs window of the Rajneesh ashram. She stood listening to the music for what seemed like ages until Raymond came. It was safe to return.

'He left this for you in case you turned up,' Raymond said, producing a sealed envelope with her name on it.

On a single sheet of paper, he'd written *Grace, come back. I was drunk. Simon.*

The lack of an apology or even a shred of remorse made her furious, and from that moment on she stopped torturing herself. What had happened was not her fault. The self-recriminations and guilt disappeared. She imagined what Marigold would say – that flirting was not an invitation to molest someone, and what a bastard act it was. She ripped up his note and flung the scraps in the garden. It was a turning point.

She had to find Marigold. Which meant finding Ed. Without a telephone number there was only one option.

On her way to the tube station, through the streets of squats and boarded up houses, she saw that the season had changed. Trees were coming into vibrant green leaf, and just where she turned the corner, for two or three steps she caught the heady scent of jasmine, hidden from view in some neglected garden. It reminded her of Melbourne – the same harbinger of spring, sprawling in promiscuous abundance over inner suburban fences. She felt an unexpected pang, a sudden nostalgia for Melbourne's four seasons in one day: gusty winds and blazing sunshine, mellow mornings and brief afternoon storms; the way the temperature could plummet from summer to winter in a matter of minutes, blindsiding visitors to the city.

Climbing the steps to Ed's front door, she was overtaken by a sudden reluctance. What if he refused to tell her anything? It would mean the end of hope. She forced herself to bang the knocker.

For two hours she sat on the top step, until a middle-aged woman carrying a lumpy string bag full of groceries stopped at the front gate.

'If you're waiting for the Irish, pet, you're too late. You won't be the last to come looking, I'll be bound,' she said, in a knowing tone.

She was already moving on when Grace leapt down the steps.

The woman, Edith, lived in a flat next door. The four Irish fellas had up and left a few days ago. It wouldn't surprise her if they'd shot through owing a month's rent. They were navvies, working on building sites like the rest of them. The Irish, she meant. And no, she didn't know where they'd gone. She didn't know their names, although there might have been a Sean, or a Seamus. She didn't think there was an Ed.

'Was there a girl, a woman, staying here?' Grace asked.

Edith shook her head. 'Course, they might have had girlfriends. I wouldn't know.' She was about to move on again and paused. 'There was a girl. I saw her once or twice.'

'Marigold?' Grace burst out.

'No, Stella, I think it was.'

'You're sure? You're positive it wasn't Marigold?'

'Positive, love, I would have remembered a posh name like that.'

It had happened. She had reached a dead end. Dead end, dead end, dead end. The words resounded in her head, beating time to the rhythm of the train as it sped through the tunnel. Ed, or whatever he was called – Seamus or Sean or something else – had vanished, just like Marigold. Grace did not doubt his existence. He'd rung Primo Press. Still, he seemed more and more like a phantom. And Marigold too. A phantom, a ghost, an unreliable memory.

Changing trains at Tottenham Court Road she stopped in the middle of the walkway, ignoring the looks of annoyance and muttered curses of those forced to abruptly alter course. Something was nagging at her. What was it? The house meeting interrupted by a knock at the door. *A bloke looking for someone called Stella,* Gerald said. Someone called Stella. Could Marigold be Stella? It didn't make any sense but with the idea fizzing inside her she began to run.

'I don't see what it proves,' Gerald said. 'Even if Marigold is Stella, or vice-versa, she's still gone. Using a false name makes sense in a way. She was slumming it and didn't want her parents finding out. Now she's had enough and gone home.'

'What about that guy at the door? What did he look like?'

'Ordinary. I don't remember.'

'Was he Irish?'

'He could have been.'

'What does that mean? Couldn't you tell?'

'I wasn't taking much notice, Grace. We were in the middle of a meeting. What does it matter?'

It mattered because of the Irishmen at Lady Somerset Road. Because they had disappeared, and she was sure that Marigold had disappeared with them. It mattered because of all the things she had noticed and put out of her mind – things she could no longer shrug off. The night everyone had been arguing about the Red Brigades and the Red Army Faction. Gerald had come in and told them about the bomb in the soldiers' pub, and Marigold said soldiers were never off-duty. She said it was empty talk unless you were prepared to kill for your beliefs, and Annie asked her whether she would ever kill anyone – it was a rhetorical question, a way of underlining that none of them ever would. Instead, Marigold had fixed Annie with a chilling look. She was always scornful of Gerald's politics, his leaflets, and the meetings he attended, saying it was childish and wouldn't achieve anything. Put together, it suggested that Marigold believed in far more radical action. And then, at the eviction of Pewsey Street when she'd insisted that Grace take her cloak. Had she been avoiding Ed, or had she simply let Grace believe it? Was she on the run from someone or something more dangerous than a part-time boyfriend?

What had happened at Pewsey Street played on her mind and she remembered Gerald saying that the Special Branch had raided some of the squats suspected of having IRA connections. He said it was bullshit, they were just harassing anyone on their left-wing hit list. What if he was wrong? What if Marigold had some kind of link with the Pewsey Street squatters? What if she had been living a double life? Was Ed really her boyfriend? Or was he her contact, her link to the IRA?

She told Gerald everything she could remember. Now and then, he asked a question, a clarification. The more she spoke, the more certain she became that Marigold was a member of the IRA and had gone off with Ed and his companions.

'Can't you see?' she said. 'It's the only thing that makes sense.'

"You're adding up wrong,' Gerald said. 'Two and two don't make five. Think about it, Grace. A member of the IRA wouldn't take that risk. They wouldn't write down that address. They'd memorise something like that.'

'There was no time. If she hadn't swapped her cloak with me, she would have destroyed it. Something was freaking her out that day, she was desperate to get away. The more I think about it, the more I think she remembered she'd left it in the pocket and that's why she came back. See, it fits with what you're saying. She had to get rid of it.'

Despite Grace's 'evidence' Gerald remained unconvinced that Marigold was a member of the IRA. She was an English toff, there was no way they'd trust her.

'I'm not saying she wasn't somehow involved,' he said. 'The Provos might have had a use for her. That translating job she was always secretive about, maybe it was connected somehow.'

'So, you'll come with me?'

'Where?'

'Back to Kentish Town. See if we can find other neighbours who might have known them. Talk to Edith again.'

'What's the point? She's gone. That's all there is to it. If she wanted you to find her, she would have left you a message that night she came back. But she didn't. What do you want from her, anyway?'

She heard the irritation in his voice, his question implying that whatever she wanted was unreasonable and too much. She shook her head and did not answer, remembering his words that day in the kitchen. *Anyone would think you were in love.*

'You're chasing shadows, Grace,' he said. 'Let her go.'

Forgotten since the confrontation with Ingred, the ironic aspidistra lay on the floor of Marigold's room, surrounded by bits of pot and scattered soil. Its leaves had become limp and were beginning to shrivel. Grace took it down to the garden and went about the task of re-potting it in a blackened saucepan that Martin had boiled dry months ago. She told herself that if she could save the plant, Marigold would return. It was magical thinking and while she had given up the idea of going back to Kentish Town on her own, she couldn't accept Gerald's advice to let her go.

As she tamped down the soil, Vanessa called out to her, waving from the direction of the Orange People ashram. Her heart sank. She liked Vanessa and since Marigold had left, they'd become closer. But Vanessa was always urging her to express her feelings and confront the truth, and she didn't feel up to an encounter group session. Too late to escape, she continued to fiddle with the soil, attempting to convey that she was busy and didn't want to be interrupted.

'There's a house dinner tonight,' Vanessa said. 'We'll all be there. You too Grace. There are things we need to discuss.'

'I don't want to talk about it.'

'Not you. Things about the house, about the future.'

'What things?'

'Tonight. Okay?'

Vanessa didn't wait for an answer and disappeared into the kitchen.

They had taken their places when Grace slipped into the last empty chair. To her dismay, Ingred was directly opposite. Since the confrontation in Marigold's room, they'd avoided each other by mutual understanding. Now, with only the width of the table separating them, she dreaded Ingred's critical gaze and kept her own eyes lowered.

'It's good you are here, Grace. We've been worried about you,' Ingred said. She spoke in a kindly tone, and Grace felt her composure slipping. Being an object of pity was almost worse than Ingred's condemnation.

'Oh, I'm fine,' she replied, gaily. 'I've had a low iron thing. I'm over it now. So, what's the meeting about? Vanessa said there's something we need to discuss. If it's Marigold's room—'

'No,' Gerald interrupted, 'it's not that. We've had an offer from the council.'

There was a chorus of groans and exclamations of *fuck the council*. What was the point of discussing their bogus offers? But Gerald was not to be put off. The council, he said, had passed a resolution that Belton Road was to be demolished and replaced with new housing. Yes, they had heard it all before, it was the same old story with local government authorities everywhere, and all they did was wreck existing houses and let them stand empty for years. But this time, the council had offered them an amnesty, and rehousing for everyone who wanted it.

The news of an amnesty did not satisfy them, and a fresh outburst of criticism broke out. The council would never offer anything decent; they'd end up scattered to the four winds in neglected estates if they got anything at all. It was just more of the same lies.

Gerald began to look angry.

240

'Listen,' he said, 'of course we should investigate what the offer amounts to. But we can't just dismiss it. What about Dave and Tina? And Jen and her kids from number fourteen? You think they're going to turn up their noses? We've got three weeks to decide. After that, they're withdrawing the offer.'

Everyone began talking at once, demanding more details from Gerald and putting forward opinions and making various declarations. It was soon clear that if they accepted the council's offer, the household would be split up. Couples could apply for rehousing, otherwise each person had to make their own application. And if they refused the offer, then they had to find another squat. The only other option was to make a stand and fight the demolition order. Gerald said it was likely to fail, but there were times when even hopeless battles had to be fought because they were part of something bigger.

'Does that mean you're going to stay and fight?' asked Annie.

Whether Marigold had liked it or not, Gerald was the unofficial leader of the squat, and everyone was keen to hear what he planned to do.

'I'm not sure,' he replied. 'I need a few days to think about it.'

It was decided that everybody else should take a few days to think about it too, and then come together to discuss it again before a general street meeting. It wasn't just a question of their future. It was also the future of the Free Republic of Beltonia.

28

The dominoes tumbled one after the other. Alan and Annie were the first to declare their plans. Alan, who had always seemed out of place in his suit and whose job nobody understood, had been promoted.

'We've found a flat in Clapham,' Annie said, 'and Alan can afford the rent, so we're moving there.' She looked embarrassed and defensive. 'We'll still be involved, it doesn't change anything. You know … our politics.'

Except for Gerald, everyone reassured Annie that it didn't change anything. Nobody mentioned that Alan's politics had always been suspect. After Annie and Alan, the next domino was Raymond. He had decided to return to France and resume his university studies. Then Martin announced that he was moving to the Findhorn commune in Scotland where they grew enormous vegetables with the help of nature spirits. It was part of his personal enlightenment quest, although the relevance of the big vegetables remained obscure. Vanessa was also on a spiritual trip and had booked her flight to India. She was going to Poona to meet the Bhagwan. Ingred, meanwhile, had already moved her possessions across the road to the separatist house (and into Thea's arms, Grace supposed) until they found somewhere in Hackney.

'What about you, Grace?' Annie enquired. 'You haven't said anything.'

'Come to Poona with me,' Vanessa said. 'I promise, it will change your life.'

Surrendering to the Guru was the only way to be fully alive and achieve bliss. It was, Grace noted, the third such proposal Vanessa had made to her, preceded by astrology and encounter groups, neither of which had lived up to the life-changing promise. For a second, she was tempted. Why stay in London? What was there here for her? Maybe, in India, she'd find what she was looking for. Then she remembered Janine and Cathy, the pubic hair fungus, and dead people on the streets. The hordes of Australian travellers.

'I've decided to stay and oppose the demolition order,' Gerald announced, before Grace had the chance to reply to Vanessa. 'There's a few of us in the street. We're not giving up.' It wasn't that he expected to win, but he couldn't let Beltonia be destroyed without a fight. They had tried to build something new, to liberate themselves from capitalist slavery and the old class hierarchies and even if it was imperfect, he wasn't going to give it up for the convenience of the council. Expounding on his reasons for staying, his face took on an almost ecstatic expression. Grace wondered if the others noticed.

'I think I'll stay too,' she said. The lure of India had been fleeting. Staying wasn't really a decision, it was more of a breathing space.

Of those who had decided to go, Vanessa was the last to leave. In the final days, she dyed her clothes orange, having decided to take sannyas when she got to Poona. Grace helped with the dyeing, thinking of Linda who had become Shanti, and whom she'd never met. She imagined Marigold helping Shanti dye her clothes, and it was both comforting and sad to think of her performing the same task that she was now doing with Vanessa. On the day of her departure, Gerald and Grace drove her to Heathrow. When it was time to say a final goodbye, Vanessa wrapped her arms around her.

'Bhagwan says *be, don't try to become,*' she whispered.

With only Grace and Gerald left, the squat had an end of year, gone home for the holidays atmosphere. In fact, it was worse, Grace thought, as there was no prospect of anyone returning. The house was too quiet and the bedrooms, stripped of possessions, seemed to forbid entry. Often, she found herself hovering in the doorless doorways without knowing why. There was no reason to hover, no reason to enter. Most of the time Gerald was out, engaged in the fight against the evictions. At first, he tried to include her, having assumed that she would want to be involved. She had assumed the same thing, hoping that it would give her purpose and a focus, that she might even become a leader, which made her think of Rosa Luxemburg, the Polish revolutionary who was shot dead and flung into a Berlin canal in 1919. Back then, women were not allowed to be leaders.

'I'm not feeling up to it,' she told Gerald, who soon gave up asking.

Since leaving Primo Press something fundamental had changed. She didn't mean the thing with Simon or leaving the job. When she tried to identify what it might be, there was nothing specific. Only that there was no going back, and the future had yet to be written. Everything was on hold. She was waiting, no longer sure whether it was for Marigold. Day by day, she began to sink further into a depression. Left on her own, she ate porridge for breakfast and dinner. Sometimes she went to the local pub and had a pie and mash, thankful that she'd kept Simon's money. She had to think about the future – where she was going to go and what she was going to do when the eviction battle was lost – and kept putting it off.

It was mid-morning when Gerald marched into her bedroom and stood at the end of the bed, arms folded, glaring at her. 'Get up,' he said, 'you've been moping for fucking ages. It's enough, you've got to snap out of it.'

'Really?' she said caustically, attempting to disguise the shock she felt at his intrusion. 'What's it got to do with you?'

'I'm living with a sad sack and I'm fed up of it. Stop feeling so sorry for yourself and get up.'

'Leave me alone. Get out of my room,' she cried.

'Forget it, I'm not leaving. You need to snap out of it. Ever since Marigold left you've been a misery guts.'

He moved forward and ripped the eiderdown off the bed. She screamed at him to leave her alone and that Marigold had nothing to do with how she felt.

'Oh, yeah?' he said. 'Pull the other one.'

His disbelief increased her fury and she leapt up, fighting for control of the bedclothes.

'That's it,' he shouted, 'fucking go for it.'

When she realised that Gerald was egging her on, she stopped and let her end drop.

'Good,' he said, 'now get dressed. Meet me downstairs in five minutes. We're going out.'

After he left the room, she sat down on the bed, determined to deny him the satisfaction of obeying. She had no intention of going out. Two minutes ticked by. When four minutes had elapsed, she scrambled for her clothes.

Gerald ordered her into the van and to be quick about it. He didn't gloat for which she was grateful. Nor did he say where they were going, and she didn't ask. It felt good to let him take over. A tiny, yet perceptible sense of excitement flickered, something that had been lacking for ages. She wasn't disappointed when the destination turned out to be Hampstead Heath. He said she needed fresh air and to be in nature and after a walk they would find a pub for lunch.

'Thank you,' she said, teary because of his kindness which she hadn't expected and didn't feel she deserved.

'Don't start blubbing,' he said.

245

They meandered across the Heath, Grace following where he led. The spring day with its light breeze and gentle sun was perfect for walking. Gerald told her that they were not going to win the eviction battle and that the houses would be demolished.

'Do you know where you'll go?' he asked.

'Not yet,' she replied.

After their first excursion they began to spend more time together. The campaign to save Beltonia was winding down. Beltonians were leaving, finding new squats, or taking up the offer to be re-housed. In the evenings she and Gerald cooked and afterwards went to the pub and played darts. They laughed a lot and there was an ease between them. Grace liked his passion about things, and his sharp intelligence. Often, she joined him in his room where they listened to music and he told her stories about his past, like getting busted with a tab of acid and doing two weeks in remand in Brixton jail. How most of the others were black guys who couldn't raise the money for bail. He told her that the experience opened his eyes. The more you look, the more injustice there is.

This night, after smoking a joint, they lay on his bed, listening to John Martyn's *Solid Air*. Someone was leaving, the words of the song all too resonant and Grace's thoughts turned to Marigold. She remembered what Gerald had said – how Marigold could have left her a message that night she came back, but she didn't. *What do you want from her?* he'd said, and she hadn't answered. Now she wondered if she'd meant anything to Marigold, or whether she was just a convenience who'd outlived her usefulness. Someone easily discarded. Was the closeness she'd felt all in her imagination? A pathetic, one-sided thing. What had Marigold ever revealed about herself beyond those few hard won crumbs extracted that night at the pub? Was her secrecy one more piece of evidence pointing to her involvement in the IRA, and if not the IRA, something equally clandestine? Gerald was right in one way at least – Marigold was an outsider. Like me, she thought suddenly, and it occurred to her that perhaps that was why Marigold had chosen her. Someone whose history and family resided on the other side of the world, who was vulnerable and in need of a friend, ready to overlook half-truths and evasions. The feeling that she'd been used caused a resurgence of bitterness to rise up, until, unexpectedly, she recognised something else. If Marigold had used her, wasn't it just as true that she had used Marigold, making her the object of fantasy, the object of desire, for the very reason that she was safely straight? And if Marigold had kept secrets, so had she. What right did she have to feeling bitter and abandoned when so much of 'her' Marigold was a fantasy?

'Don't think I'm marvellous,' she'd said, 'because I'm not,' and Grace had ignored the warning. It made her reconsider Marigold's failure to leave her a note or warn her that she was going to disappear. Maybe, after all, none of it mattered. Then, surprising herself, she changed her mind. She wasn't going to let Marigold off so lightly, remembering all the times she'd made promises and not kept them. The way she had taken Grace for granted. This time, she wasn't going to excuse her, even if it was only in her imagination, because she no longer believed they would meet again. But she wasn't going to hold a grudge either. What mattered was to accept that Marigold – whether she was Stella, a member of the IRA, a revolutionary, a rich girl defying her parents, or all of those things combined – was not perfect and only occasionally marvellous. Being occasionally marvellous was more than enough. The recognition of it made her smile.

'Grace, did you hear me?'

She turned to look at Gerald; she'd been so absorbed in her thoughts that it was a shock to find him there.

'We could apply together.'

'Apply for what?'

'A flat. Weren't you listening?' He went through it again – how they could apply as a couple and get somewhere decent.

'But we're not a couple.'

They were lying side by side, their heads turned toward each other when he leaned in and kissed her. She responded and when the kiss ended, he said, 'We could be.'

'No, we couldn't.'

'Why not? I like you, and I know you like me.'

'Because—'

'Because what?'

She was going to say that he was right, that she liked him a lot, only she didn't quite know what she wanted to do, that she might go travelling and didn't want to make a commitment to anything. It was all true, and she knew he would understand, but at the last minute, something unexpected happened.

'Because I'm a lesbian,' she said.

Gerald laughed. 'No you're not.'

She sat up, and he sat up too.

'Yes, I am.'

'I don't think you are, Grace. You can't be.'

'I am.'

He was staring at her intently, as if he had never really seen her.

'Why didn't you say so ... before?'

'Because I didn't want it to be true.'

'And now you've changed your mind?'

'I can't go on pretending to be something I'm not. I just can't go on doing it. I can't go on fighting myself. I don't want to do that anymore.'

'You're not like those women,' he said, a pleading tone in his voice. 'You're not one of them.'

'I am one of them. I'm a dyke.'

She knew it was true, and in saying it she felt something release inside her. It was extraordinary, the anguish she'd been carrying for so long was already lifting. She was a lesbian, a dyke, possibly even a butch, and not even the combined spectres of Miss Moore, Sister George or Childie could terrify her out of it.

'So, I was right. You were in love with Marigold. Are in love with her,' Gerald said.

'Yes,' she replied. To say it aloud was liberating.

'And she—?'

'Oh, god no. She's totally straight.'

'Did she know?'

'That I was in love with her? I think she suspected. We talked about lesbians once and I told her I wasn't gay.'

'That's why you've been so upset. About her disappearing. I mean, not just that she was your friend.'

There was no need to reply, and for a while they didn't speak, each absorbing what had been revealed. Grace was thinking about Gerald's refusal to believe she was gay.

'Is my being a lesbian disgusting to you?' she asked, at last.

'No. Course not. It's just that I'm not even in the race.' He grinned. 'Sure you don't want one final fuck before going over to the other side?'

She laughed and told him to fuck off. 'I'm baring my soul and that's all you can think about?'

Later, unable to sleep, she kept murmuring to herself, *I'm a lesbian, I'm a dyke*, feeling a sense of liberation instead of the usual revulsion. How could such a transformation have happened? It seemed so unlikely that she panicked, terrified that the feeling was temporary and by tomorrow, being gay would become unbearable again. She went on torturing herself for a while and discovered that her heart wasn't in it. The words lesbian, dyke, gay, homosexual no longer had the same awful ring to them. Words that had filled her with such dread had taken on a glow. She wanted to roll them around in her mouth and say them aloud. What had happened was a sort of miracle and in a confusedly blissful state, she drifted off to sleep.

The next day, she went across the street to see Ingred and apologised for being such an idiot. She explained about how she hadn't wanted to be gay. It had taken her ages, but now it was okay.

'Actually, it's more than okay,' she said.

Ingred congratulated her on coming out and gave her a hug, which turned into a kiss. Tempted though she was to give in to it, Grace pulled away. She wasn't sure it was what she needed right now. Ingred said she understood and was not offended. There was a lot going on in their lives.

She returned to the squat and finished clearing out Marigold's room. The aspidistra had miraculously survived, and she gave it to Gerald. He had rejected the council's offer of a flat on the seventeenth floor of a tower block and was moving into a building off Edgware Road where the squatters were trying to set up a housing co-op. It was a new tactic in the ongoing battle for decent housing and he wanted to be part of it. They said goodbye on the street, beside his van.

'If you change your mind about being a lesbian—'

'I won't. But it's not really goodbye,' she said, 'you're not getting rid of me that easily.'

She waved until the van turned the corner.

Once Gerald had gone, she wandered through the empty house, her echoing footsteps making her more aware than ever of the silence that had wrapped itself around the building. In every uninhabited room a few discarded objects remained, ghostly reminders of those who'd left. A bundle of clothes that had resisted Vanessa's orange dye; some French books that Raymond couldn't fit in his backpack; Martin's badly scratched Tangerine Dream album and a pair of black silk stockings; Annie's torn poster of *La Môme Piaf* and pages of Alan's computer printouts. In Gerald's bedroom she found a leaflet. *To squat is to challenge authority. Beware of authority. Beware of doublespeak.* The Orwellian echo made her think of Marigold and the aspidistra.

She let the leaflet fall to the floor and closed the door behind her. Upstairs in the front room, the velvet curtain that covered one half of the window hung limply. She smiled, remembering Marigold lying on the couch, swathed in her velvet curtain dress.

There was nothing more to do. Council workers had disconnected the electricity and cut off the gas. She was almost ready to leave. One final night and then in the morning she would close the front door for the last time. She sat down at the kitchen table. Gerald had arranged to pick it up later, after she'd left. An unused aerogram lay open in front of her. This time, she'd write a proper letter to her parents and tell them about her life. Not that she was a lesbian – not yet. She wanted to hold it to herself for a little longer. After scrabbling unsuccessfully in her bag for a pen, she upended the contents onto the table. Wallet, passport, the elusive pen, notebook, hairbrush and more, tumbled out, followed by the unopened letter from her father. Seeing it, she was flooded with a sense of panic, a foreboding that something terrible had happened at home. Why else would he have written? And how could she have let it languish in her bag, unread for so long?

At first, her eyes skittered over the page, expecting words like *illness, come home*, or even the word *death*. When some part of her brain registered that none of those words were present, she started at the beginning again.

My darling girl,

You will be surprised to get this letter from your old dad. I should have written earlier because it's been on my mind, the way we left things. I want to tell you I was wrong. I wanted you to stay here in Australia where I could protect you. Well, what could I protect you from? You see, I keep thinking of you as a child, but you're a grown woman now. It's not my job to hold you back but to let you go and trust you'll find your own way. Do you remember how we read Kipling's Kim together? I remember it goes something like this: Life is brief, but in that time, it offers us some splendid moments and meaningful adventures. That is what I hope for you my dear girl. Splendid moments and meaningful adventures.

The letter continued in a more conversational mode, giving her news about the farm, her mother, and Will. She couldn't focus and folded it up to read later. Then she bent her head, resting her forehead on crossed arms, and wept.

29

Ingred invited her to stay at the separatist squat for the last night.
'I won't jump on you,' she said, 'unless you want me to. It will be cold and lonely over there, Grace.'

Ingred was right, it was cold and lonely and impossible to sleep when every sound, every creaking board and rattling window made her heart race. All she had to do was cross the road to her new tribe. But she didn't go, feeling that it was important to stay in the squat that had been her home, and where she had become a Beltonian. She had to spend the final night alone, keeping a vigil, a way of marking the end of an era. Calling it an era sounded too grandiose, but she couldn't think of another way to express it. She knew something special was ending.

Her room was empty except for the mattress and the poltergeist wardrobe that nobody wanted. The candles she'd lit earlier flared as wind puffed through the gaps around the window frames, rattling the wardrobe door, reminding her that she had forgotten to wedge it shut, and that sooner or later it would swing open and bang against the wall. Reluctantly, she got up to fix it. On this occasion the latch wouldn't hold and in frustration, she gave it an angry shove. The wardrobe rocked back and forth before settling again. A piece of white fabric fluttered down from the top and landed at her feet.

She picked it up and seeing that it was just a boring white handkerchief, was about to drop it again, when something caught her eye. A monogrammed letter stitched in one corner. She blinked, almost expecting it to disappear. It took her breath away, and she sat down heavily on the mattress, staring at the letter S. How the handkerchief came to be on top of the wardrobe was one more unresolvable mystery. But its existence was a partial answer to a bigger question. The S, Grace was sure, stood for Stella.

30

The Night Ferry train pulled out of Victoria station, bound for the Gare du Nord with Grace on board. It was a last-minute decision, a way of honouring something in herself and of remembering Marigold. She no longer cared about not speaking French or where she'd stay. Things would work out somehow. She was going to wander Paris like a flâneur, following Celine and Julie's meanderings through Montmartre, beginning in the little park where Celine dropped her scarf, before riding the funicular to the summit and Sacre Coeur. There, she'd look for a bar and drink a toast to Marigold who was probably the mysterious Stella who, in turn, was possibly a member of the IRA. 'Maybe,' Grace thought, 'I'll even have a fling with a French girl,' then corrected herself to think 'woman', because girl was infantilising.

The Night Ferry train was crowded. Some people were speaking French, which reminded her of Raymond – his Deleuze-inspired ravings that none of them understood and the delicious croissants he used to buy for Saturday breakfasts. More memories flooded back, of Beltonia and everyone at the squat. Bonfires in the back garden, getting stoned in the upstairs room, listening to trippy music, and going to Holland Park with Annie, collecting money from people while she busked. Friday night curries and argumentative discussions around the kitchen table because everyone was passionate about something. The way Gerald and Marigold annoyed each other and then turned out to be having some kind of fling. Was it a one-night thing, she wondered, feeling a twinge of jealousy before laughing at herself because it was ridiculous to feel jealous like that. Her time in Beltonia had been short, not even a year, and yet it felt as if she'd lived a whole lifetime of experiences. Splendid moments and meaningful adventures. Which brought a lump to her throat and a promise to herself that she'd write home very soon.

She had decided that after a week in Paris (spending Simon's money) she would go back to London and move into the Hackney women's squat. Ingred said there was plenty of room and they both agreed it would be fine. Monogamy was boring and if they felt like it, they could sleep together. It didn't mean they were a couple. Grace wasn't as confident as Ingred about casual sex and the jealousy that might go with it, but she had catching up to do and Ingred was experienced.

She thought about Primo Press and wished it hadn't ended like that. It was Simon's fault, but she didn't hate him. She didn't hate Rita either, although possibly because she was no longer being persecuted by her. Even though the job of Girl Friday hadn't lived up to much and was disappointing, she'd learnt a few things and improved her typing. The things she'd learnt were less tangible but just as important – to stand up for herself; to ask questions and not to pretend she knew things when she didn't. Ingred had mentioned something about a feminist publishing house run by women and said she ought to check them out when she got back. She had nothing to lose, and they might offer her a job. A real job, this time, with real things to do.

She thought about everything that had happened to her since arriving in London and spent a few moments cringing, remembering how desperate she'd been to reinvent herself, get rid of her accent and pretend she was English. And how it hadn't turned out that way because the reinvention was really an acceptance of who she was in the first place. It was okay that she would never be a true Londoner. For better or worse, she was an Australian. And after all the torment, it was okay that she wasn't straight. In fact, being a lesbian already felt marvellous.

Acknowledgments

Thank you to Susan Hawthorne, Renate Klein, Pauline Hopkins and the team at Spinifex Press for your energy, expertise and wisdom, and your collaborative approach.

Thank you also to those who read early drafts of the novel and gave insightful feedback, in particular, Judy and Peter Hall, Carrie Tiffany, Terri-ann White and Lou Ryan. To Nadine Davidoff, many thanks for expert analysis and advice. And to Kelly Gardiner, Michelle Wright and Kate Davies, for your generous support.

For the many conversations about writing, and for friendship, thank you to writer-neighbours, Trish Bolton, and Belinda Probert. And, as always, thank you to Antoni Jach whose master classes were invaluable.

To friends in London – especially Lizzie, John, David, Kris, Tony, Richard, Brodie and Lee – I'm so glad to have met you all and for the intense years we shared when we were young.

To my sisters, Rosey and Penny, nieces, Emily and Anna, aunt and uncle, Judy and Peter, I can't thank you enough for the love, support and encouragement.

And of course, most of all, thanks to Ana Kokkinos.

Other books available from Spinifex Press

The Leaves

Jacqueline Rule

Faith and Evelyn are close friends, neighbours, and single mothers of Luke and of Mitch – and both bear the scars of the trauma of colonisation and the Stolen Generations. When Faith dies unexpectedly, Luke's childhood in Sydney is severed into a 'before' and 'after' and a chain of catastrophic events unfolds that will alter the course of his life.

Navigating the upheaval of a broken foster system (that serves as a pipeline to poverty and incarceration in 'juvie'), *The Leaves* is a bittersweet meditation on motherhood and loss, on the power of female friendship, and the role of the state in perpetuating violence.

Luke's journey exposes the aftermath of colonisation as the nature of punishment, historical trauma and healing are examined. In doing so, the novel reveals the cruelty and futility of the youth detention system, and the violence of the law itself.

Through the pursuit of unattainable justice for Luke, *The Leaves* raises larger questions about a society that is yet to take responsibility for its own historical crimes.

The Leaves is where literature meets activism, and one would hope that by triggering the emotions of the reader, it may compel an understanding.
—Jess Whaler, *The Weekend Australian Review Magazine*

It's a small book in length, but big in intensity and effect … Every time this book is read, Rule's hold on the axe will strengthen. A highly recommended read.
—*Law Society Journal*

ISBN 9781922964021

The Floating Garden
Emma Ashmere

Sydney, Milsons Point, 1926. Entire streets are being demolished for the building of the Harbour Bridge. Ellis Gilbey, landlady by day, gardening writer by night, is set to lose everything. Only the faith in the book she's writing, and hopes for a garden of her own, stave off despair. As the tight-knit community splinters and her familiar world crumbles, Ellis relives her escape to the city at sixteen, landing in the unlikely care of self-styled theosophist Minerva Stranks.

When artist Rennie Howarth knocks on her door seeking refuge from a stifling upper-class life and an abusive husband, Ellis glimpses a chance to fulfil her dreams. The future looms uncertain while the past stays uncannily in pursuit.

This beautiful novel evokes the hardships and the glories of Sydney's past and tells the little-known story of those made homeless to make way for the famous bridge. Peopled by bohemians and charlatans, earthy folk and fly-by-nighters, *The Floating Garden* is about shedding secrets, seizing second chances, and finding love amongst the ruins.

… beautifully detailed … finely crafted … an elegy for the forgotten … a subversive counter-history to the tumult of rapid progress.
—*The Sydney Morning Herald* and *The Age*

… a beautiful meditation on grief, guilt, and regret, set against the backdrop of Milsons Point, Sydney, 1926.
—Judges' report, MUBA Prize

ISBN 9781742199368

Remembering the Tarantella
Finola Moorhead

Remember The Tarantella is a remarkable work. It's learned and frivolous, female not feminine, silly and serious. Written in several strands of narrative, the many characters create a space as if reading were a dance party. Story is not the main objective. Private conversations and thoughts are always within earshot of the rhythm of others, like the stamping of feet and the beat of the music. This is concerto-like poetry; many instruments of different tones assist the reader to know who is who.

A visionary and questing novel of startling energy, intelligence and passion, its form shaped to its own image, it is the work of a major writer.
—Helen Daniel, *The Sydney Morning Herald*

Moorhead's novel then, is a major achievement by anyone's standards. Its expansive scope and its complex yet intricate structure sets it apart from much of the more mundane mainstream literary activity in Australia during the late eighties. It is to be hoped that the next few years will see it receive the recognition it deserves – both in Australia and overseas.
—Mark Roberts, Rochford Street Review

Finola Moorhead's *Remember the Tarantella* is … a strongly optimistic cluster of female myths, in beautiful prose, whose interweaving narratives and characters entice and delight.
—Jeff Doyle, *The Canberra Times*

ISBN 9781876756932

If you would like to know more about
Spinifex Press, write to us for a free catalogue, visit our
website or email us for further information
on how to subscribe to our monthly newsletter.

Spinifex Press
PO Box 105
Mission Beach QLD 4852
Australia

www.spinifexpress.com.au
women@spinifexpress.com.au